THE OTHER WAY AROUND

THE OTHER WAY
AROUND

SASHI KAUFMAN

🌿 carolrhoda LAB
MINNEAPOLIS

Carolrhoda Lab™
An imprint of Carolrhoda Books
A division of Lerner Publishing Group, Inc.
241 First Avenue North
Minneapolis, MN 55401 U.S.A.

For reading levels and more information, look up this title
at www.lernerbooks.com.

Cover and interior photographs: © iStockphoto.com/amygdala_imagery (sky); © iStockphoto.com/Sara Egner (cracked playa texture); © i love images/Cultura/ Getty Images (driver); © iStockphoto.com/spxChrome (notebook paper).

Main body text set in Janson Text LT Std 10/14.
Typeface provided by Linotype AG.

Library of Congress Cataloging-in-Publication Data

Kaufman, Sashi.
        The other way around / Sashi Kaufman.
            pages   cm
        Summary: To escape his offbeat family at Thanksgiving, Andrew West accepts a ride from a band of street performers who get their food and clothing from dumpsters, but as he learns more about these "Freegans" he sees that one cannot outrun the past.
        ISBN 978–1–4677–0262–1 (trade hard cover : alk. paper)
        ISBN 978–1–4677–2404–3 (eBook)
        [1. Runaways—Fiction. 2. Street entertainers—Fiction. 3. Homeless persons—Fiction. 4. Mothers and sons—Fiction. 5. Family problems—Fiction.] I. Title.
PZ7.K16467Oth 2014
[Fic]—dc23   2013017670

Manufactured in the United States of America
1 – SB – 12/31/13

For Dad and the
shared love of stories

PART ONE

THE PAST IMPERFECT

WHEN DO GIRLS FART?

When do girls fart? I know guys let it fly basically all the time. Any time it's funny, when they feel like it, as a weapon, to clear a room. But girls don't seem to do this. In fact if anything girls seem a lot more attuned to avoiding anything that smells bad. They have a lot of products directed towards this purpose. But they have to let it go some time. Everyone does, right?

The whole topic has become a lot more interesting to me since I've become one of a handful of male students at St. Mary's boarding school. It actually stresses me out a little bit. I mean, I've never been one of those people who enjoyed gassing people with my flatulence. Most of the time when I fart, it's in the bathroom. But at St. Mary's there's only one bathroom that's designated for male students, and it's on the first floor next to the custodian's supply closet—which is, incidentally, also the boys' locker room. So I've become kind of a furtive farter, letting them fly in the hallways and then moving swiftly from the scene of the crime.

Back when I was in public school, I knew this guy Rick who called that crop-dusting. He was my lab partner in seventh grade science class, and he used going to sharpen his pencil or getting a drink as an excuse to wander the classroom and let the gas fly. It was actually kind of funny to watch people react and accuse each other after he had just passed by. I'd probably be the one blushing and shaking my head. *It wasn't me, man, not me.*

You might think ending up at an all-girls high school would be a guy's idea of heaven, but it's not that simple. Sure, they're everywhere; brushing up against me to get to their lockers, flipping a silky ponytail in my face as they file out of homeroom, or even worse, adjusting their clothes—skirts hiked up and shirts unbuttoned as they walk out of class and buttoned back up when they walk in. I have to keep my eyes on the floor unless I want to walk around semi-hard all day. All day I'm surrounded by girls my own age. The problem is not that they're mean or rude to me, or that they resent me for infiltrating their arena of female empowerment. The problem is that they don't see me at all. They sweep past me every day, immersed in conversation, captivated by one another, and totally oblivious to my human presence.

Alex explained it to me this way. "You're like a floor model, Andrew West." For some reason, Alex insists on referring to me by my full name, as if there were more than ten other boys at St. Mary's—much less other Andrews. "You're like a cardboard cutout version of a typical male. They see you, you're acceptably groomed, decent to look at, you'd probably fit in with anyone's living room décor, but you're the display model. And let's be honest, no one really wants to go home with the display model if they can afford something better. It's nothing personal, Andrew West."

"How is it not personal?" I asked.

"This is a cloistered life they lead here at St. Mary's. Boys are something that exists on the outside. The fact that there are a few of us here on the inside doesn't really change that idea. You're not so much male as you represent the males." He sighed loudly. "Unfortunately that makes us brother figures or best friends with bad acne. They'll confide in us and befriend us. You might even get one to practice making out with you if she gets drunk. But they'll never date you. We've seen too much. You know what I mean?"

"Kind of," I said. "Not like you care anyway."

"True," he agreed. "I have no interest in the female of the species. I suppose in some ways it's worse for you. At least I don't have temptation waved in front of my face every day. No offense," he added, giving me a cursory once-over.

"None taken," I said, blushing furiously.

He explained the concept as we changed into our clothes for gym. The custodian's closet was a big enough space for the three of us. Alex, Willem Beech, and I are the only male students in the sophomore class. There are a few others in the freshman class, but they don't have gym at the same time as we do.

Willem always changes quickly. He stands in the corner and throws his clothes on and off with lightning speed. This is both a function of his shyness and his eagerness to get back to whatever fantasy or science fiction novel he's reading at the time. Willem reads all the time. He reads under his desk in class, walking through the halls, and at his solitary table at lunch. The cafeteria is a brutal place to be friend-lacking. For a while I mooched off Alex's popularity, silently sitting with him and his friends on odd days and on even days eating as I walked to the school library. I didn't think anyone noticed until

I sat down with Alex one day and he winked and said, "Must be Thursday." Willem's father is the gym teacher—a fact I frequently compare to my own situation. It's hard to decide which is worse; being the unathletic son of the gym teacher or the unstudious son of the headmistress.

Due to my age, this is the first time that I'm attending school at the place where Mom is working. When I wasn't directly under her wing, it was easier to act like it was the system that was failing me and not the other way around. But at St. Mary's, I'm like an ugly red zit on Mom's otherwise smooth skin. Mom was headhunted by this school—at least that's the way she likes to put it. They needed someone to oversee the integration of male students. It was conveniently inconvenient. Mom said St. Mary's was a chance at a fresh start for both of us. For her that meant the chance to be in the top position at a fairly prestigious high school and for me, I guess I was supposed to embrace the opportunity to blossom into the Rhodes scholar everyone seemed to believe was lurking behind the years of mediocre report cards. I was at St. Mary's so she could monitor my studies more closely in these critical "college preparatory years," as the brochure described. Nancy West is not going to have a son who doesn't attend college—this I'm well aware of. Unfortunately for her, her first year as head of a new school is a bad time to take a sudden renewed interest in her son. For both of us.

Alex is an excellent student *and* a superb athlete. At his old school he played soccer in the fall, basketball in the winter, and tennis in the spring. It's obvious he excelled at all three. He sinks three-point shots with ease and has a fierce backhand that makes Mr. Beech, who also coaches tennis, salivate. There is currently no use for his skills at St. Mary's since all the schools we play are other all-girls schools. Alex doesn't seem to mind. For being such a superior athlete, he's oddly uncompetitive. Whenever we scrimmage at anything in gym class he always goes out of his way to pass to everyone, even the least coordinated players. Win or lose, he doesn't seem to care.

Alex will tell anyone who asked the story of how he ended up at St. Mary's. An illicit affair with a student teacher led the public school system to politely ask if he wouldn't consider attending school somewhere else, on their dime, of course. I'm not entirely sure if I believe it, but if it's a lie, it's an entertaining one, so I'm willing to let it slide. Besides, my roster of friends at St. Mary's isn't exactly overflowing.

I don't mind Alex's floor-model theory. It's better than anything I've come up with on my own. Before I met Alex I chalked up my complete lack of any success with girls to something I referred to privately as the curse of Analiese Gerber. Analiese was the last girl to express any interest in me whatsoever. In fifth grade a posse of her giggly, gum-smacking, ponytailed friends accosted me in the lunch room.

"We need to ask you something," Tracy Jennings, the ring-leader of their small group, announced.

I remember being stunned. It was rare that one girl spoke to me deliberately, much less an entire gaggle of them.

"Who do you like?" she asked, pointing her small chin defiantly in my direction.

I knew what this question meant. I heard the popular girls asking it of each other all the time, but no one had ever asked it of me.

"I don't know," I said. This apparently was an acceptable answer because it sent a wave of whispers and giggles through the small group. The only one untitillated was Tracy Jennings.

"You don't know, like you don't want to tell us, or you don't know like *you don't know?*"

"I don't know," I said blankly. Here's where things began to go badly. The other boys I normally ate lunch with were scuttling to the side like so many crabs frightened by a shadow.

"Because Analiese likes you," Tracy said.

"Oh," I said. Over the course of the next few weeks I would contemplate a hundred other ways I could have responded to that declaration. Ways that would have continued the mystery of whom I might like, ways that might have granted me entrance into the popular kids' circle. It was a turning point, I know that now.

"So do you like her?" Tracy asked with all the subtlety of a police interrogator.

"I don't know," I said, and this time I really meant it. I had never thought about Analiese Gerber in this way. She wasn't an unattractive girl. She had straight, brown, shoulder-length hair and large, brown, doe-like eyes. She always wore shiny pink lip gloss, and sometimes it ended up smudging above her lip.

"Because she likes you," Tracy reiterated. She was starting to sound annoyed. Clearly this interaction was not going the way she had envisioned.

"Okay," I said finally, hoping that the conversation might end so I could finish my peanut butter and jelly before our brief lunch period was up. Tracy and her posse walked away, a little deflated, but I was just starting to process the conversation that had taken place. *A girl liked me! This was great!*

At recess I walked the perimeter of the kickball field alone, thinking about the implications of the whole conversation. I thought about Analiese and decided that the way she wore her lip gloss was actually pretty cute. I envisioned us going to the movies together, waiting outside when the movie was over for my mom or her dad to pick us up. The other kids would walk by us and give us knowing glances. I had never gone to the movies with anyone besides my mom.

At the end of the day, while we waited for the buses to be called, I walked nervously over to Tracy Jennings, who was tilting forward across her desk and blowing enormous bubbles with her gum.

"Yes," I told her.

"Yes what?" she said, staring at me like I was a cartoon monster—weird but not really scary.

"Yes, I like Analiese too," I said. I could feel myself blushing.

"Oh," said Tracy. "Well she likes someone else now." She gave me a look of feigned sympathy mixed with scientific curiosity. "Are you really sad?" she asked. "'Cause I could tell her that if you want me to."

I couldn't even answer her. I walked away from her desk stunned. All my plans were destroyed. And I was sad, truly sad—or so I told myself. "You shouldn't mess with a girl's feelings like that," Tracy called across the classroom.

I stared back at her in disbelief. Tracy just shrugged and went back to her gum smacking.

I tried to catch Analiese's eye as we boarded the bus to go home for a long weekend. I wanted to give her what I imagined to be a soul-searching glance. But she was happily chatting with Billy O'Brien as she got on her bus. I guess if I learned anything from the whole incident, besides that girls were completely baffling, it was not to imagine a future for myself that was dependent on anyone's feelings, even my own. Especially when it could be so easily shattered by uttering a simple, "Oh." And I couldn't help but wonder if I had lost my one shot at love to a kid who always chewed with his mouth open.

MORE TROUBLE WITH GIRLS

Margaret is not a hot girl's name. But there she is, sitting two rows in front of me in English class. And she is undeniably hot. They always know it too, the hot girls. They always know they're hot. I wonder how they know? Does it come on their birth certificate as a designation? Caucasian, six pounds eleven ounces, nineteen inches long, hot girl. Margaret was named after the anthropologist Margaret Mead. She told us this on the first day of school. I don't think there's anything sexy about anthropologists, not even in a bare-breasted *National Geographic* kind of way. But I'm willing to make an exception.

She is chewing on her pencil eraser. And even that's hot. If anyone else did it, it would be disgusting, but Margaret looks all nervous, and while she's chewing on her pencil eraser, her silky red hair starts falling out of her ponytail blocking my view of her incredibly hot neck. I start thinking about running my hands through her hair, or how it would feel to have her head in my lap. That goes nowhere good. I shift uncomfortably in my seat, glad that there's another half hour left before I have to stand. I try and focus on the test: an essay on *Romeo and Juliet*. Embarrassingly, all I can think of is that scene where Romeo says he wishes he could be the glove on Juliet's hand so he could touch her cheek. I don't think this particular line of thinking is going to help me complete my essay on the individual versus society. I'm also pretty sure that sharing this thought with Margaret would not turn out much better for me than it did for Romeo.

Something pings me in the back of the head. I picked up tiny piece of paper off the floor and unroll it.

"Look up, moron," it says in Alex's tiny penciled scrawl.

Ms. Tuttle is staring at me. She is sitting at the front of the room, correcting papers while we take the test. She waggles her green pen at me (Ms. Tuttle thinks that red pen is too punitive) and points down at the test. I smile and do my best to look appropriately sheepish. When I turn around to give Alex a head nod he rolls his eyes in my direction and then in Margaret's. He shakes his head sadly. *Out of your league,* he mouths. I shrug my shoulders and we both go back to the test. It's not long before I'm spacing out again, staring out the window at the bare gray branches and the white November sky. Did I grab my jacket today on the way out the door? I'm wondering how cold it is when Ms. Tuttle coughs loudly. I look up and see that she is beckoning me with one hooked finger. Reluctantly I get up from my seat.

I follow her into the hall. She sighs before she says anything and touches her neck the way a religious person might finger a cross. But there's nothing there. "Andrew, I assume you're aware that this test counts for fifty percent of your grade this quarter." Teachers always think things are more important than they really are. But I nod anyway to satisfy her. And it's true, I am aware of that fact. She's only said it about fifteen

17

times a day for the last three days, as though bludgeoning us with this fact might get us to actually study. "Did you even prepare a note card?" she asks.

I pull a crumpled 3x5 index card from my pants pocket and hold it up briefly for her inspection. Ms. Tuttle may be a teacher, but she's no dope. "Does it have anything on it?" Her voice is patiently sarcastic. I can't believe it's only November. Usually it takes teachers at least six months to figure out that I'm a terrible student. I smooth the card open and show her. It's titled *Romeo and Juliet Theme Essay*. Underneath that are the words *Individual versus Society*, followed by *Romeo versus society* and *Juliet versus society*.

"It seemed like kind of an obvious theme so I didn't think I needed a lot of notes," I say without meeting her eyes.

"Well, you've got about twenty minutes left of class time, and I can't wait to see what you come up with once you conquer that first sentence." Again with the sarcasm. I just nod and make like I'm going back into the room. Ms. Tuttle must have a moment of weakness, because she puts her hand on my shoulder and asks in a softer tone. "Is this about your meeting this afternoon?"

Honestly, I had forgotten, but I know an opening when I see one. "I guess I am a little distracted."

"Well, I suppose if you need more time on your essay," Ms. Tuttle relents.

No! I want to shout. Don't do it! I thought for a minute you were different, but you're a sucker just like the rest of them. "Yeah," I say. "That might be good."

"I'm not going to hang you out to dry, Andrew," Ms. Tuttle assures me. *In front of your mother the Dragon Lady*, I think. I wonder if Ms. Tuttle is afraid of my mother the way so many teachers are. It's pretty much the reason I passed first quarter. Nobody wanted to piss off the new headmistress early on. I don't hate my mother, but I hate when she plays the headmistress. I'm smart enough to know when she's throwing her Ivy League vocabulary in someone's face, and it makes me want to vomit and run in the opposite direction from whatever future she has in mind for me.

"We just want to find a way to help you be successful," she adds. It's hard not to cringe. I remember this is Ms. Tuttle, not Mom, but it seems like I've heard these words a hundred times over the course of the last three or four years. This is not my first parent-teacher meeting, nor will it probably be my last. On my way back into class I catch another smirk from Alex. I manage to at least write a passable introduction to my essay before the bell rings at the end of the period.

TEACHER MEETINGS

My first teacher meeting was a result of my first-ever trip to the principal's office. We were living in Geneseo, New York, so Mom could finish her Ph.D., and I attended the local elementary school. I remember this first teacher meeting quite clearly. Every other one since then kind of blurs together.

The unit was called Understanding Handicaps. Each week several well-meaning volunteers came to our school and provided a lesson designed to better help us understand what life was like for people with different disabilities. We liked it because it interrupted a rather tedious social studies unit that involved the mass memorization of all the land forms in Europe and Asia. Our teacher, Mrs. Wilcox, liked it because she got to sit at her desk and let the volunteers run the class. After a few initial head nods, probably meant to underscore the importance of whatever we were learning, she would grade papers and drink her Lemon Lift tea.

The first week we got to push each other around the hallways in borrowed wheelchairs. The second week we were paired off and had to lead one another around the school blindfolded. We were given several tasks, such as opening a locker or washing hands in the bathroom. Roz Parker chipped her front tooth when her Seeing-Eye friend let her lean too close to the fountain while getting a drink. Pushier parents, the kind who send their daughters to St. Mary's, might have investigated the use of curriculum time that led to the unfortunate dental incident. But Geneseo was a different kind of town, and Roz's parents probably had problems, dental and otherwise, far worse than a chipped tooth.

After each of these experiential activities, we had to answer some questions in a workbook about what it felt like to try out the disability for the day. Week three was called Developmental Disabilities, which someone had figured out was grown-up code for retarded. By the time the volunteers arrived the classroom was buzzing with anticipation. How were they going to simulate this? Everyone was trying out their best retard voice—surely not what the program initiators had in mind when they wrote the curriculum. Andrea Peterson's cousin told her that they had a machine that could turn your brain retarded for short periods of time.

Much to our disappointment, our task was a lot more mundane than what we had all imagined. Pennies were spread out on the desk—this was a good start. And we were given oven mitts to wear and told to pick up as many pennies as we could. This, we were told, was what it felt like to be mentally retarded. In my own defense, I think we were *all* a little disappointed. I raised my hand and asked what I felt was on everyone's mind: "Why does picking up pennies make you seem retarded?"

"People who are *developmentally disabled* have to struggle to complete tasks that are simple for people without disabilities," the volunteer explained patiently.

"Yeah, but why are they picking up so many pennies?"

The volunteer stared at me, screening my expression for any possible signs of cheekiness or insubordination. "The pennies are just an example," she said, this time a little less patiently. It wasn't really the explanation I was looking for, but I knew enough about adult signals to let it go. The lesson went on without interruptions until one of the volunteers tried to explain to our class that people with Down syndrome are often sweet, good-natured, and childlike. This time it was Matt Hider who objected.

"No they're not," he blurted out without raising his hand. We all looked smugly at the volunteers. We knew something they didn't.

"Well, actually," the volunteer began.

"My sister's got that and she's a real brat," Matt announced. "Especially if she doesn't get her way. She hits all the time too." Matt was the second youngest of seven. His family squeezed into the tiny ranch at the end of our street. I knew for a fact that he was the one who took care of his younger sister every day after school until his parents came home from work. I nodded as he spoke, as though living on the same street as the kid with Down syndrome lent me some sort of secondary authority.

"Well, I'm sure she doesn't mean it," the volunteer said and smiled brightly at Matt.

"Oh yes she does," Matt insisted. "Once when I took away the potato chips because she was going to make herself sick, she bit me." He rolled up his sleeve to reveal the distinctive scars of bite marks. Now it was getting good. We all jumped up from our seats to look at Matt's wounds. Mrs. Wilcox, roused from her stack of papers by our sudden movement, stood up to retake control of the class. "All right everybody, that's enough," Mrs. Wilcox said in an elevated tone. Disappointed, we began to drift back to our seats. The best part of the class was clearly over.

"I bet she doesn't sit around all day picking up pennies either," I blurted out louder than I meant to.

"No way, man, she's not *that* retarded," Matt replied. The whole class snickered, and for a moment, I reveled in being the kid who had cracked up the whole class.

"Andrew West." Mrs. Wilcox drew herself up to her full height. A piece of hair had come loose from her otherwise un-flappable bun. "You can take your smart mouth directly to the principal's office, young man."

I remember the heat that rose up instantly in my face and the way everyone else dropped their eyes to their desks, as if disobedience might be contagious. It wasn't like junior high, when kids were sent to the principal's office all the time and everyone just kind shrugged in a too-bad-for-you kind of way. This was elementary school. The principal was a mythic figure who appeared only during holiday assemblies and national emergencies. This was serious.

As I slowly walked down the polished stairs, my sweaty palm gripping the banister for support, it occurred to me that if anyone had been smart-mouthing, it was Matt Hider. I guess it wasn't as easy to send the kid with the retarded sister to the principal's office.

The secretary looked up from her teddy bear catalog long enough to give me a shaming look and direct me to the wooden bench outside the principal's door. I sat there and watched the office comings and goings for about twenty minutes before anyone else spoke to me. I could hear the muffled tones of Mr. McGinty on the phone inside his office. I watched as a third-grader's mother came to sign her out for a dentist appointment. Two kids, only one who actually looked sick, came down to go to the nurse's office. Mrs. Bolduc, the school nurse, came out at one point and smiled at me until she realized why I was sitting where I was sitting. She exchanged her smile for a troubled look and went back in her office.

Finally Mr. McGinty came out and kneeled next to me so that his head was at my eye level and I could see his yellowing teeth and smell the Scope on his breath. "I suppose you know why you're here," he said.

"I was rude to the teachers," I offered, hoping for a brief moment this might be as easy as confession—which I had only seen in movies, since Mom's family thinks too much religion is tacky and Dad describes himself as a recovering Jew.

Mr. McGinty nodded. "I've called your mother, and she's on her way in. She's trying to get ahold of your father so he can be here too." My blood froze. They were calling my parents? Over this? My face grew hot again, and a few fat, embarrassing tears began to well up in my eyes. Mr. McGinty seemed satisfied with this response. He stood up with some difficulty and spoke to the school secretary. "He can wait in the conference room. Why don't you set him up with something to do until everyone gets here?"

I was ushered into the conference room next to the principal's office, a stale, windowless room with a table, five chairs, and a tower of extra folding chairs stacked in one corner. Month-at-a-glance calendars detailing the schoolwide events and planned field trips covered the walls. I was given a coloring book and some crayons. Once I grew tired of staring at the calendars, I turned my attention to the coloring book, which turned out to be a series of cautionary tales about a misbehaving frog who makes bad choices. The book had clearly been used before, and I halfheartedly enjoyed whoever had given the frog a yellow Mohawk and a cigarette hanging out of his mouth on each page. I turned to a blank page and began to color the frog purple.

The buildup to the meeting was worse than the meeting itself. By the time my parents got there, school was over and Mrs. Wilcox could attend, along with Mrs. Richards, the school social worker. I was asked a few times if I understood why I what I had said was wrong and inappropriate, and I was able to get away with answering by head nod and sorrowful expression. What I remember most about the meeting were my parents. My mom seemed to actually enjoy the meeting and suggested several times that we might need to reconvene if there wasn't any progress in my behavior or attitude. She mentioned several times that I might have seemed moody lately. It was clearly an invitation for further questions, and she seemed disappointed when no one took her up on it.

My father said nothing, his mouth pursed with tension. He tapped one end of a ballpoint pen lightly on the table throughout the entire meeting. I already knew my parents were splitting up, even though neither had said anything directly. I assumed this was what my mom was getting at. She actually seemed disappointed when Mrs. Richards told her she didn't think weekly social work appointments would be appropriate at this time. "Andrew seems to have a pretty good understanding of what he did wrong," she explained. And then it was over.

Outside in the parking lot there was an awkward moment as my parents walked purposefully toward their separate cars, and I was unsure of whom to follow. My father turned around first. "You want to go to Friendly's?"

"Sure," I said.

"David, I hardly think taking him out to lunch is appropriate to the occasion."

"Did I or did I not just hear you say an hour ago that I need to spend more time with him?"

Mom looked like she wanted to say more. But she didn't, so I followed my father to the car and we went to Friendly's, where I ate a chicken finger basket and he drank Diet Coke and folded and refolded his straw wrapper while trying to explain the basics of the divorce to me.

WHAT I'M COMING TO

I know what pity looks like. I've seen it enough to recognize it when it's staring me in the face. Which is why I'm not smiling at the sad half-smile that my mom's secretary is giving me while I'm waiting outside her office. I'm trying not to think about whether some part of breakfast is staining my school uniform. I want to smooth down the cowlick that inevitably pops up on the back of my head by the end of the day, but I resist the urge to act in the face of this sad woman with lipstick on her teeth and a misbuttoned cardigan.

Before I can really get going on my mental rampage, Mom buzzes through to ask if I'm still waiting.

"Sheila, will you ask him if he can find a ride?" the tinny voice scratches out on speaker phone. Sheila looks at me awkwardly. I enjoy her embarrassment as she buzzes back through and reminds my mother that I'm here for a meeting with *her*—for the not-so-dreaded teacher meeting with her and the rest of my teachers. "That's today?" Mom asks rhetorically. "I had it down for next week." No response is needed.

It's ten of three, and slowly my teachers begin to drift in and make their way to the conference room just off the main office. Miss Simms, my biology teacher, Mr. Carroll is geometry, Mr. Kunitz from world history, and of course Ms. Tuttle, who smiles sympathetically as she walks past. Even Mr. Beech shows up, and phys. ed. is the one class I'm passing. Mrs. Byers, my guidance counselor, ruffles my hair as she walks by.

I like Mrs. Byers. She's the only African American person on staff at St. Mary's; she refers to all her students as "her babies"; and she's unbelievably optimistic. When Mom expressed some concern earlier in the year about my grades, Mrs. Byers said, "Who, Andrew? My baby? Uh uh. I'm not worried about Andrew. He's going to be just fine once he settles in and makes the transition. He's going to be just fine." Plus she always has chocolate, and she never questions you if you want to make an appointment to come see her. You can pretty much stop by anytime, which I've made an occasional practice of on test days. She knows I'm not doing that well, but she never pushes me or asks me why.

I already know how this is going to go. Mom will begin by making a little speech about how we can all agree that I'm not living up to my potential. Then there will be teacher reports where everyone says how surprised they are because I seem really smart but the quality of my work is pretty poor. Mr. Beech will be the only exception here when he announces that I'm passing gym with flying colors. He will punctuate this by giving me a dirty look for wasting his time. Then everyone will agree that overall I'm not making enough effort and I need to do better.

Next everyone will look at me, and someone, probably Ms. Tuttle, will ask if there's anything that the teachers can do to help me be more successful. At which point I'll shrug and say that I don't think so. And if I'm feeling especially sanctimonious, I'll add something about how I know my education is my responsibility. I'd probably be more likely to care if any one of them could demonstrate the usefulness of what they're teaching for life after high school. Dad never bothered to finish his degree—he claims his thesis got held up in committee, but Mom says he wasn't motivated enough to see it through—and he's got a job and a pretty decent life, I guess.

Sometimes they'll ask me for some kind of review or assessment of how my time at home is spent. Mom usually jumps in here and assures everyone that I do not have access to video games and my television time is strictly limited. Which of course makes everyone wonder if I have a life at all.

The truth is, I don't have answers to their questions, and I don't think they do either. I hate when adults look at you like you're some kind of puzzle just waiting to be unlocked by the right question. I like to read—mostly biographies and survival stories. It's cool when people are actually fighting for their survival. I bet no one ever asked Ernest Shackleton to write a five-paragraph essay on the individual versus society.

I rarely like the assigned readings. We read *The Grapes of Wrath* earlier this year, and I kind of liked that. It's sort of like a survival story. I'm remembering it now because I'm thinking of this one scene where Tom Joad gets annoyed at this guy, who works at the gas station during the Great Depression when basically the whole country was going to hell, because he just keeps saying how he wants to know what the country is coming to. According to Tom, the guy is just talking to hear himself talk. That's how it is with these meetings. Everyone sits down and wants to know what I'm coming to.

Then it's time for solutions. Ms. Tuttle suggests that I keep a journal for extra credit in English. I'm not going to tell her that I'd rather have my fingernails removed by some Gestapo guy than spend any more time alone with my stupid thoughts. Instead I just nod, like this might be doable. Mr. Carroll suggests that I stay after school for extra help. I nod again, knowing that I'll only have to do that once or twice before I can start blowing it off. Kunitz recommends some website with a bunch of study skills ideas, and Mom makes a show of writing it down. I've got to give Kunitz credit for that one. The guy's got four kids, there's no way he's staying after to work with someone like me, and I don't blame him. And then the meeting is pretty much over. I'm almost out the door when Mom asks me if I can still find a ride home at this hour because she needs to stay at school and get caught up. She never bothers to ask who I get these mysterious rides from, and I never bother to tell her that 99% of the time I walk. We wouldn't want to shatter the illusion that I actually have friends at St. Mary's.

THE AFTERMATH

That night I wait until Mom's had her second glass before I come out of my room. She's still wearing work clothes, but she's put on fuzzy slippers and she's leafing through a women's clothing catalog at the top of a stack of unopened mail.

"The board is giving me a really hard time about the curriculum," she says out loud.

I reach into the cabinet and grab a handful of Cheez-Its from the box. "Uh-huh?" I say, while munching the crackers.

"I mean, they hired me because they wanted change and now they're dragging their feet every time I suggest something. We can keep Latin and classical studies, but religious education has got to go—at least the way it's being taught now. Maybe we could revamp it into some kind of a world religions class . . ." Her voice trails off. She pushes aside the catalog and scribbles a note on the back of some unopened mail. Then she looks up and, as if suddenly realizing who she's talking to, frowns. "That was embarrassing for me today, Andrew."

"Sorry."

"But I mean that's really not the point. The point is your future, Andrew."

Maybe, but it's not the first thing that popped into your mind. "I know," I say.

"I mean do you think about the future, honey? I'm not going to be able to take care of you indefinitely."

"What's for dinner, Mom?"

Mom looks annoyed and reaches for the stack of takeout menus in the middle of the table before she gets my point. "What is that supposed to mean?"

"Nothing. I was just wondering what's for dinner."

Mom stands up from the table quickly. Her chair tips back but doesn't fall. "Order what you want," she says and huffs down the hall to her bedroom. "Your father called," she says over her shoulder. "He wanted to know if he could postpone your birthday dinner until next weekend. I figured you wouldn't mind since it's already a month past your birthday."

I guess we're both fighting dirty now.

After Italian takeout and her third glass of wine, Mom tries again. "What do you want out of life, Andrew?"

It's definitely her third glass of wine if we're getting into the open-ended existential-type questions. Hmmm, how to answer? To live in the same place for more than two years at a time? Friends who actually speak to me outside of school? A hand job by somebody other than myself? Somehow I know none of these answers are what she's looking for. "I don't know." She sighs. But I'm really not trying to be irritating at this point.

I just don't have the answers she's looking for. For someone who has worked for so long in education, she's really pretty dumb about kids.

"What did you want out of life when you were my age?"

I say it kind of quietly. I don't want her to think I'm being completely serious, but maybe I am.

"I wanted to go to college so I could get a good job and make my parents proud," she fires back at me with almost frightening automaticity.

Seriously Mom? I'm thinking. That's the best you can do? Did she not realize I was asking her a legitimate question? I know that Mom was the middle kid, and her older sister, Madeline, married a rich guy, lives like twenty minutes from their parents, and has this total high-class lifestyle. Uncle Kris kind of did the rebellious thing, so I guess Mom just got stuck in the middle. I know she likes her job. She likes being head of the school and all that. But I'm not just any screwup student. I'm *her* kid. She's staring at me now. Not in a mean way, but really staring, as if the intensity of her gaze is going to unlock my secrets. This is when I start to feel uncomfortable. What if she's right? What if there's something wrong with me because I don't have a college in mind or a career I'm planning for? What if I have some freak version of like mental mononucleosis, and I'm destined to be lazy for the rest of my life and like work in a Laundromat folding other people's underwear while making up weird stories about them and listening to my iPod? I really want to believe there's more than just Mom's version of how to be a successful human being. But I have no proof and so far no definable skills beyond what seems to be an above-average power of observation. If given a choice, I think I'd rather be living a semi-decent life than just hyperactively observing everyone else's.

I get up and start loading my plate into the dishwasher. I'm trying to ignore The Stare, which threatens to burn a hole in the back of my head. When I look up again she's pulled out her overstuffed weekly calendar, and she's flipping ahead, marking something down.

"Your Uncle Kris and Cousin Barry are coming for Thanksgiving," Mom says.

I let the fork fall from my hand into the sink. It clatters into the disposal. "What? Seriously? What about Mima's?"

"It's just one year, Andrew. We can go to Mima's next year. I really think Kris needs me to reach out."

Why? You'll spend the whole weekend doing work, and Kris and Barry will eat all our food, sit on the couch, and watch football. "Well, maybe I can go with Dad," I suggest. As soon as it's out of my mouth I wish I could suck it back. That kind of comment has to be carefully researched or else it elicits the pity look.

"I think your father has plans," Mom starts.

"Okay," I say quickly, hoping to stop her. I look down and intensify my search for the fork in the disposal.

"He's going to the Bahamas."

"Okay."

"With that fitness instructor of his."

"She's a physical therapist," I mumble.

"What?"

"Nothing." What's the point? Mom loves the idea that Dad is like this middle-aged cliché who drives a sports car and dates a younger woman. Truthfully, Dad's car isn't that nice and Melissa isn't that much younger than he is. But maybe it's easier for Mom to think that way.

***

Back in my room I flip briefly through my copy of *Romeo and Juliet*. Flirting with the idea of writing a killer essay that will

34

make Ms. Tuttle swoon, I turn on my laptop and open a new file. But then I check my e-mail a few times, nothing there, and surf Google Images for pictures of the Bahamas. It's way too early for most of the puny mountains around here to be making snow, but out of habit I check the ski and board report for upstate New York. My snowboard is hanging unloved and unridden in the garage. All those hours of raking leaves and shoveling sidewalks, just hanging there out of reach.

I love that release at the top of the trail where I surrender my momentum to gravity and whatever coordination of skills I can put together. My toes squish into the front of my boots and all my organs seem to press forward. Once I'm heading down the trail, I just move my body and react to whatever obstacles come my way. Skiing used to be something Mom and I actually liked to do together. But every time I bring it up, Mom just sighs and talks about how busy she is and wouldn't it be nice to have time for things like skiing.

I check a travel site for plane fares to Indiana, where Mima lives. Too late and too expensive. There's the bus, but the bus is smelly and full of weirdos. It's really a last-ditch option. I click back over to my Word document and stare at the blinking cursor for a while. Finally, I decide I'm too tired to start writing anything now, and I close the lid.

I can't fall asleep right away. I'm still kind of annoyed about Kris and Barry. I was looking forward to a few days off from school, although I really can't say why. Now I guess I'll look forward to Christmas, but that feels really far away. Maybe I'll see if Dad wants to take me *and* Melissa somewhere cool. Doubtful. But I close my eyes and think about a steep slope and two feet of fresh powder.

THANKSGIVING

"You know how I know you're gay?" Barry says.

I shrug, knowing there is no way to avoid the punch line.

"You go to an all-girls school," he says and barks out a short, choppy laugh, sending a round of Doritos splinters all over the front of his shirt.

"You know how I know you're gay?" I counter.

Barry looks uncomfortable. He's not used to me turning his favorite jokes back on him.

"Your name is Barry," I say and go back to what I'm writing.

Barry looks puzzled. "That doesn't even make any sense," he says. Without giving it too much more thought he launches into the next assault. "Hey, you know how I know you're gay?" He doesn't wait for a response. "You write in a diary!" He grins at me triumphantly. The orange Dorito dust encrusts the corners of his mouth. I should know better than to respond, but I do anyway.

"It's not a diary; it's a journal. And if you must know, it's an assignment for school." My face burns a little, even if it's only Barry.

Barry doesn't miss a beat. "You know why you're gay?"

he continues. "Cuz you're doing homework, and it's not even Sunday."

Now I'm just annoyed. It's not like I was even writing anything profound. I was mostly just doodling in the margin of a blank page just to avoid conversations like this one. "Wouldn't that just make me studious, diligent, fastidious, or even conscientious?"

Barry stares at me, his mouth hanging ever so slightly ajar. "Whatever, dude." He selects a particularly large Dorito chip from the bag and stuffs it in his mouth whole. The crunching noise seems to be his punctuation mark. He goes back to watching some rerun of *That '70s Show* on TV and leaves me alone for a little while.

Barry's dad is my mom's brother, Kris. My annoyance about their visit is twofold. For one thing, Barry is pretty much the bane of my existence. He's annoying, and he smells, and he seems to be pretty much incapable of having a conversation that strays beyond the following topics: classic rock bands, reality TV shows, boobs, and anything at all related to the playing or watching of ice hockey. There's only one of those subjects that I find remotely interesting, but hell if I'm going to talk about tits with my Neanderthal cousin. Besides, he probably wouldn't believe it and would use whatever I said as an excuse to ask me if I'm gay.

The real reason that Barry and Uncle Kris's visit is so annoying is that it supplanted one of my the few family rituals I actually like. Every Thanksgiving my mom and I visit my dad's mother at her assisted-living home in Indiana. My grandmother Mima is pretty much the coolest member of my family. She refers to my dad, who happens to be her son, as "the schmuck," even when Mom asks her not to.

"Why?" she'll say. "He is a schmuck." And then Mom will get all quiet and leave the apartment for a little while. When Mom gets pissed at Mima, I usually find her down by the pool. It's pretty much the best part of that place besides the food. The pool at Shady Acres is enclosed in this giant glass dome. It's all steamy and warm in there, almost like a greenhouse. It's like our own little tropical vacation.

I don't know if Mima gets too intense for Mom sometimes or if it's just that she knows she doesn't have a leg to stand on in that argument. I appreciate what she's trying to do. You know, protect some sainted image of my father in case he decides to show up again someday and attempt to have some kind of relationship with me. But it's a little hypocritical, considering that Mom does her fair share of Dad-bashing when we're at home. She's just a little more passive-aggressive about it. But really I just prefer the honesty; I mean, it's not like I haven't noticed that he's been pretty much AWOL for the past seven years. It's not like he's been off climbing Mount Everest or saving the children in Africa or in prison, for god's sake. He's the development director at a history museum. Which, when he's in a pissy mood, he describes as schmoozing people for money. When he's feeling good he gets all starry-eyed about "going back into the field someday." I'm really not sure what he's talking about. I mean, what field? I think this is just something he tells himself so he doesn't have to admit he hates his job.

It actually might be kind of cool if he were in prison. I wouldn't mind visiting him. It would be kind of interesting to visit someone in prison. I bet you could get a lot of those meals that come in partitioned trays. I used to love eating Lunchables, before Mom figured out they had the nutritional value of the cardboard they were packed in. That's the way the food comes at Mima's house. Every night we fill out this little card saying what we want for our meals for the next day, and then they deliver them, just like that. All you have to do is heat stuff up sometimes. I guess I kind of like things when they're neat and organized. Somehow I don't think that's the kind of mind-blowing revelation that Ms. Tuttle is looking for.

It would really annoy me if anyone read this and thought that I was a bad student because I'm lacking a male role model in my life. Because I really don't think that's the case.

Having two parents is kind of an outdated model family at this point in the twenty-first century. In fact, most of the kids I know live with one parent or the other, or are part of some kind of blended family. They used that term in our eighth-grade health class back in public school. It's kind of a nice way of labeling a whole bunch of people who don't necessarily want to be family but are forced to think of themselves that way. The term always made me think about putting a family in a food processor and chopping it up until the parts were even and indistinguishable from one another. Which, frankly, doesn't sound all that great to me.

Mom and Dad and I aren't really part of any blended family. We're just like three extra ingredients that ended up in the world. We don't belong to anyone else, and we barely belong to each other anymore. Back when my parents first split up, Mom and I lived with her parents while she figured things out. That wasn't so bad. Norma (my mom's parents wanted to be called by their first names) used to take me on outings to the Boston Museum of Fine Arts, which I nicknamed the Boring Museum for Adults, or to see a youth concert at Symphony Hall. The latter were a little better since she usually brought candy in her purse. Plus there were naked statues. It wasn't ideal, as far as entertainment goes, but it felt good to be part of something a little bigger than just me and Mom, or me and Dad at his condo in New York City.

I used to spend half the time with Dad at his condo. But then we moved to Boston and getting back and forth became more and more of an issue, so I just stopped seeing him as much. I kept waiting for him to make it an issue with Mom—you know, that he was being denied his parental rights or whatever—but he never did.

I overheard them on the phone once. Well, I overheard Mom's end, anyway. I could tell she was complaining about his lack of involvement with me because she was saying "he" and "his" with extra emphasis combined with phrases like *schoolwork* and *Boy Scouts* Then I could tell he was arguing with her because she said, "Well, I'd like to have some time to find myself too, David, but some of us are busy raising a child."

I never thought about myself that way before—like somebody's burden. I just figured that parents felt about kids the way they do on TV: like they were the best thing that ever happened to them. Wasn't it your responsibility to sort all that "who am I" crap out before you had kids? I don't know how they can expect me to have the kind of answers that they don't even have when they've got like twenty-five years on me.

I was never a very loud or needy person, I'm pretty sure of that. But after I heard that conversation, I made an even bigger effort to lie low and stay out of Mom's way. It was weird. I expected her to notice and react one of two ways. I thought she would compliment me on what an easy kid I was to raise, or I thought she would say something about how she missed spending time together. But she never said anything. So I just kind of kept on disappearing little by little. And it was never really a big deal until I started messing up in school. And even then, Mom's never really put two and two together.

THANKSGIVING PART 2

Barry and Uncle Kris have been here for approximately twenty-eight hours and forty minutes. I don't know how much more I can take. Tonight Uncle Kris came into my room while Barry was brushing his teeth. Barry gets my bed while he's visiting, and I sleep on this pull-out futon on the other side of the room. Kris sleeps on the couch in the living room. Personally, I think if we're going to have a strict policy here, that Mom should give up her bed for Kris and take the couch, seeing how they're brother and sister and Barry and I are only cousins.

I can tell by the look on his face that Kris wants to have some kind of heart-to-heart with me. "Barr Barr is really kind of a sensitive guy, Andrew," Kris begins. "And when you put him down it really kind of bums him out. So if you could try and go easy on him this weekend, I'd appreciate it. He's in a lot of pain."

I want to scream, "Are you serious? Are we talking about the same kid here? The one who just spent the last six hours telling me how and why I'm gay?" But I just nod and say, "Sure." It seems to be the quickest and easiest way out of the conversation.

Uncle Kris has always been a little deluded when it comes to his progeny. He used to get all excited and proud when Barry would rip a good one, like Barry's flatulence is some kind of proof of his masculinity. But then at the same time he expects the kid to memorize Shakespeare or have like this deep emotional side. I just don't see it.

Mom did mention something about Aunt Allison not showing up for Thanksgiving. I just figured she was still pissed off at Mom for making fun of Martha Stewart at their house a couple years ago. It turns out that Aunt Allison is on a cruise with some of her girlfriends and made the conscious choice to avoid all of us on this holiday, including Barry and Kris.

The last time Barry and Kris were at our house for Thanksgiving, Allison was with them. Mima came out from Indiana and even Dad was there. It was right after the divorce was finalized; Dad had his new place in the city, and Mom and I were back at our house. I guess they thought it would be less jarring to try and celebrate the holiday all together, but the whole thing was forced and awkward. Mima was staying with us, and Dad was staying in a hotel.

I got up early on that Thanksgiving morning to go swim in the heated pool while Dad slept in one of the plastic chaise lounge chairs, the newspaper covering his face and his hangover. I remember being worried about leaving my cat alone in the house with Barry. Merlin had recently had surgery to remove a fatty deposit from his leg. He was loopy from the pain medicine and kept bashing the plastic cone he was wearing to prevent him from pulling out his stitches into the furniture. Every time he crashed into, something Barry would laugh hysterically and say, "Hey, Andrew, even your cat is retarded."

We ate dinner early because Dad said he had to get back for a work thing. Mom was extra irritable because she was only on her second glass of wine. Aunt Allison had made these candle holders out of cut-up magazines and seashells collaged onto paper towel rolls. Whatever she used to glue them together must have been flammable, because when she went to light the candles, the whole thing went up in a ball of flame.

Barry burst into hysterics; meanwhile, Kris was waving his hands, trying to put out the flames but only fanning them further. Under the table, Merlin was yowling and bumping his cone into the table legs. Finally Dad leaned forward and blew really hard on them, which put out the flame but sent a spattering of hot wax all over Mom's turkey. So Mom was pissed, and Aunt Allison was pissed, and everyone had to pick little wax blobs off their turkey.

It didn't get any better from there. After Mom had her third glass of wine, she started talking about food prices and how expensive everything was getting. She and Aunt Allison got on a rant about how much kids cost, all of which, I knew, was a semi-veiled attack on Dad because Mom and Allison never agreed on anything. Then Dad said, "Great, Nancy, why don't you make him feel even better about his existence?" At which point Mom told him not to put me in the middle of things, even though she kind of already had.

***

Later that afternoon, while Kris and Barry snored off their pie and ice cream on our couch in front of a football game, I caught Dad trying to sneak out unnoticed. "Where are you going?" I asked as he slung his travel bag and briefcase into the passenger seat of the Volvo.

"I'm sorry, Andrew, but I've got to get out of here. Your mother is making this impossible for me."

"She doesn't seem that happy either," I mumbled lamely.

"Yeah, this was a dumb idea," Dad said. I guess he was interpreting my comment as agreement. *Anyway, what was a dumb idea? Having Thanksgiving together? Or having a kid together?*

That afternoon I played card games with Mima and lost every one, even though I could tell she was going out of her way to let me win. "No offense to your mother, Andrew," Mima said. "But this is a drag. Next year the two of you should come out and see me instead."

"But what about Dad?"

"He can come if he wants to," Mima said. "But I have a feeling he'll be busy."

PART TWO

THE
CONDITIONAL

RUNNING AWAY

I didn't intend to run away. I just threw some stuff in my backpack and started walking. I guess I intended to make a statement. My face is still burning, and the whole way down Evergreen Street I keep glancing over my shoulder, looking for Mom's car. But it never comes. This just pisses me off more, and I walk faster. I had figured on Kris and Barry wanting to do turkey and all that, but I had forgotten about football. After the third game in a row, I felt the yellow and white lines swimming in front of my eyes. Every time I got up to do something else, Mom would shoot me that look like I was deserting the family.

Finally I managed to ignore her death stare and I found refuge in my bedroom. I pulled out one of the books on colleges that Dad sent me as a means of communicating about my future. I figured now was that moment when there was absolutely nothing else I would rather be doing. I flopped down on my bed, brushing aside Barry's dirty T-shirt and boxer shorts. It was wet.

"Jesus Christ!" I screamed and hopped up off the soggy sheets. I stuck my head out in the hall. "Barry!" I yelled. "You freakin' slob, what the hell did you spill on my bed?"

Barry didn't even look away from the football game. Kris shot my mother a distraught glance, and before I could say anything else she was dragging me back into the room by my sleeve.

"Your cousin Barry is going through a very rough time right now, Andrew, and I need you to be a little more compassionate."

"Fine," I said exasperated. "But does he have to be such a slob? Why does going through a rough time give you the right to dump soda or whatever on somebody else's bed?"

My mother glared at me. "I don't think it's soda, Andrew."

It took me a minute to figure out what she meant. "WHAT?! He pissed the bedmmph?" Mom thrust her hand over my mouth before I could get the words out and dragged me into her office "That's disgusting," I said. "And why didn't he say anything?"

"I don't know, Andrew. He's probably mortified. Kris says he's been having a lot of trouble at school with kids picking on him."

It didn't really fit with my ideas about Barry. I guess I just figured, from the way he talked about girls and hockey, that he had friends. He seemed to me like someone who would fit in pretty well. But what do I know about fitting in?

Mom went over to the bed and pulled off the comforter and the sheets. "It's not that big a deal, Andrew. You did it when you were little. It's mostly water anyway."

I looked at the wet mark on my mattress. It vaguely resembled the mitten-shaped state of Michigan. "Easy for you to say," I said. "You're not the one sleeping in piss."

"*Compassion*, Andrew," she said as she went through the door, carrying the bundle of soggy sheets to the laundry room.

Sullenly I walked back into the living room, where Kris

and Barry were transfixed by the men moving on the screen. I even felt a little bit bad for Barry. Until he opened his mouth again.

"Hey," he said without glancing away from the screen. "You know how I know you're gay?" I couldn't believe he was starting in on this shit again. "You don't like football," he said, and then he choked on a swallow of soda so it came out his nose.

"Come on Barr Barr," Uncle Kris said, still staring right at the game. "Don't make a mess."

A MESS? I wanted to scream. *How about the mess you already made in my bed?* I stormed back down the hall and into my room. That was when I packed my bag.

I dumped out my backpack onto the bare mattress, careful to avoid the wet spot. I had brought home most of my textbooks in an effort to impress upon Mom my interest in improving my grades. I scooped up all the books and loose papers and looked around the room for somewhere to put them. I used my big toe to nudge my desk chair away from the desk and dumped the pile there. When I pushed the chair back in, you could hardly see the stack. As an afterthought I went back and grabbed the notebook I'd been doodling in and my copy of *Into the Wild*.

Into the backpack went a couple changes of clothes, some clean underwear, my toothbrush, and my extra glasses. I grabbed all the cash I had, which wasn't much, and the emergency credit card Mom gave me but told me never to use. I also had a check from Mrs. Grindle down the street, who'd paid me for raking her leaves the last two Saturdays. It wasn't much, but I figured it was enough to get me a bus ticket to Indiana. If I had to use the credit card, that wasn't a big deal. It wasn't like I was trying to hide where I was going. I planned to call Mom and tell her where I was—just not until it was too late for me to turn back.

When I turn the corner of Evergreen Street and Washington Avenue, it really kind of hits me. No one is coming to stop me. I'm really leaving town on my own. The bus station is on the far end of Washington, and even though there's a public bus that runs along Washington, I'm pretty sure it doesn't run often on holidays so I just keep walking. It feels good to walk. I'm kind of afraid if I stop walking to wait for the bus I might lose my momentum all together.

I keep trying to rationalize my escape in my head as I walk. Going to Mima's isn't such a big deal. I'll be back in a few days, and Kris and Barry will be gone. Mom will be pissed, sure, but she'll get over it, or at least forget about it when the first post-holiday crisis erupts at school. I'll just have to fly under her radar for a little while, which is what I do most of the time anyways.

***

The Glens Falls bus station is really just a holding room with uncomfortable plastic chairs, bad fluorescent lighting, and a few snack machines. Mom and I spent some time here waiting for Mima's bus the last time she came out. There's not even a real public bathroom. If you want to use the bathroom, you have to ask for a key and then they buzz you back into this other room that's like a break room for the employees.

It's pretty quiet, even for a holiday. There are just a few people in the seats waiting for the bus: an old lady with an enormous pink scarf wrapped and rewrapped around her head, and a fidgety guy wearing a mechanic's uniform and tapping on his leg with a rolled-up newspaper.

In the corner there's a group of kids who look about my age. They're kind of clumped up, sitting on their sleeping bags and backpacks even though there are plenty of chairs free.

The man behind the glass at the bus station window has mahogany skin flecked with lighter brown birthmarks. He has a double chin and a couple rolls where the base of his skull meets his neck. He's eating a tuna fish sandwich; I can smell it through the glass, and he has a tiny bit of mayo smeared on his upper lip. His eyes are glued to a tiny color TV and what looks to me like a Mexican soap opera.

"Can I help you?" he says, still watching his show.

"Yeah," I say nervously, "I need a ticket to Bloomington," I pause, "Indiana."

"Can't do it," he says. My heart sinks a little bit. "Furthest I can get you tonight is Cleveland. Bus leaves in an hour. You can catch the first bus to Bloomington in the morning."

"That's fine," I say, relieved that there is a bus at all. "I'll take a ticket, round-trip, I guess."

For the first time the man looks up at me. He takes a bite of his tuna sandwich and chews it carefully as though considering both. "How old are you?" he asks.

"Sixteen," I answer, too quickly to lie.

"Your parents know where you are?"

"Of course they do, silly!" A girl has suddenly appeared beside me and links her arm through mine. She's much shorter than I am and has short, spiky black hair and an upturned nose with a little bump on the bridge. She reaches up and ruffles my hair.

"Please don't do that," I say.

She ignores me and looks up at me with dark brown eyes. "You don't think we'd let him get on the bus all alone, do you?" She smiles winningly at the man behind the counter, who looks as confused as I do. "Mom's in the car." She holds her hand up to her head mimicking a phone and tosses her head back and forth in fake conversation. "On the phone again. She wants you to come out and say good-bye once you get your ticket."

I nod bewildered. "Okay?"

"Okay," she says and pinches my cheek the way the old ladies at Mima's place always like to do. I pull away, annoyed. She smiles, winks at the man behind the counter, and saunters away.

This bizarre display is enough to convince the man behind the counter to print out the ticket. I push sixty-four dollars underneath the glass partition and get back a bus ticket and thirty cents in change. This, along with a few crumpled dollar bills, will have to last me until Mima's.

I have an hour to kill until the bus leaves, so I pick a chair in the corner near one of the snack machines and settle in to wait. I pull my copy of *Into the Wild* out of my backpack and open up to the page where I left off. But I'm not reading. I'm watching the bus-ticket girl and her friends in the corner.

THE FREEGANS

There are five of them hunkered down in the corner of the bus station, sitting on backpacks and rolled-up sleeping bags. In addition to the bus-ticket girl, there's another girl with long blonde dreadlocks facing away and lying across the lap of a kid wearing an army vest with an enormous anarchy symbol drawn on the back. An Asian-looking kid wearing a giant pair of headphones over his fauxhawk is talking too loudly to a tall guy with a short, scraggly beard as he makes peanut butter sandwiches.

My stomach growls as I watch him dip a pocket knife into this jar of peanut butter and then drip gobs of it onto the bread. Every once in a while he stops to lick the excess off the top of the knife where it swivels and folds in. I ignore the obvious hygienic problems here as I watch him distribute the sandwiches. He's sitting cross-legged as he does this—a way I've only ever seen girls sit. He's also smiling so sweetly—like one of those naked babies that fly around in those giant Italian paintings. He just keeps smiling and handing out sandwiches. I'm so busy watching him that I don't notice when the bus-ticket girl reappears at my side.

She slams herself down into the seat next to me, rocking

the entire row of interconnected plastic chairs. She has two sandwiches in her hands.

"You want one?" Her voice is deeper and scratchier than before.

I shake my head. "No, thanks, I just ate at home."

"Okay," she says, almost smirking. "Suit yourself. I just know that when I first ran away, I learned pretty quickly that you should take food whenever it's offered. You don't know where your next meal is coming from."

"I thought I wasn't supposed to take candy from strangers."

She gives an appreciative chin nod and takes a bite of her sandwich. "Good one. How about a puppy?"

"Anyway," I say, "I'm not running away."

"Sure, traveling alone on Thanksgiving is just more convenient and hassle-free because everyone else is sitting down and eating with their families. Plus there's nothing more pleasant than an empty bus station on a cold night. I get it."

I ignore her sarcasm. "It was a last-minute decision . . . to go to my grandmother's house."

"Does anyone know where you are?" she lifts the softened paper American Airlines tag still looped around my backpack strap, left over from Mom's and my last trip to see Mima, and reads it. "Andrew?"

I shake my head again. What was the point in lying?

"Then you, my friend," she says as she jerks the tag off the strap and crumples it in her hand, "are running away."

She shoots the crumpled tag at the nearest waste can. "You're old enough that most people won't bother you about being on your own. But until you get where you're going, it's better to avoid being identified if you don't want to be. If you don't give the police or anyone your name, the worst they can do is throw you into state or foster care. And that sucks, but it's not that hard to get out of."

"Your area of expertise?"

"It used to be." Her voice hardens slightly. "I'm nineteen now, so I'm pretty much free to go wherever I want and do whatever I want. I'm G, by the way," she says and sticks her hand out for me to shake.

"Andrew," I say as I accept her firm handshake. She's small but solid. And I can't decide if she's pretty or not. She's not unattractive, but there's something about her looks that's kind of serious, almost severe. "Just G?"

"Yeah, Maria Regina actually. It's terrible isn't it? Sounds like a nun or a pasta sauce. So I'm just G. What about you? Do you go by Andrew? Andy? Drew?"

"It doesn't matter, whatever is fine."

"What do you mean it doesn't matter?"

"I really don't care." And it's true. Well, up until this moment it's always been true. Andrew, Andy, Drew, whatever. It's all the same to me. Moving so many times, I kind of got to the point where it was enough if someone remembered the basic gist of my name.

"Whoa. This is your name we're talking about here, not the condiments you put on a sandwich. This is how people greet you in the world. How they form their first impressions of you. How they decide if they're going to walk all over you or not."

I just shrug the way I always do when I want uncomfortable conversations to end. But G isn't going to let me off the hook that easily.

"Okay," she says. "We're going to decide this right now. I'm going to introduce myself to you again, and whatever you say this time, that's your name. Okay? I'm G," she repeats and sticks out her hand.

"Andrew," I say and shake it again. She seems satisfied with this.

"Good. Drew's okay, but Andy's a little weird. It always reminds me of those dolls. Remember Raggedy Ann and Raggedy Andy?" I don't really, so I just shrug my shoulders again.

Over in the corner, the girl with the long blonde dreadlocks gets up from the floor and walks out of the bus station. She comes back carrying an enormous Hula-Hoop covered in black and white stripes.

She sets the Hula-Hoop down and proceeds to remove several layers of clothing. Off comes a rather large, black hooded sweatshirt. Underneath is a brown cardigan sweater that Mima might wear. That sweater comes off and underneath that is a smaller sweater; that only comes halfway down her stomach. She's wearing a short skirt, like the field hockey girls wear, a pair of red-and-white-striped tights, and black combat boots.

Altogether she looks like a grungy version of Pippi Longstocking. G and I watch as she picks up the Hula-Hoop and begins to swing it around her stomach. Everyone in the bus station is staring as she gets the thing going faster and faster. It's hard not to. Even the guy behind the glass is temporarily distracted from his show. He looks like he's trying to think of a reason to tell her to stop but can't come up with one. This girl has the most amazing stomach muscles I've ever seen, not that I'm an expert. I try not to stare at her midsection but it's next to impossible. I focus instead on her face, her brow furrowed in concentration. Her eyes are focused on the floor and the spinning hoop on her hips. Underneath her dreadlocks, which I've always thought were pretty tacky and gross on white people, she's really pretty. She has sharp cheekbones and perfectly shaped pink lips. She's like a hot girl in disguise!

"That's Emily," says G, sounding a little annoyed. "I guess she's just practicing. It's not like we're going to make anything here."

"Is that what you do?" I ask without ever taking my eyes off Emily and her undulating midsection.

"Sort of. That's Lyle over there," she points at the boy with the anarchy vest. He has light brown hair that looks like it's on the verge of thinning and enormous sideburns as if to compensate. "He and I do a trapeze and ropes act. Jesse made these." She holds up the peanut butter sandwiches and offers me one again. This time I take it and bite into the squishy wheat bread. The peanut butter sticks to the roof of my mouth, and I shovel it off with my tongue. Jesse's hands are stretched over his head, and the sole of one foot is pressed into the opposite leg in what looks like some kind of yoga pose. "Jesse's kind of like the MC. He's a storyteller. He's just kind of got a way with the audience. You'll see what I mean."

I cock my head to the side, wondering if they're actually going to perform here in the bus station. With my mouth full of peanut butter I gesture at the ruddy-cheeked Asian kid in the headphones.

"That's Tim Lin. He's kind of new. So far he's just along for the ride. He's been recording us for some college project he's doing. He seems all right. And you're pretty much seeing what Emily can do." There's that hint of annoyance again.

Emily has the hoop up around her neck. Her dreadlocks are flying out in back of her like a janitor's mop. She wiggles a little bit, and the hoop drops down over her shoulder and out onto one arm. She keeps it going there for a little while, but then grabs it suddenly and stops. She sets the hoop down next to Lyle and grabs a sandwich, which she rips into two uneven chunks. With part of the sandwich in her hand, she walks over to me and G. Yup, she's a hot girl all right; she even eats with confidence.

I sit up in my chair and brush the crumbs off the front of my jacket.

"Hi," says Emily. She squats down in front of us, balancing with one hand on my knee and one hand on G's knee. A girl has never touched my knee like that before—intentionally, I mean. Her nails have chipped purple polish on them. I try really hard not to notice that her tights are the kind that stop at mid-thigh. Maybe that makes them socks? I'm no expert. "I'm Emily," she says, grinning in my direction. There is a smudge of peanut butter on her teeth, and she has a single freckle exactly above the middle of her top lip.

"This is Andrew," G says, but I can hardly hear her over the crackle of electricity that seems to be coming from the place where her hand touches my leg.

"So is he coming with us or what?" Emily asks.

G rolls her eyes. "I hadn't really gotten that far."

"Come with you where?" I say, my heart suddenly racing.

Emily takes her hand off G's knee and crosses her arms, leaning forward on both my knees. I can see straight down the front of her shirt. I stare up at her eyes. I try really hard to stare at her eyes. They are warm and blue. "You should come with us, Andrew. It's going to be crazy, a crazy good time."

If my phone hadn't rung at exactly that second, I think I probably would have gotten up and gone wherever with Emily. But the buzzing in my pocket breaks the spell.

I look at the phone. It's Mom. "I should take this," I say, but Emily doesn't move. "I gotta stand up." I move to get on my feet. She hops back gracefully and walks back over to the others. I shake my head clear and answer the phone.

"Hi, Mom."

"Andrew, where the hell are you?"

"Yeah, about that. I needed to leave." I look at my watch and calculate the time it would take her to get out of the house and drive to the bus station. It's not quite long enough to tell her where I am.

"Andrew, you didn't answer my question. Kris and Barry and I were about to sit down to dinner. I sent Barry to get you in your room, but you were gone. Now where the hell are you? This is incredibly rude and awkward for me, Andrew."

"As rude and awkward as someone pissing in your bed? Or telling you every five minutes that you're gay?" I walk a little farther away so that G and Emily can't hear every word of our conversation.

"Look, Andrew." Mom's tone is conciliatory now, but I've heard her talk to enough parents on the phone to know an act when I hear one. "I know this has been a difficult weekend for you. I know Barry is not exactly your cup of tea." I resist the urge to shout *More like a cup of pee*. "But this is family time. So I need you to tell me where you are so I can come get you."

I want to ask her about family; about how much she even likes her so-called family; about what even makes us family anymore. But I'm not going to get into it now. "I know it's family time, Mom. That's why I left." I take a deep breath. "I'm going to Mima's. I'm on the bus," I improvise.

"You're on a bus?" she says quietly. This is surprising. I'm expecting more of a freak-out.

"Yes."

"How did you get on a bus?"

"I walked to the bus station and got on a bus."

"To Bloomington?"

"To Cleveland, actually. But I'll get the first bus to Bloomington in the morning."

There is a long silence before she speaks. "Oh, sweetie," she said. "You can't go to Mima's"

"I'm going, Mom. I'm already on my way."

"Oh shit, Andrew, I'm so sorry. I don't know how to tell you this, sweetie. Mima's dead."

THE REFUND

No one close to me has ever died before, so I'm not sure how to react. When people in the movies die, their loved ones always cry and scream and roll around on the floor. But the only thing I'm aware of is that my feet start to sweat, like really sweat. In fact, my whole body seems to go up about a hundred degrees. Holding the cell phone in one hand, I wriggle out of my jacket and toss it on the chairs in back of me.

"She's *what?*" I finally say.

"Andrew, please tell me where you are. I don't want to explain this over the phone."

"Well maybe you should have thought about that earlier? Besides, I told you, Mom. I'm on a bus to Cleveland. I can't see any road signs because it's dark outside. If I had to guess I would say we're somewhere outside Utica. Now please tell me what happened to Mima?" My voice breaks a little.

"She had a stroke, Andrew. She died peacefully in her sleep."

"When?"

"Tuesday."

"You've known since Tuesday, and you didn't tell me? I don't understand. What were you waiting for?"

"Andrew, I screwed up here and I'm so sorry," Mom begins. "It was the day before vacation, and you know how that is at school—"

I cut her off. "You were busy? You couldn't tell me about Mima because you were busy?" My voice is getting higher and louder, but I don't care. "And what about Wednesday? Or sometime today perhaps? You were just too damn busy to tell me that my grandmother died?"

"I know, Andrew. You're right, you have every right to be upset. But honestly, I was hoping your father was going to call you. I thought you should really hear it from him. I loved Mima very much, but she wasn't my mother. Part of me didn't think it was my place to tell you."

Her voice is sad and small. But whatever honesty is coming through is eclipsed by my rage that she is bringing her beef with Dad into this. "That's just perfect," I hiss. "Blame him for this—and everything else—why don't you? His mother just died. He's probably making funeral arrangements and calling people, and he's grieving. He's probably in shock or something."

"He's in the Bahamas." Her voice is flat. "He called me from Nassau, from the hotel. He asked me to tell you. He asked me to tell you that the funeral will be postponed until he gets back from his vacation."

I hear the words. I hear "Nassau" and "Bahamas" and "hotel." Each one stacked up on the other. Stacked up on my eyelids like cinderblocks trying to squeeze the hot tears out of my head. Mima is lying cold and alone on a tray in some morgue somewhere while her only son cavorts on a beach with his girlfriend.

"Really shitty," I finally say, when I think I can speak without crying.

"I know, sweetie. I really thought he would call you himself."

The rage boils up in my gut again. "No, Mom," I say between clenched teeth. "The both of you are really shitty. So thanks, thanks for being two shitty parents." I hang up without another word. I walk back over to my seat and collapse into it. Emily has wandered off, but G is still sitting there, looking concerned.

She doesn't say anything for a while. She just sits there, which is okay. I don't want to talk about it, but I don't exactly want to be left alone. And somehow even the presence of someone I barely know is still comforting. After a few minutes my body temperature returns to normal and I can take a full breath without whistling through my teeth.

"So what are you going to do?" G asks a few minutes later.

"I don't know." I don't really want to go to Cleveland only to have to turn around and take the bus back again. But without Mima, there really isn't anything for me in the Midwest. The thought of waiting here for Mom to come pick me makes the blood beat in my ears and my stomach churn. I don't really see what other choice I have. I flip open my phone to call her back, and that's when it hits me. Barry and Kris are still there.

I know I can probably suck it up and forgive my mother for yet another botched episode of parenting. But having to share my grief over Mima with Kris and his troglodyte bed-wetting son—that just isn't an option. I can just picture Kris actually wanting to talk about Mima and how I *feel* about the whole thing. I flip the phone closed again and stare at the digital time display, hoping for some answers.

"You should come with us," G says.

"Where?"

"Rochester, or maybe Syracuse. Well, that's for tonight anyway. We'll be able to make some money there tomorrow and then we'll head south."

"What's south?"

"Burdock," G says. "It's a big festival in New Mexico for people like us."

"Street performers?"

"Sort of."

At this moment I have no intention of going anywhere with G or her strange friends. But the conversation is a good distraction. "So if the money's so good in Syracuse, what are you guys doing hanging out in the Glens Falls bus station?" For the first time in our conversation G looks a little bit uncomfortable.

"We're broke," she says simply. But I can tell she hates saying it. Her face is flat, tough, like she's waiting for someone else to throw the first punch. She sighs. "We had a pretty good thing going in Burlington for a while. But it's a small town, and pretty soon the police were on us every time we tried to set up. You can get a license to perform there, but it wasn't worth the money. Anyway, we stayed at a friend of Jesse's place for about a week, camping in the backyard, but I guess they got kinda sick of us coming in and out to use the bathroom and all. So now we're here. The gas light came on about fifteen miles north of here, and it seemed like this was the first decent-sized town for a while so we decided to stop. Obviously it's pretty bad timing, being Thanksgiving and all. But don't worry," she adds. "We'll figure something out in the morning. We always do."

I look down at the bus ticket in my hand. I don't need it anymore. I don't even really need the sixty-three dollars. It feels like what Mima would have wanted me to do. She liked people with a sense of adventure. "You should take this," I say and hand the ticket to G. "They'll give you a refund, and you guys can use it for gas."

"We can't take your money."

I look at her skeptically. "Yes you can. I mean isn't that the point?"

"We *earn* our money," she says indignantly. "Look, you should come with us and then it's an exchange. You give us gas money, and we provide a vehicle for a weekend of parent-free rebellion. When you're ready to go home, we'll drop you at the nearest bus station and you can call your mom. I'm sure she'll send you money for a ticket. You look pretty well taken care of. Unless of course I'm wrong and you're ready to go home right now."

There's something in the way she looks me up and down. Like she knows my whole life. I'm not sure whether to be offended by her judgment or follow her to find out what she knows that I don't know. But I do know I'm not ready to ride home next to Mom like a chastened fourth-grader who made some bad choice out of the cartoon frog book. I'm not. But am I really ready to just head off with these people, three of whom I haven't even met yet? G stands up and I stand up next to her.

"Okay," I say, moving quickly before I can think this through any further.

"Okay, then. Let's go cash that ticket in."

THE BUS

G goes up to the ticket counter with me and uses the same "talking to adults" voice that worked with the man behind the counter before. I don't even really know what she says to him this time. I'm not really listening because my mind is jumping back and forth from fury at Mom, to sadness about Mima, and the whole time there is a high-pitched buzzing noise in my ears, like suddenly I can hear the hum of fluorescent lights above everything else. Whatever she says, it works, and pretty soon I have sixty-three dollars back in my hand and the man behind the counter goes back to his soap opera. With my money and my backpack in hand, I follow G over to meet the rest of her friends.

I have low expectations. I've been the new student four different times at four different schools, and meeting new people just never seems to go that well. The school I was at before St. Mary's was a public middle school On the first day of seventh grade I wore this black T-shirt with some band logo on it. It was Fall Out Boy or something—I don't even remember. But somehow this rumor got started that I was a goth. Later that week I got dragged into the guidance counselor's office for a talk about how my personal appearance could be off-putting to others. He asked me a lot of questions about whether I thought about death a lot or hurting myself or others. It sounded to me like he was reading out of a manual on how to talk to kids. I managed to convince him that I was not a danger to myself or others, but somehow the goth label stuck. I didn't have many friends at that school either.

Meeting G's friends is different. For one thing, they all shake my hand like adults. Jesse, the guy who made the peanut butter sandwiches, stands up, smiles, and looks me in the eyes like he's really genuinely happy to meet me. His eyes are a deep blue and seem like they're also smiling, if that's even possible. He's wearing a velvety-looking shirt that just barely meets the waistband of his pants: purple corduroys with a stripe of multi-colored patches going down the outside of his leg. Lyle, the kid with the anarchist vest, hops up and shakes my hand too, but he isn't quite as friendly. The Asian kid wearing the headphones doesn't get up. He pulls the headphones down around his neck and holds his hand up from his place on the floor.

"Tim's always like that," G says.

"Like what?" I ask.

"Lazy."

"Hey," Tim says from down on the floor, "It's a medical condition." He pulls somewhat self-consciously at his sweatshirt so it's not so snug around his stomach pudge.

G smiles. "No adrenaline," she explains. "*He claims* his body doesn't make it so he has to take medication to substitute. I like to give him crap about it though." I nod, wondering if I'm being put on. "And you already met Emily," G says, gesturing down at the dreadlocked girl, who is perched cross-legged on one of the duffel bags. Emily is swaying back and forth as though she's listening to music that no one else can hear. She gives a little wave, and a smile that makes my stomach flip-flop, without interrupting her rhythm.

"So, Andrew," Jesse says, "I hear you're going to be joining us on our magical mystery tour?" He smiles at me again like I'm a fuzzy kitten or a big-eyed puppy.

"Uh, yeah, I guess I am." Is this guy messing with me? Or is he on something? I guess if I were broke I'd be psyched to see sixty bucks walk through the door in any form. But his eyes are clear and his smile seems genuine.

Jesse stretches his arms over his head; his already short shirt rides up and reveals a hairy belly. "Well, gang, what do you say? Should we hit it? Andrew here is going to front us some cash until we get to the next big thing."

I smile an awkward, closed-lip smile, swing my backpack over one shoulder, and follow as Tim, Emily, Lyle, and G gather up their belongings and traipse out of the bus station. I focus hard on putting one foot in front of the other while ignoring the voice in my head that's screaming at me to reconsider.

Out in the parking lot Jesse stands next to an old orange VW camper van. "This is Shirley," he says proudly.

"Hi, Shirley," I say.

Jesse grins and runs around to unlock the driver's door. "You buy, you fly, man. You want to ride shotgun?"

"It doesn't matter." Being an only child, I never really fought with anyone over that kind of stuff. But Jesse looks a little disappointed by my indifference. "I mean, sure, if you don't think anyone would mind."

"No way, man; it's all yours," he says.

I open the passenger-side door and climb inside, sticking

my backpack at my feet. Shirley's mustard-yellow seats are cracked and patched with duct tape. The van smells like spices. Cinnamon and garlic powder were the two that I could identify. The rest just melds into a funk that drifts somewhere between pumpkin pie and bad body odor.

The remaining bags and people sort themselves out behind me, and then the metal door slides shut with a resounding thud. I'm still trying to ignore the part of my brain shouting for a reassessment of my decision-making process. It reminds me of bungee jumping, which I did at camp the summer we lived with Mom's parents. I didn't even really want to, but Norma said it was what everyone did in the summertime. Anyway, once you got up on the platform, wearing the harness and the helmet and all that, there really wasn't any other choice but to jump.

Jesse turns the key and the van starts on the first try. Everyone else bursts into applause.

"It's tradition," G shouts from the back of the bus.

Behind the driver's seat is a small sink filled with bags of bulk macaroni, rice, and a gravelly-looking grain I don't recognize. There are smaller bags of spices, boxes of instant oatmeal and instant mashed potatoes, some darkening bananas, and the bread and peanut butter from the bus station. Underneath the sink is a wood-paneled cabinet, which is overflowing with more foodstuff.

The sink is the only sign that the bus was once a camper. All the other seats have been removed, and G, Lyle, Emily, and Tim are sprawled or sitting cross-legged on the floor of the van. The back of the van is packed with duffels, tote bags, and sleeping bags. There are a few garbage bags bulging with clothes. These items form a wall that prevents the driver, or anyone else, from seeing out the back of the van. I'm glad to be sitting up front, strapped safely into the passenger seat.

We stop at the Irving station on the outskirts of town—the only thing we pass that's open. I wait uneasily for Jesse to pump the gas—eager to be moving again. When we're stopped I start to think about Mom sitting at home waiting for my call—or, more likely, frantically dialing and redialing my cell phone, which I have since turned off.

I hand Jesse the money so he can pay for the gas. When he gets back in the van he gives me that strangely sincere smile again, and then we are off.

In the back of the van, everyone is settling in to what seems to be a familiar routine. Lyle is wearing a headlamp and reading a small paperback of *1984*. Emily is wearing Tim's headphones, and G is shuffling a deck of cards. Suddenly I feel a moment of panic, and out of nowhere I shout, "I don't do drugs!"

Lyle looks up from his book an amused smile on his face. G is grinning too. Emily pulls off her headphones and says, "What?"

"He doesn't do drugs," Tim repeats.

Emily looks confused. She shrugs her shoulders and puts the headphones back on.

"Neither do we," G explains. "We're all straight edge." She twists around and lifts up her short black hair so I can see the black *X* tattooed on the back of her neck. "Do you know what it means?" she asks.

"Kind of," I lie.

"I don't think they have straight edge in Glens Falls," Lyle says. He has a way of punctuating all this sentences with a condescending smile that's half a smirk.

"It's a commitment," G says, ignoring him. "No drugs, no booze, no cigarettes. Clean living, pure and simple. We're also vegetarians."

"Or vegans," Emily shouts loudly, her ears buffered by the headphones.

Lyle reaches over and pulls one of the ear covers away from her ears. "You're shouting," he says.

"Oh, sorry," Emily says. She smiles sweetly and lies down with her head in his lap. Lyle picks up his book again and begins to gently rub her back.

"You want to find some tunes, Andrew?" Jesse asks.

"Sure." I lean forward to adjust the buttons on Shirley's radio. The van is old. The buttons for the radio are the kind that you push in and the needle slides over to find the pre-programmed station. When none of these produce a signal I begin to gently twist the knob to find a station.

"Those don't usually work," Jesse says. "They're programmed to the stations up near Lake Placid. That's where my dad lived. The van was his. I haven't bothered to figure out how to change them yet."

"So he gave you the van."

"Kind of," Jesse says. "He died this year, and I got the van."

"I'm sorry."

"Yeah, me too. Now that I think of it, I may never change those stations. It's kind of cool that no matter where we go, my radio is trying to connect to those stations back home. Even if all I get is static."

I twist the dial until I find the classic rock station playing a Van Morrison tune. It wouldn't be my first choice, but it seems like something unlikely to offend anyone.

"My grandmother just died," I say, trying out the words for the first time. They don't even seem right. Dying isn't something Mima would do.

"Yeah," Jesse says. "G mentioned something about that. She said your moms didn't handle it all that well."

I shake my head. Even just thinking about it, my throat begins to tighten with anger. It feels really good to be moving away from her at sixty miles an hour.

"You'll deal with it when you're ready," Jesse says, like he's seeing the future. "That's the beauty of the bus, man. No past, no future, just today."

I nod. It's cheesy, but I can tell he means it. What would my life look like with no past; no stupid divorce or disappearing father? And no future? Well, not much lost there.

"Were you close to your dad?" I ask.

"Yes and no," Jesse says. "He had all these ideas about what I should be studying at college. He was supposed to go. He was going to be the first one in his family. He was all set up at this little community college in Portland, Maine. And then his first week there, the apartment building where he was renting a room burnt down. He didn't have anything saved. So he came back home and started working in the mill."

"Whoa," I say. It comes out before I can help it. I've never really known anyone who didn't go to college or even worked in a mill. I kind of thought that was just something people did before there were colleges. But thankfully Jesse doesn't hear it that way.

"Yeah," Jesse says, "the fire completely wiped him out."

"What was he going to study?" I ask.

Jesse looks thoughtfully ahead at the road. The white and

yellow lines whizz by us on either side. "I don't know," he says. "Business, I guess. That's what he was always on my case about."

"He wanted you to major in business?" I try to sound polite.

"Yup," Jesse says. "You've known me for half an hour, and you can already see that wouldn't work. I don't know why *he* couldn't figure it out."

I shake my head with disgust. "It seems like parents should know their own kids a little better."

Jesse nods. "Yeah, you would think so. But I don't hold it against him." He pauses thoughtfully. "Well, maybe I did for a while. But it's kind of different now. I guess he was just doing the best he could, you know, the way he'd been brought up."

"After he died, I found out he was way in debt trying to pay for school. He never told me. He got hurt a few years ago at the mill, and he always made it sound like they gave him some big settlement. I probably shouldn't have believed him. My grandmother sold his place, but the bank owned most of it anyway. All that was left was Shirley." He pats the steering wheel affectionately. "That was last spring. I finished the term, but there was no way I could go back to school on my own dime." He shrugs his shoulders. "So here I am."

"Where's your mom?" I ask, hoping the answer wouldn't be dead.

Jesse shrugged. "She's around," he says noncommittally.

"My dad's like that," I say softly.

Jesse nods, but he doesn't pry. I shift in my seat so my head falls back into the bucket headrest. I know I can still go back. I know we aren't that far from Glens Falls and that Jesse would pull over in a heartbeat if I asked him to. I also know that my cell phone has a full charge on it, and that it will last at least another day. A slightly queasiness comes over me when I realize that I didn't stuff the charger into my backpack. I look at my watch; it's a little before eight. I could probably call Mom right now and be back in my living room by ten thirty. But I don't. My skin is prickling, and I'm suddenly conscious of my breathing in a different way. I've crossed a line into a genuinely new experience—something I don't do very often.

I close my eyes, but the bumping and shifting of the van, not to mention my unease in this new situation, make sleep just a bit out of reach. Mom hates heights—she even had to take a Xanax to go skiing. One time when Mima was visiting, we drove up 87 because Mima wanted to go leaf-peeping. She convinced Mom to go on this gondola ride up the side of some family-run ski resort. Every time we hit a little bump passing one of the poles, Mom gripped the side railing with white knuckles. Mima just laughed and told her to lighten up. She stood as close to the windows as possible and said she could think of worse ways to die. She just loved to go for a ride. I squeeze my eyes tighter, holding back memories and tears.

I try and stay awake, just in case they're secretly planning on harvesting my organs, but my head lolls forward on my shoulders and periodically my eyelids flutter closed. I wake up as we are pulling into a Walmart parking lot.

"I'm bushed," Jesse says. "Anyone else want to drive?" There's no response. "All right, then who's up and who's down?"

"I'm up," G says, "and you drove," she adds.

"That means there's three of us back here?" says a male voice, either Tim or Lyle.

"I don't have to," I start to say as I sit up.

Jesse puts his hand on my shoulder. "Nah, man, stay where

75

you are." He reaches in the back for a sleeping bag, which he stuffs in my lap. I shake it out of the stuff sack and arrange it around me as best I can. The bucket seat goes back so I'm almost horizontal. The rest of them shuffle around in the back, and I hear the sounds of the top of the bus creaking open. There's some thumping overhead as G and Jesse climb up to sleep. And then it's quiet for a few minutes until the sound of a loud, rippling fart splits the air.

"Jesus Christ!" says a voice that I'm pretty sure is Lyle. I'm starting to recognize the nasal tension of his voice.

"Sorry, man," Tim says.

"If you didn't eat all those weird mushrooms it might not smell so bad," Lyle complains into the darkness.

"Hey," Tim says, "let's not make this an Asian thing."

"They stink when you cook them, they stink when you eat them, and they sure as hell stink when they come out your ass!"

Tim responds with another tiny rocket-fire fart. He giggles like I've never heard a boy, man, whatever, giggle. It's all high-pitched and really funny. Suddenly we are all giggling in the darkness. All except for Lyle, who is still grumbling about the smell. I try and tell myself it's just like the first night of camp. The first night sleeping anywhere different is always a little weird. But it's not just the new sounds and the weird smells. I'm about to close my eyes and submit to a state of complete and total vulnerability within arm's reach of five people I barely know. I'm going to do it, and not because someone else signed me up. I choose to do it.

DUMPSTER NUMBER ONE

When I finally drift off, it's into a restless sleep. It feels like every few minutes I wake up and have to feel around to figure out where I am again. I wander in and out of dreams filled with bus stations and airports. In one of these moments I find myself back in the huge, carpeted playroom of a house we lived in when I was five. Dad had a dartboard and an air hockey table, and I used to build forts underneath it. In the dream someone was handing me the phone, and when I listened to the receiver it was Mima. "Oh," I say. "I didn't know you could call."

"Of course I can," she says. "I just wanted to tell you that I'm fine. Everything's fine here." In my excitement I hand the phone over to my mother so she can say hi too. But when she takes the receiver she looks at me quizzically.

"There's no one there," she says above the droning dial tone.

Close to morning, I dream that Mima and I are walking down the sidewalk, holding hands. I have an ice cream cone and she asks me for a lick. I hand it over and she winks devilishly as she devours half of it in a single bite. "You're sweet enough already," she says.

I'm the first one up the next morning. The sadness of my dreams lodges like a piece of stiff cardboard in my throat. It's cold. My eyes open slowly, taking in the gray morning light. I try not to move too much, to avoid both waking people and coming into contact with the parts of my clothing that aren't warmed by my body. My neck is stiff from being twisted up against the bucket seat, and there's a strand of dried drool on my chin. I wriggle out of my seat, shedding the sleeping bag like a snakeskin, and carefully pull the metal door handle, pushing the van door open. The sun is up, but it's obscured by a blanket of gray clouds and has barely the brightness of a full moon. Still, it seems warmer outside the van than in it.

The Walmart parking lot is big but not empty. Apparently we aren't the only ones to use it like a motel. A few RVs are parked together in one corner, and a rusting sedan stuffed midway up the windows with clothes and papers sits two rows over. I can't tell if there's a human in it. I put my hands over my head and try to stretch out my back by bending first to one side and then to the other. It's a mistake. The second I put my hands over my head, my shirt comes untucked and a draft of late autumn air sweeps up under it. I shiver and jump in place for a while to warm up.

There's no avoiding it; I need to call Mom. I'm sure she's losing it, and every minute is probably making it worse. As far as she knows I'm arriving in Cleveland this morning where I will get on another bus that will bring me back home. Except that's not going to happen, and I'm not sure how to tell her. I look back at the van nervously, hoping and fearing that someone will wake up and come out to interrupt me.

I pull my phone out of my pocket and press the power button waiting for the lights to come on and the phone to beep. I take one more look at the van but no one is stirring. So I dial.

"Andrew," she says. With that one word I can tell she hasn't slept.

"Hi, Mom."

"Andrew, where are you?"

"I'm in Cleveland," I lie.

"Andrew, we need to talk about this, and we *will* talk about this when you get home. But right now I just need to know what bus you're getting on and whether or not you need to me call in a ticket for you."

Here's the jumping-off point. I stand on the platform, staring straight down at the ground. I can't do it. I'm not going to jump. I need to be pushed. There's a long pause while she waits for me to say something.

"Andrew? Are you there?"

"Yeah, Mom, I'm here."

"Do you have any idea how irresponsible and dangerous your behavior is?"

I roll my eyes. There it is. That's the push. "Mom, I'm not coming home. Not right away."

Her voice gets instantly cold. "What do you mean, Andrew?" I can hear the headmistress coming out in full force.

"I met some people, some kids, and they offered to give me a ride so I'm going to go with them." Even *I* realize how bad this sounds. I try to make it a little better. "Don't worry, Mom; they're straight edge," I tell her, trying out my new terminology. "You know, no drugs, no alcohol, they don't even eat meat."

"And this is supposed to make me feel better? You're getting a ride home with complete strangers, and I'm supposed be glad that they're vegetarians?! Where in God's name did you meet these people?"

"In the bus station."

"In Cleveland? But you just got there."

"My bus got in early," I cover quickly. "I was hanging out talking to them. They gave me a sandwich and offered me a ride."

"Andrew, this is ridiculous. You don't even know these kids. Who are they? Where are their parents?"

"They're around," I say. "Look, Mom, I know this doesn't make a lot of sense, but it's just what I need to do right now."

"What makes you think you know anything about what *you need* to do right now?"

I'm silent because we both know I can't answer that. All I know is that something about what I'm doing right now feels right. But I know there's no way Mom is going to get that.

"You know who you sound like, Andrew?"

"Dad," I say. There's a pause. I'm sure she's surprised. But I'm not going to let her beat me to that punch line. It's just too obvious.

"Is this about Mima?" Her voice is softer now.

"Partly. Yeah, partly it is."

"This isn't going to bring her back, Andrew."

"No kidding, Mom, I'm not a moron. Look, you always said I was sensible, right? And you always say I'm mature. Do you really think I'd go running off with a bunch of terrorists or child traffickers?"

"This is ridiculous. I can't believe we're even arguing about this. You need to march yourself over to that ticket counter and get on the next bus home. Immediately."

I don't answer right away. I know and she knows that I am about to openly defy her. I try to keep my voice calm. "I'm not going to do that right now," I say simply.

"I could call the police, Andrew."

"Yeah, you could. But I wish you wouldn't, Mom."

"When will you come back?" she asks. Her voice sounded small and broken. I have to get off the phone before I lose my nerve.

"I don't know, probably Monday, okay?"

"No, it is most certainly not okay," her voice bristles. "I insist that you be back in this house by Monday, and I will expect to hear from you every night between now and then."

"My cell phone doesn't have that much power left, and I didn't bring my charger."

"There's still such a thing as pay phones, Andrew."

"Right," I say. "Well, I'll try to call."

"Do you even know their names? These people you're running off with. What are their names?"

"Jesse, Lyle, Tim, Emily, and G. I don't know their last names," I admit. "But I'm fine, Mom, everything is going to be fine." I try to sound as reassuring as possible.

She sighs loudly into the phone. "I hope you know this is the worst decision you've ever made." *This is the only decision I can remember making in the last three years.* "This is certainly not how I raised you."

"Yeah, right, Mom. Look, I gotta go. And I'm going to turn my phone off so the battery lasts longer. So don't freak out when you can't get through."

"Don't tell me how not to freak out. Not when my teenage son has just decided to run off with some vagrants he met in a bus station. I understand that you think you've got all the power in this situation. But *do not* tell me how to feel about it."

"I gotta go, Mom."

"Andrew," she says sadly, "Please call." I nod, but of course she can't see that, and hang up the phone.

The van door slides open behind me. Tim steps out wearing a long-sleeved T-shirt, boxer shorts, and a pair of thick wool socks. He stretches his hands over his head and rips another cataclysmic fart. I snicker and walk over to the van, hoping the odor will dissipate before I get too close.

"Don't worry," he says, "my morning farts never stink."

"No, but there's enough left over in here from last night to make up for it," Lyle's voice comes out muffled from inside the van. He and Emily are still curled up together. His arm is wrapped around her middle. I feel a tiny pang and a tug under my ribcage at the sight of his hand resting on her bare stomach.

"Hey, you know it's freakin' cold out there. You could shut the door," Lyle says.

I reach for the door, but before I can close it, Emily throws Lyle's arm off and sits up in the van. "Don't bother, Drew, we should get up anyway."

Her eyes are gray in the morning light. Last night, under the bus station's fluorescent lights, they looked blue. She's wearing a tissue-paper-thin white tank top, and I look away so I won't stare at her nipples poking out the fabric.

"I'm hungry," Emily comments. "Anyone want some oatmeal?"

"Me!" five voices, including my own, call out.

Emily pulls a thick wool sweater out from one of the duffel bags and slides out of the sleeping bag and into a pair of jeans that are more holes than fabric. She uses a green elastic band from around her wrist to lift her thick dreads off the back of her neck. "Ah, that's better."

I smile and look away, hoping she hasn't seen me staring.

A camping stove emerges from underneath the passenger seat and she proceeds to assemble it in the parking lot. Slowly Lyle, Jesse, and G emerge from the van in various stages of undress. They pull on layers from what seems to be a communal clothing supply. I jump up and down wearing a thin fleece jacket—the only coat I had bothered to bring with me.

"Here, throw this on." Jesse chucks a thick wool shirt my way: a button-up with green and black checks. It's the kind of thing a lumberjack wears; a little itchy around the collar, but it's warm. It smells like wood smoke and the spicy smell of the van. Lyle produces a soccer ball, and we all start to kick around while Emily makes the oatmeal. I can't juggle, but I can pass the ball around without embarrassing myself too badly. Lyle can bounce the ball easily from one foot to another, on his knees and off his chest. In daylight I can see that even though he's short, he's pretty well built. Jesse and G seem pretty athletic too. Tim passes the ball along if it comes near him in kind of a disinterested way. His pants sag off his hips, and when he trots to get a missed ball he has to hold them up with one hand to avoid losing them altogether.

As we wait for the water to boil, the morning clouds begin to thin and breaks of blue sky are visible overhead. A few cars begin trickling into the parking lot, and Walmart workers in their bright blue smocks file into the store.

"Come and get it," Emily yells. She is pouring the steaming oatmeal into an odd assortment of ceramic and plastic bowls. There are only four.

"You can share with me, Drew," she says. "I always eat out of the pot."

"It's *Andrew*," G says a bit forcefully.

Emily ignores her. "Do you mind?" she asks me.

"Not really," I say truthfully. I look away to avoid catching G's eyes.

Everyone grabs their share and finds a corner of the van to eat in. Emily thrusts the pot handle and two spoons into my hands and grabs a sleeping bag out of the van.

"Come on," she says. I follow her around to the other side of the van, where she sits down next to the back tire and spreads the sleeping bag over her lap. The sun is shining brightly now, and on this side of the van it's actually warm. I just stand there like an idiot, holding the pot of oatmeal.

Emily looks up shielding her eyes from the sun. "Put the pot down, *Andrew*, and come sit next to me." She holds the sleeping bag up on one side like an invitation. I put the pot down on the ground and sit down next to her. She pats the sleeping bag over our laps, closes her eyes, and leans back against the bus. "The sun feels good."

"Uh-huh," I agree. It's the only response I can manage. Our legs are touching under the sleeping bag. Actually, to be more specific, her knee is touching my thigh. I close my eyes and let the sun warm my face. If this is life on the road, I think I could get used to it.

We sit there like that for several minutes until Emily says, "It's probably cool enough now."

"What?"

"The oatmeal." She giggles. "It's probably cool enough to touch the pot."

"Oh, right," I say. I grab the pot by the handle and hand her one of the spoons. With my free hand I spoon warm oatmeal into my mouth. I always thought oatmeal had a bad, slimy texture, but this is incredible. It's sweet and warm, and as it slides down my throat it seems like every painful moment of the past twenty-four hours is erased. I smile at Emily. "It's really good."

"Yeah," she says in between mouthfuls, "I got a way with the Quaker Oats Man. That, and maple syrup. Maple syrup makes everything taste better. Nature's candy."

"I thought raisins were nature's candy," I joke.

"What?"

"Never mind," I say, embarrassed by my dorkiness. "So how did you meet these guys anyway?"

"Oh, you know," she says, like this is a perfectly normal way to live. "I was hanging out in Burlington, and Jesse and G and Lyle were busking and doing their act. I can juggle and do the hoops, so I started working with them. When they decided to leave, I went with them."

"So is that where you're from? Burlington?"

"No, I'm from a little town called Kingfield. It's near Burlington, but it shouldn't even really be called a town. It's like a town hall and a convenience store and a volunteer fire department. It's the kind of place people go to get away from it all." She holds up her fingers in quotations and rolls her eyes. "I had this boyfriend for a while and he lived in Burlington, so I started staying at his place a lot. Then we broke up, but he still let me crash there. It was all right, but I was ready to move on."

There's a mechanical way in which she recounts this information that makes me think there's more to the story. "Do your parents know where you are?"

"Bird and Darryl?" Emily snorts. "Kind of."

"Do they care?" I ask quietly. Suddenly I'm feeling sorry for myself, and I can't really explain why. "Wait, your parents' names are Bird and Darryl?"

"Bird's my mom. I've never met my real dad. I don't even think Bird really knows who he is. Darryl's like her common-law husband. They met on a Phish tour. They had the twins and then they just had another baby. So yeah, they kind of know where I am. I'll send them a postcard when I get around to it. They've got their hands full at home anyway."

"What about school?" I'm guessing that Emily is close to my age.

"Neither of them is in any position to lecture me about dropping out," she says. "School's overrated anyway. I *was* going to this pretty amazing place called Milestone. It's like this alternative school where you pick what you want to learn about and the teachers—well, they don't call them teachers, they're called facilitators—so the facilitators help you figure out how to access that knowledge. And that was all right. But then after Baby Lucille was born my mom had to quit her job. The health-care system in this country is completely messed up. You know there are some places like in Europe where women get a year off from their job so they can raise their kids?"

I nod like this is something I might be even remotely aware of. Emily goes on, "They couldn't swing the tuition, so I had to go back to public school. I can't take the institutional bullshit of those places. So here I am. The school of life. Accessing the knowledge of the world."

We lean back against the van, eating mostly in silence, enjoying the sweet oatmeal and the warm sun. After we scrape the pot clean, Emily sighs and rests her head on my shoulder. I always thought dreadlocks would be dirty and smelly, but Emily smells great—like really strong peppermint soap. I breathe little shallow breaths so I won't move and end the moment. This could be me. Me and Emily and no institutional bullshit. I think I know what she means by that. Either way, this is definitely the closest a girl has ever been to me in my life, and I'm not going to break the spell for anything.

HELLMART

"Andrew!"

I jerk my head up at the sound of G's voice and shield my eyes so I can see her. Emily doesn't move. G's eyes flick over to Emily and then back to me. She sighs loudly.

"Come on. we're going in."

"In where?" I ask.

"Hellmart," G says. "I wish there was some way around it, but you need your own sleeping bag. I shared with Jesse last night and either his feet were sticking out or my head was completely covered. It wasn't fun."

"Sorry. I didn't know I was using his sleeping bag."

"It's not a big deal, but we need to get you your own for tonight. If you're staying with us, that is," she says.

"Yeah, okay." Reluctantly I slide out from under Emily's sleeping bag and walk away with G.

"You guys check out the back while we're in there, okay?" G calls to Lyle, Tim, and Jesse. Before I can ask her what she means, the magical mechanical doors swing open and the smell of stale air and fake buttered popcorn assaults my nose. We both smile politely at the elderly gentleman assigned the task of greeting us.

"I hate this place," G mutters as we study the blue-and-white signs hanging from the ceiling at the entrance to each aisle.

"How come?"

"On a corporate level, the pay sucks, they sell cheap plastic crap made by children with lead poisoning in China and that will probably end up in a landfill in less than six months. On a personal level, my Aunt Ginger used to work at one of these places. She hurt her back, and they hired a big lawyer to convince her she wasn't entitled to worker's comp. After that she couldn't work for a while, and she and my Uncle Paul couldn't afford to have me live at their house any more. So that's how I ended up at foster home number one."

"Oh," I say. I had never really thought of Walmart as anything more than a big store that sold a lot of stuff. "I think camping gear is down here." We make our way down the aisle filled with coolers, fishing gear, tents, and camping stoves. At the end there is a small section devoted to sleeping bags rolled up in neat spirals. The cheapest one is $49.99, about twenty dollars more than I have left. I could use Mom's credit card, but I really don't want to. I don't want her to hold it over me that I was on my own for less than twenty-four hours before I was dependent on her again. I also don't want G or anyone else to know I have it, for a couple reasons.

As we're standing there, a blue-smocked employee with a tight ponytail lacquered to her head walks briskly past the end of the aisle.

"Excuse me," G calls after her. "Are these the cheapest sleeping bags you have?"

"Yep, that's it," she says. "Except for the kids' ones." She eyes G up and down. "You might be able to fit. My son still uses one and he's fourteen."

"Where would we find those?" G asks.

"Around the corner." The woman points to the next aisle over.

***

"Ooh," G exclaims as she unties the knot and unrolls a Strawberry Shortcake themed bag. It's covered with pink and green cupcakes, but it's only a little bit smaller than an adult sleeping bag. "There's this, Spiderman, or Superman."

I try and imagine crawling underneath this thing with Emily, and thoughts of Analiese Gerber make my stomach turn. Who am I kidding? "I guess I'm more of a Spidey guy."

"I can see that," G says. "There's definitely something a little secretive and nerdy about you."

"Thanks."

We pay for the sleeping bag and a large bag of Twizzlers at the register. I stuff the last of my money, all two dollars and seventy-two cents, back into my pocket.

Back in the parking lot I'm surprised to see the bus is running and everyone is packed inside. "Come on," G says nervously, "Let's run."

"Okay, but it's not like we stole this stuff or anything," I joke.

"Right," she agrees. But her eyes are scanning the parking lot.

We start running towards the van. Lyle is riding shotgun, and Jesse is driving again, so G and I jump in the back. As soon as we slam the van door Jesse burns a little rubber peeling out

90

of the parking lot. I get up on my knees and look behind us. Two agitated-looking Walmart security guards are pointing at the van as we drive away.

I sit down, feeling a little bit thrilled but mostly confused. Emily is organizing a pile of stuff including a loaf of bread, two large containers of orange juice, a couple bags of Sun-Maid raisins, a family-size bag of baby carrots, several large bags of tortilla chips, and what looks like a child's paint set.

"Where did all that come from?"

"The excesses of capitalism," Emily answers without looking up.

"Did you guys steal that stuff from the store?"

"Hell no," Lyle says. "I wouldn't set foot in there if you paid me."

"Well then where did all that come from?" I thought the question had been pretty clear the first time.

Lyle turns around in his seat and looks me straight on. "The dumpster," he says simply. "Pretty sweet, huh?"

I can tell he's waiting to gauge my reaction. I take a moment giving myself a little more time to process this information. "So you're going to eat this stuff? Out of the trash?"

"Where do you think your peanut butter and bread came from last night?" Lyle asks. "Or this morning's oatmeal?"

"A store?"

"It *was* in a store," Emily explains. "They have to pull the stuff off the shelf before it expires. Most of it hasn't even expired the day it goes in there, and in a big store like that it doesn't sit there very long. Almost everything in there is perfectly good food." I'm not totally horrified, but there must be some displeasure in my facial expression.

"See, I told you he was going to freak out," Lyle says.

"Shut up," Tim unexpectedly chimes in. "I thought it was a little weird at first too. But it's really all perfectly good food, and sometimes you find other cool stuff."

I look curiously at the bread, carrots, and tortilla chips. They seem okay. "Isn't it kind of sloppy and gross in there?"

"Sometimes," G says. "But most stuff is in bags. We can pull the bags out and see what's in them before we even open them up. We live in a really sanitized world. Even our garbage is pretty clean."

"It's not just about getting food out of the trash," Emily says. "It's a movement, an anticapitalist movement. It's Freeganism."

"Freeganism?" I look up in time to see Jesse and G meeting eyes in the mirror. G is rolling hers. "So does that make you Freegans?"

"Yes," says Emily definitively.

"If you like labels," Jesse says. "I just like getting stuff for free." He smiles at me in the mirror. "It fits my budget."

I think about the two dollars and seventy cents left in my pocket. Who was I to be complaining about the origins of a perfectly good peanut butter sandwich? "Okay with me, I guess," I say.

"See!" Emily says triumphantly. "I told you he wouldn't be weird about it. Andrew is open-minded. He's a highly evolved male of the species." She leans over, wraps her arms around my neck, and kisses me on the cheek. My face flashes bright red, and Lyle looks annoyed as he turns around to face front again.

Emily continues putting away the food, and Tim puts his headphones back on. G starts arranging the bags behind her into a little nest. I grab a couple of duffel bags and lean them up against the side of the van. The last time I was intentionally in a car without my seatbelt on was when I was seven and our neighbor used to let me and his son stick our heads out the sunroof of his Porsche on the way home from soccer practice. Somehow Mom found out and forbade me from ever getting a ride with them again. It's an odd feeling to be hurtling down the highway at sixty or so miles an hour with no restraint, when my whole life had been belted in and buckled down. I kind of like it. "So where are we going?" I ask.

"Rochester," Jesse says from the driver's seat.

"How come?"

"College town, lots of young people around," he says.

"On Thanksgiving break?"

"Yeah, there won't be a lot of students. But it's got a little downtown area. People will be out and about today and tomorrow."

"Biggest shopping day of the year," I say offhand.

"You know, today is actually International Buy Nothing Day," Emily chimes in.

"Wait, let me guess," I say. "Is that a day when everyone is supposed to buy nothing?" As soon as I say it I wish I could take it back. Emily ignores my sarcasm and keeps talking. "International Buy Nothing Day was created in response to Black Friday. You know the day after Thanksgiving when they have all those sales and people line up and get crushed to death in order to get the new Tickle Me Elmo for their precious little kid?"

"Uh-huh," I say.

"Well International Buy Nothing Day is all about showing corporations that they don't have power over us and they can't tell us what's going to make us happy."

"I don't know," I say, "That Elmo is a pretty funny little guy." I'm only kidding and trying to lighten the mood in the van. But Emily just glares at me. G gives a little snort, and Jesse stifles a grin with the back of his hand. It's the second time in an hour that I have no idea what they're talking about, but I want to prove I can think for myself. "All I'm saying is people like buying stuff. Some people clip their coupons for that day like a month ahead of time. They love the idea that they're getting something for nothing, or something for really cheap. Why rain on their parade?" Now I'm just playing devil's advocate. I don't want Emily to be mad at me, so why can't I shut up when she's talking about something that's obviously really important to her?

She looks at me fiercely. "They're raining on Earth's parade," she growls with a clenched jaw.

That's all G can take. She snorts loudly and doubles over laughing. Emily glares at her and retreats into a corner of the van. It's quite awkward, since there really isn't anywhere to *go*. She turns her face toward the wall and tries her best to look dignified.

"I'm sorry," I say. "I'm not trying to make fun of you. I just don't really get how getting people to buy nothing for a single day will really make any difference?"

"The goal is to raise people's awareness about consumerism and the effects we're having on our planet," Lyle rejoins the conversation. "It's not really about not shopping on that day so much as it's about getting people to realize that their way of life is corrupting their souls and ruining the planet."

"Whoa, seriously, corrupting their souls? Isn't that a bit heavy-handed?" I don't like that he's taking Emily's side against me.

"I don't think so," Lyle says.

"Neither do I," Emily declares from her corner.

***

My face is warm and my butt is starting to go numb from sitting on the van floor. I glance once around the van, but no one besides Emily seems that mad. Maybe I haven't completely blown things after all. I'm surprised to realize that I care. I pull my copy of *Into the Wild* out of my backpack and pick up where I had left off last night. I'm not really reading, though. I just keep running my eyes over the same sentence again and again. It's actually the second time I've read it, so I know what's going to happen. I just love the buildup, his life on the road, and all the little details about the weird, unhappy people he meets. Periodically I glance up at Emily, who is ferociously clacking away on some wooden knitting needles. Whatever she's making is large and gray and shapeless. The wool gives the whole back of the van the smell of dirty hay.

At one point I catch Tim watching me as I watch Emily. I quickly look away. "So what's going to happen when we get to Rochester?" I ask him.

"They'll do their show, we'll try and make some money for gas, and then we'll keep going," he says.

"What's the show all about?"

"It's a little different every time. Usually Emily dances or does the hoops. Jesse juggles and usually tells a story, and then Lyle and G do their thing."

"Which is what?"

"Hmm," Tim says. "Really better seen than described."

The road hums along, and it's quiet in the van for a while. I turn to my backpack and rifle through the contents again. I take out my notebook and turn to the back, thinking maybe someone will want to play hangman or something. I'm surprised to find a shakier block-letter version of my handwriting is there on the back of the inside cover. My name and an address I haven't lived at for almost seven years. I turn to the front and flip past a couple blank pages until I come to a title. It says *Divorce Diary.* Nine- or ten-year-old me has given it a subtitle too. "Stupid stuff I don't want to write about Mom and Dad's stupid divorce which has nothing to do with me." It's long and, I recognize now, plainly a falsehood, but I'm still impressed by the literary technique.

It also triggers a memory. For a couple months at the beginning of fifth grade, Mom and Dad had me visit with a counselor to talk about my feelings around the divorce. The counselor suggested I write things down in a journal. And here it was. I flip forward, but there are only a few pages with writing on them, each one a short list. One of them simply says, "pedofile priest = nothing."

When I was in fifth grade, the teacher announced that our class was going to adopt an orphan for our class holiday project. The teacher held up one of those packets with the starving child on it. You know, the one with sad, soulful eyes and a distended belly. The other kids were really excited about it and a conversation immediately began about what we would name our orphan. "The kid probably already has a name," I said to no one in particular. But I was ignored amidst an excited buzz of gift ideas for the new class pet. "My mom says these programs are all a big scam," I announced, louder this time.

The class quieted. The kids were looking at me with interest. Only slightly more exciting than picking out names for the class orphan was the possibility that an adult might be shown up in some way. Mrs. Pettengill gave me a tired stare. But it was quiet, and I had the floor. "I mean you might as well hand over your money directly to some pedophile priest." Now it was very quiet. The kids didn't know what I meant. *I* didn't even know what I meant. It was just something my mom used to shout at the TV every time those ten-minute ads came on. That, and "There are plenty of starving kids right here in our own country." In retrospect the second comment might have been the better choice. Especially since I had no idea what a pedophile was. Mrs Pettengill did. Her jaw just about hit the floor as she hustled me out of the room and down to the principal's office.

It was a lot different than the first time I got sent to the principal's office. There were no punitive consequences except Mom had to come pick me up. It was a couple weeks before Christmas vacation. I remember Dad was on the computer a lot, trying to find a new place to live. Mom got pretty red in the face when she found out about my comment, but even she didn't bother to punish me. It was the first time, throughout the whole divorce, I remember thinking she had really let me down. Needless to say that class project was canceled. Something the other kids held against me for the rest of the year. I was the Grinch who stole their orphan.

***

Just then Tim shouts out, "TENS!!!"

"All right," Jesse says. "I think there's a rest stop up ahead."

"Tens is like ten minutes until you need a bathroom," Tim explains. "Fives is like five minutes. And if you yell turtles, that means it's an emergency and whoever is driving should pull over at the nearest good-sized bush or tree."

This is good information to have. I flip ahead a few pages in the notebook and make a new list that I title *Useful Information*. I like to title things. Maybe because it seems to be an indication of something promising. I write down Tim's explanation for getting the van to stop when you have to crap. A few minutes later the bus pulls in at a gas station and everyone piles out to stretch their legs. Tim jogs off to find the key to the bathroom. G follows Tim, while Emily and Lyle walk over to a picnic bench. I lean back against the side of the van, trying to get my back to crack.

"I think I pissed Emily off," I say off handedly to Jesse. "I feel bad."

"Really?" he says and cocks his head to one side.

"Well, I feel bad if she's upset. But I don't really feel bad about arguing with her," I clarify.

"Good," Jesse says. "You shouldn't. Emily's got to learn that she can't just shout her opinions at people to make them agree with her. She can get really preachy sometimes, and more often than not, it has the opposite effect. She ends up turning people off to the things she's saying because the way she's saying them is so . . ." he pauses.

"In your face?" I offer.

"Yeah, pretty much," he says. "Still," he offers after a few minutes have passed. "If you think you might have hurt her feelings, it never hurts to apologize."

"Yeah, I know." I was kind of hoping Lyle was going to head for the bathroom so I could talk to Emily alone. "I really liked talking to Emily this morning."

"I bet," Jesse says.

I look up quickly to see if there's any hint of suggestion in his comment. But there's none. He simply gives me another ultra-sincere smile and then gestures to Lyle with a wave of his hand. "Hey, man," he shouts. "Can you take a look at the exhaust pipe for me? I think I heard a clunking noise that last mile or so."

I look curiously at Jesse. Did he read my mind? I walk casually over to where Emily is sitting and sit down next to her. I clap my hands together nervously, unsure of what to say. "I'm sorry," I start. "I'm sorry if I was too sarcastic or whatever, and I pissed you off."

"Thanks, Drew," Emily says. She's twisting one of her dreadlocks back and forth between her fingers. "I shouldn't have gotten on your case either." She sighs loudly. "Jesse says I can be too preachy, and it turns people off from what I'm saying."

"I'm interested in what you're saying," I say. "I'm just not sure I agree with it all. Not yet, anyway."

"That's cool," Emily says. "I respect that. You have to find your own path."

"Well," I say, wondering if that's something I'm looking for or running from, "I'm not sure that's exactly how I would put it, but yeah."

"So we're cool?" Emily asks. She sticks her hand out to shake.

"Absolutely," I say and shake it firmly. She holds on to it for a second and then gives it a little squeeze

"Good," she says and lets go. My palm, where she squeezed it, is warm and tingly. Apologizing to girls I like. I make a mental note to add this to my list of useful information.

G comes back out of the bathroom, and we all drift back over to the van. We wait a few more minutes for Tim, and then slowly one by one we assume our spots inside the van. I take out *Into the Wild* again, but instead of reading I amuse myself by flipping through the pages and letting my finger land on a single word. This word will be a sign for what's to come.

The first time I get "polish," but I can't figure out how to make a prediction out of that one so I flip the pages again. This time my finger lands on "pursuit." Somehow that seems more meaningful, but before I can contemplate the full ramifications of this prophecy Tim is back and we're ready to roll.

"Dude," he says as he climbs into the van, "Killer a.m. BM."

"I'm sorry, what?" I ask, thinking I've misheard him.

"A.m. BM," G repeats. "That's what he calls his morning dump."

"Don't knock it," Tim says. "I am, if nothing else, a killer pooper. Smooth and regular every day."

"Your mother must be proud," I say.

"Mama Lin knows, man. She's the reason for all this fine peristalsis."

"Yeah, and the reason I can't breathe through my nose at night," Lyle snaps.

"Dude, you're just jealous because you're so stopped up. Maybe if you'd let go of some of your anger, you could let go of those hard little pellets you're hanging on to."

It goes on like this for the next twenty minutes. It's definitely the longest, and maybe only, conversation about pooping that I've ever been privy to. Even the girls get into it. Emily claims of course that even though vegetarians fart more, their farts aren't as smelly as those of meat-eaters. I try and imagine any of the girls at St. Mary's having this kind of conversation, but I can't. It would be like one of those weird Chinese lip-dubbed movies that come on late at night. It's refreshing in a really weird way. What's even more refreshing is that I haven't thought about Mima or Mom or any of the mess back home for at least a couple hours.

PARABLE OF A BUMPER STICKER

Lunch is in the van, more peanut butter and jelly, and we roll into Rochester around three in the afternoon. Jesse finds a spot for the van in a little park down by the Genesee River. It seems like it would be a nice spot to hang out in the summer. Right now, its only inhabitants are a few homeless people wrapped in blankets or sleeping on the benches. I look at them curiously. There are no homeless people in Glens Falls, none that I'm aware of, anyway. And whenever I saw them in Boston, I just kind of thought of them as a feature of the city. But there's this one guy curled up on a bench, a heavy vinyl-wrapped bike lock connecting a shopping cart to one ankle. I wonder what his path in life was, or if he ever had one.

No one knows the area too well, so we split up to scout places to perform and possible food sources, aka dumpsters. "Come on, Andrew," G says as Emily walks off with Lyle and Jesse heads off with in the other direction with Tim. G and I wander around the downtown area, crossing streets and strolling the sidewalks with no particular agenda. Emily was right about one thing; there are a lot of people out shopping. We're possibly the only ones not laden with bags and boxes. Behind a Finagle a Bagel store, G harvests a couple of bags of day-old bread and pastries while I stand guard. I'm glad I don't have to go back there and root around quite yet. I know it's hypocritical when I'm eating their food all the time, but I'm not quite ready for the reality of where it comes from.

While I'm waiting for G, I turn on my phone. Only one bar of battery left and three new messages. The first two are from Mom. Nothing new, she's just checking in and hoping I'll call. In the second one she asks specifically what bus I'll be on so she can plan on picking me up. The last message is from Dad. He sounds annoyed and rushed. Hopefully he didn't have to disrupt his vacation too much to make this phone call. He tells me he thinks I'm being irresponsible and immature. At the end of the message he doesn't even leave a number; he just tells me to call my mother and get my ass back to Glens Falls. He doesn't even say anything about Mima. My eyes burn and my stomach churns. I shut the phone off again and shove it in my pocket.

"Do you miss them ever?" I ask.

"Who?"

"Your family."

"Oh," G says and stops walking for a minute to think about it. I shift nervously from foot to foot. I didn't think it was a big-deal kind of question, but I'm realizing a little too late that it might be. "Not really in a general way. But sometimes little things make me remember them—that they're out there doing all sorts of things we used to do together. And then I feel a little weird. Is that missing them? I don't know."

After walking a while, G starts talking again and it takes me a minute to realize she's still answering my question. "Like today. Seeing all these people Christmas shopping reminds me of how stressed my mom used to get around the holidays because my parents never had any money. I remember going over to this girl's house when I was in third grade and her mom brought us juice boxes and real Oreos with the name stamped on them. And that was like the first time I realized that juice didn't all come frozen in a can. When we had food in the house, it was always No Name juice and potato chips. Seriously, that was what the generic brand was called. For a long time I thought you really had it made if you could afford Tropicana and Tostitos.

"Anyway, so Mom would try and put some money aside so she could get us some kind of Christmas present, and inevitably my dad would get it from her one way or another. He'd tell her we were late on some bill or that he needed it for an investment." G shakes her head. "So this one Saturday we were out shopping with my grandma and my sisters, and my grandma was pestering Mom about what she was going to get us for Christmas and Mom was trying to avoid telling her that Dad had once again made off with all her money. Grams thought Dad was a total deadbeat anyway. She loved conversations like these and trying to get my mom to admit that she married a total loser. So my sister Elise saw some jelly shoes in the store. They were like these rubbery slip-on shoes; totally useless in the winter. Anyway Elise started whining at Mom about how she really wanted them, and so of course my little sister started in on her too. And then Grams was saying how they were a really good deal, but I could tell that she just wanted to get Mom to admit that she didn't have the money.

"So finally my mom caved and bought us each a pair. I remember she said, 'I should be able to buy my girls a pair of shoes if I want to.' I didn't even want them, but she just told me to pick a color and I knew I didn't have a choice. When we got home I hid them under my bed so Dad wouldn't see and flip out on her. But it didn't matter. Elise put them on as soon as we got home and . . ." G drifts off and then suddenly looks up at me embarrassed. "Sorry."

"No, it's okay," I say almost a little too insistently.

G looks even more embarrassed. "I guess that's why I don't think about them too much. Most of the memories are like that one."

I wonder what G sees when she looks at the homeless people sleeping on benches by the river. We don't talk a whole lot more as we scope out the Midtown Plaza as a possible performance space. It's busy now, but G is concerned that it will be too quiet after five o'clock. When we get back to the van, Jesse and Lyle announce that they've found a good spot. The Village Gate Square is a shopping area with artists' studios, and they're having an open house that evening. Jesse talked to a guy about performing in front of his gallery and the guy said it was okay.

"It's a lot more relaxing when we don't have to worry about getting busted by the cops," G says.

"Right," I say, like this is one of my everyday concerns too. By the time we get over to the Village Gate Square and park the van it's time to set up the show. Tim has enlisted me to hold the microphone while he films, so my job is pretty much taken care of. I watch as the rest of the group gets ready to perform. G uses a public bathroom to change, and when she comes out she's transformed. She's wearing red-and-white-striped tights underneath a black velvet leotard. A green velvet skirt completes the look. She's put something on her face to make it whiter, and her cheeks have bright red circles on them. A few black freckles dot her nose.

"You look like a giant doll," I say before I can think about whether this is a compliment.

"Yeah, that's kind of the idea."

"A buff doll," I say and poke at her arm muscles, which are clearly visible beneath the stretchy fabric. G smirks and leans forward into a bodybuilder pose. Lyle is wearing a similar outfit but has shorts that go over his tights. He's busy rigging up some ropes to hang from a streetlight. "Do you need any help?" I ask.

"It's kind of complicated," he says without looking away from the knot he's tying. "I could probably show you some knots when I have more time, but tonight it's probably better if you just stay out of the way."

I try not to take his brusque tone personally. "You can help me," Emily volunteers from inside the van.

"Sure," I say, and wander over, but not before I see Lyle scowl down at his knots. Inside the van, Emily is still getting dressed. I look away quickly when I see that her shirt is only partially pulled over her head.

"Drew, you're so sweet," she says. "But I'm not ashamed of my body. Can you tie this in the back?" The back of her shirt has laces that pull together and make it clear that she's not wearing a bra. I try not to think about this too much. The sight of her naked back is enough to turn the twitch in my pants into a full on hard-on. Once she's dressed, Emily has me throw juggling balls at her while she spins the giant Hula-Hoop around her waist.

I'm not an expert on street performers, but I have to say I'm surprised by how good the Freegans' show is. Lyle and Emily warm up the crowd with a combination of tightrope walking,

Hula-Hooping, and juggling. Lyle moves with agility along a thick rope strung between two parking signs. He has several clubs that he's able to light on fire and juggle while walking back and forth. Meanwhile Emily keeps the hoop going; first around her waist, then her neck, and then out to each arm. A decent-sized crowd has gathered, at this point and they seem to be really into it, especially the kids. They all gasp when at one point Lyle teeters back and forth on his rope while keeping three torches going in the air.

Jesse comes out next, and he really works the audience. His smooth and gentle voice, which I've kind of gotten used to over the last twenty-four hours, takes on a new, commanding presence. He sounds like one of those late-night radio DJs who give people advice about their love lives. He gets all these kids out of the audience and gives them fish puppets to hold, and then he tells this story about a bigger fish who was ganging up on all the little fish. Emily wears the big fish costume and struts around in front of the audience, playfully pushing the little fish out of the way. Then Jesse gets all the kids to get in a group and chase the big fish away. It reminds me of a bumper sticker I saw once with a school of little fish chasing a bigger fish. It said "Organize," or "Fight the Power," or some other hippie slogan. What's really amazing is how Jesse keeps all of this going— the story and the little kids with their puppets—and manages to hold the audience's attention without letting everything fall into chaos. He gets a really big round of applause at the end, with the parents clapping loudest of all.

G and Lyle's act is last. While they're getting set up, a flushed Emily sits down next to me. "What do you think so far?" she asks, mopping at her sweaty face.

"It's great! Honestly, it's really great!" I don't tell her that my expectations were pretty low. That I thought about slinking to the back so I wouldn't get embarrassed by people giving them money.

She smiles. "Really? You liked it? You're not just saying that?"

"Seriously, I thought it was really good." I'm not bullshitting her, or thinking about kissing the corner of her jaw, just below her ear. Okay, I'm thinking about that too. But the show was good. It feels like the first good and real thing I've seen in a while.

"And you got it? Like, the message and all?"

"It was hard to miss," I tell her. "But not too preachy," I give her a little jab with my elbow. She smiles like we have a private joke, and my stomach gets all warm and mushy.

"Okay, pay attention now because the best part is about to start." Jesse presses play on their battered-looking CD player, and some old-timey carnival music comes through the tinny speakers. The ropes hanging from the streetlight are supporting a trapeze bar that G grabs with one arm and pulls herself up on. Twisting the ropes between her legs, she shimmies higher up until she's suspended ten feet above the bar and at least twenty feet above the ground. Tim tells me I can put down the microphone, so my full attention is focused on G. Her legs are twisted in the ropes so that she's supported on them. She does a series of somersaults down to the bar and catches herself by the legs, her upper body rocking back and forth upside down. The audience bursts into applause.

Next she begins pumping her upper body so that she swings back and forth, still hanging upside down, her knees gripping the wooden bar. After she gets a good swing going, Lyle comes cartwheeling out. They grab each other by the forearms, and G swings Lyle up above her onto the bar. Their act is about fifteen minutes of twisting contortions performed ten to fifteen feet above the ground. Sometimes one of them dangles the other, and sometimes they're both moving separately on the rope swing. Watching them, I'm aware of how similar in size they actually are. Lyle's a little bit taller, but G is actually a bit more muscular. I'll bet they're close to the same weight. The whole act is carefully synchronized and completely mesmerizing. When I'm able to look away, I look around the circle at all the kids with their mouths hanging half-open.

In one of their last moves G repeats the opening sequence of twisting somersaults down the rope, but this time she catches herself on Lyle's arms. Together they twist the ropes up and let go so they both end up spinning around for a good thirty seconds before they slow down. The audience roars with applause.

After a quick bow, Jesse comes back out to pass the hat. A lot of the little kids who participated in the fish play come forward with their parents' one- and five-dollar bills. I wonder what the headmistress would think. Probably she would make a comment about how they were all neglecting their education. Mima would like it, though.

There are a lot of people around for the art opening, and the Freegans repeat the show twice more before the crowd thins out. By the end of the third show everyone is showing signs of exhaustion.

"That was amazing!" I tell G and Lyle as they peel off the layers of black and red spandex.

"Thanks," G says. Her painted-on freckles are smeared with sweat.

"Where did you guys learn to do that?"

"I used to hang banners for the Ruckus Society," Lyle says. "You know, animal rights stuff and Earth-first. We used to do actions where we would hang banners on big buildings and bridges. That's how I learned to hang the ropes. The rest of it I just kind of picked up on my own."

"I always liked the ropes in gym class," G says. "But most of this stuff I picked up from another group I hung around with a couple years before I met these guys. They were part of this alternative circus that traveled around doing their act in little theaters and cafés and stuff.

"Someone told them I wasn't eighteen yet, so I couldn't stay with them. It wasn't like they didn't know. There was just someone who had to make a big deal about it," G says cryptically. "You know how it is. In any group there's always some people who need a lot of attention a lot of the time." Whether she realizes it or not, G is staring at Emily as she finishes her thought.

"What did we make?" Lyle calls out to Jesse, who is counting the money in his battered top hat.

"Two hundred thirty-seven dollars and change," Jesse calls back.

"Not bad," Lyle says. "You think it's worth sticking around for a few days?"

The idea of sticking around Rochester turns my stomach. All this is fine as long as we keep moving. When we're moving I don't think about Mima or Mom or school, or how screwed I'm going to be when I get home. So I'm really glad when Jesse shakes his head. "Nah, I say we keep moving, head south before it gets too much colder. We got lucky with the opening. There won't be crowds like this every night. Strong objections to moving on?"

"It's his van, but Jesse likes to decide things by consensus," G says quietly in my ear. "If anyone had a strong objection we'd talk more about it before making a decision." No one says anything, so we all pile in the van and head out to the suburbs to find a big-box store lot to camp in for the night.

"Ohhh, Butter Farms," Tim groans as we pass the ice cream chain. I glance at my watch. It's a little past ten.

"You think they're still open?" I ask.

"Nope," Tim says. "I think they're just closing up. Perfect timing!" Jesse turns into the parking lot and pulls up in front of the store. We all hop out, and Tim raps lightly on the glass. A pimply-faced kid with dyed black hair and a lip ring interrupts his mopping and walks over to the door. He points to the right of the door where the store hours are posted.

"We know man, we know," Jesse says. "Did you throw everything out already?" The kid points with the end of his mop to a sagging garbage bag waiting to be tossed into the dumpster. I look at the slogan on the Butter Farms sign, which reads, "Churned Fresh Daily," and right then I realize what Tim has in mind. "We'll take that off your hands," Jesse says and grins through the glass. The kid looks uncomfortable. He glances once towards the back of the store and then shrugs. He unlocks the door and thrusts the bag out. Tim grabs it before the door is even all the way open.

"Thanks, man," Jesse says. Can anyone say no to Jesse? He smiles at the kid with the mop likes he's done the right thing.

Meanwhile the leftover ice cream is melting quickly, so Jesse speeds off to find a place to park. He pulls the van up in the parking lot next to an empty baseball diamond.

Tim rummages through the bag, pulling out half-empty plastic containers of melting ice cream. "This one looks like sorbet," he calls out. "Maybe raspberry." He tosses it under-hand to Emily, who squeals with delight and digs around in the cabinet behind the driver's seat for six spoons. "Dibs on the chocolate fudge brownie," Tim says and puts a container beside his leg. "This one looks like Oreo cookie."

"I'll take it," I say. "I mean, if nobody else wants it."

"You're going to have to share," G says. She grabs a couple of spoons, and I follow her out of the van to the bleachers next to the baseball field. For some reason the lights are still on, the air around them buzzing with dust. I shiver and sit down next to her on the cold metal bench. The ice cream is the perfect temperature for eating: soft and creamy, but still enough re-sistance that you can bite rather than slurp it off your spoon. We take big spoonfuls and don't say anything for the next few minutes. I can feel the sugar rush coursing through my veins.

"So you and Lyle," I say between bites. "How long have you guys been doing your act?"

"I don't know. Ever since I met up with these guys, six months or something like that?"

"And were you guys ever, like, together? I mean like a couple?"

G snorts, and a piece of Oreo cookie rockets out of her mouth and lands on my knee. Still coughing, she reaches over and brushes it onto the ground. "He's not really my type, Andrew," she says.

"Oh, sorry," I say. My face flushes red, and I wait a few minutes for it to cool down. "I never get what girls mean when they say that."

"Well what *I* mean when *I* say that, is that Lyle's not my type mostly because he doesn't have a vagina." I'm embarrassed but not confused. But I must look it, because G feels the need to clarify even further. "I don't play for your team."

"Yeah, yeah, I get it. You're a lesbian." I try and say it like it's not the first time I've ever uttered the word in serious conversation. "I get it, I just didn't know."

"Huh," G says thoughtfully. "And here I thought my whole look screamed big dyke."

"Well, I don't really have a lot of experience identifying," I gulp here, "'big dykes.' You know, not in a lineup or anything."

G smiles. I think she's enjoying my discomfort and surprise. "Well, now you know."

I remember the word that popped into my head back at the bus station. I thought she looked severe. Is that a stereotype? Was I stereotyping her before I even knew she was a lesbian? I wonder if she knew I wasn't gay. I probably made it obvious the first time I stared down Emily's shirt.

A loud war whoop comes from the van. Jesse is running towards us, shirtless, his chest decorated with elaborate painted designs. My first thought is that it's ice cream, until I remember the paint set that someone pulled from the Walmart dumpster that morning. Tim, Jesse, and Lyle are all shirtless, their chests and faces decorated with intricate designs. Emily is trotting behind them, carrying the paint and wearing only a ratty-looking tank top tucked in at her ribcage like a bra. Her shoulders, stomach and face are also adorned. Jesse leads them in a victory lap around the bases, running and cartwheeling and yelling at the top of his lungs. Then they climb into the bleachers and surround us.

"Strip," Lyle says and points at both of us. G looks at me, shrugs, and pulls off her sweatshirt and puffy vest. I do the same with my top layers. My chest immediately ripples with tiny goose bumps, but I don't feel cold. Jesse takes a big glob of green paint on his finger and paints a zigzagging line down the side of each arm. Emily decorates my back with something yellow and orange, and after that I lose track of who's doing what. I just close my eyes and try to ignore the weirdness of so many unidentified fingers touching my skin. The paint is cold but dries quickly to form a crackly second skin on my arms, chest, and back. After a few minutes I open them and look over at G. I can't help but laugh. She looks like a little kid just in from a rainy Halloween.

"Come on," Jesse says, beckoning us to follow. "Let's go make a little noise." He takes off running toward the back of the baseball diamond, where he hops the short metal fence and keeps running. We all follow. I take one backward glance at my clothes, my only warm clothes, left in the bleachers. It's as though I'm leaving the bus station all over again. Every skin cell of my exposed flesh is tingling in the night air, every follicle of hair standing at attention.

We follow Jesse across the park and through some bushes into someone's backyard. I pause for a second before stepping onto private property. But no one else seems to care, so I follow the leader through their garden and over the monkey bars of a children's swing set. The only light from the house is the flickering blue glow of a television set. I swing from bar to bar, dancing on the outside of my old life like some colorfully painted, mocking monkey god. We run this way through more yards and driveways, down more sidewalks and across quiet suburban streets. The pavement of the streets is still warm and safe. *We* are what's dangerous. But no one stops us; no one calls out to us. We are running and flying.

Jesse finds an enormous trampoline in back of a huge Victorian-style mansion, and we all take turns bouncing and doing tricks. When the lights finally come on in an upstairs window, we retreat through the bushes at the back of the property. In back of another enormous McMansion, we stop for a minute to let Tim catch his breath.

Lyle sniffs the air suspiciously. "Is that what I think it is?"

Jesse's eyes go comic-book wide in the darkness. "Chlorine?" We creep through the trees to find the steam still rising from a large, kidney-shaped swimming pool. It looks like a giant aquamarine jewel shimmering in the night. "Oh, heated pool. I love this neighborhood," Jesse whispers.

"I don't know," I start to say.

"You don't have to go in," Jesse says, and it's not like a dare or a tough-guy act or anything. "We'll be quick, you can wait right here with our clothes." The rest of the Freegans are already pulling off their pants and stripping down to nothing. I shouldn't be surprised. They've definitely proved themselves to be an all-or-nothing kind of group. And then suddenly I'm standing there surrounded by five piles of clothes, and I can hear the soft splashes and sighs as they enter the warm water.

Jesse loves this neighborhood. I wonder if he would love Glens Falls. Or if he ever knew anybody with an in-ground pool. Does he love it because he senses the truth behind the heavy oak doors and alarm-sensitive windows? Does he know the houses are empty inside? These are depressing thoughts, and I don't want to be standing here in the dark all alone with them.

It's dark, I tell myself as I pull down my pants and then my boxers. I try not to look at anyone or see anything as I slip out of the trees and walk naked towards the edge of the pool. The water is within sight, and nobody is looking my way. I take a deep breath and in that same instant stub my big toe on the concrete path surrounding the pool. "Shit!" I curse loudly, and five heads whip around in my direction. There's nothing else to do in this situation. I take another big step and cannonball into the pool.

When I come up for air Jesse is laughing and shaking his head. "Come on, man, there's no way that went unnoticed. We gotta bolt." I take a minute to scrub at the paint on my skin before hopping out of the pool and back into my pants. Sure enough, we're barely dressed when the outdoor lights flicker on. We scamper out the driveway, holding our shoes and shaking our dripping heads. A few blocks away from the house, we stop to put our shoes on. I briefly examine the gash on my big toe before stuffing it back into my sock. Hopefully the chlorine sterilized it a little. We walk back toward the park and the van quietly. Jesse seems to know where he's going, and I just follow behind, floating really. These houses could be the houses of any of the towns I've lived in. The kids zoning out in front of the TV could be any of the kids I've sat beside in class for the last ten years. But they're in there, and I'm out here. As we're walking Emily skips up to me and pulls my arm around her shoulders. Her teeth are chattering wildly. "I'm fuh-fuh-fuh-freezing, Drew. Keep me warm."

I pull her in towards my body. For whatever reason, adrenaline, excitement, blood loss, I'm not cold at all. I rub her shoulder with my hand, and she wraps an arm around my waist. By the time we get back to the van I'm getting cold, but I'm still sad that our moment together is ending. And I'm a little bummed out when Lyle and Emily sleep up and the rest of us are down below, but mostly I'm too tired to care. My Spidey sack is warm and dry, and as I'm drifting off, I think about the sweetness of the ice cream and the warmth of the pool and the sensation of being painted on by a hundred different fingers. It's the oddest thing, but even though I'm miles from home and Mima's gone and Dad's a shit, the only absence I feel is the absence of loneliness.

THE SQUAT

In the morning Jesse ministers to my injured toe with some hydrogen peroxide from what looks like the world's oldest first aid kit. "Is that thing from World War I?" I joke as he pokes around in the metal tin for a Band-Aid that still has some adhesive power.

"I don't think you need stitches, but you're definitely going to lose the nail at some point," he assesses. Gingerly I place my sock over my foot, trying hard not to knock the Band-Aids.

After oatmeal and a brief cleaning of Shirley's floor, we are on the road again. It's only an hour to Buffalo, and there's some debate in the van about whether it's even worth stopping. Jesse and Lyle seem to think Cleveland would be busier and a better bet for making money, but G and Emily are concerned that by the time we get there it will be too late to scout a good location. Emily keeps talking about a squat she heard about on the outskirts of town that she wants to check out, and since I have no opinion about where we go and no idea what a squat is, I keep quiet. Finally everyone agrees to let Tim make the decision. G jabs him in the ribs, so he takes off his headphones, and explains the two choices. He listens carefully to both ideas and says, "I've never been to Buffalo, man. Let's stop there."

Jesse smiles and shakes his head. "Good enough," he says.

It's the second time I've witnessed the curious decision-making process they call consensus. Sometimes it seems as random as throwing a dart against a wall of swaying balloons. But the results are as good as any so-called adult decisions I've ever witnessed, and as long as they make decisions and we keep moving, I don't care.

I flip open the divorce journal to where there's a page called *Spending Time Together*. I know it's not my title. In fact, I don't even think it's my handwriting. But underneath two columns, labeled *mom* and *dad*, are lists of ways I spent time with my parents. There are only two things under Dad's column: shirt shopping and ice cream.

They're not bad memories. Dad used to take me with him when he'd go to Bloomingdale's to pick out a new dress shirt. He always did this before a job interview. I liked the way a man in a suit would come and ask us if we needed help, but Dad and I liked to go through the shirts ourselves, looking carefully at slight differences in stripes or buttons and checking the neck size, which I still remember was 15 1/2. Then we would go out for ice cream sundaes. It was always a school night.

There are a lot more things on Mom's side of the paper. Things like shoe shopping and groceries, soccer practice and skiing, picking out old movies at the library. But none of them have the clarity of this one memory with Dad.

***

"Okay," Tim says after we've been riding in silence for a while. "This is the game: desert island. You can only bring two movies for the rest of your life. What would they be?" He looks at me.

"I'm not going first," I protest. I know one of them right away, but I need to think about the other one.

"*Citizen Kane*," Lyle says. "And *One Flew Over the Cuckoo's Nest*."

Tim looks at him with disbelief. "Dude, that's a messed-up island you live on."

Lyle shrugs. "Whatever. "

Now I know I won't try and impress anyone with my answer. I'm tempted to say *The Muppet Movie*, just to point out how pretentious he's being, but I decide to be honest instead. "*North by Northwest* and The Lord of the Rings trilogy, I guess."

"Classy and dorky," Tim assesses. "I'm not sure the Lord of the Rings can count as one movie, but I'll let it go this time."

"Thanks," I say. G picks Lord of the Rings too, and something called *The Breakfast Club*, which I've never heard of. And then, before anyone else can respond, Tim goes into this long description of some Spanish movie he really likes where all these people are competing to see who can have the most luck. It sounds pretty weird.

"What about you?" I lean over and ask Emily quietly.

She shakes her head like she's embarrassed, but I can tell she's glad I asked. "I have really cheesy taste in movies," she whispers.

"So?" I say.

"And it's been ages since I saw one at the movie theater anyway."

"Come on. Just tell me," I nudge her.

"I really like *Grease*," she says and then looks up to see if I'm laughing. "And *Dirty Dancing*. Any Jane Austen movie, or anything with Meg Ryan. And musicals in general. I loved *Mamma Mia*," she gushes. She looks up, and I'm smiling. "You think I'm a total dork, don't you?"

"Hey, Emily," Tim interrupts. "What about you? Come on, two movies."

She shoots me a look. "I like books," she says.

"Luh-ame answer," Tim says. But he moves on to Jesse. Meanwhile Emily smiles at me like we have a secret.

Finding a place to perform in Buffalo turns out to be trickier than expected. After one sparsely attended performance the group decides to pack it in and head for the squat. In the meantime, I find out from Tim that a squat is abandoned real estate where people live without paying rent or owning the place. This is a new concept, and I write it down on my list of useful information, even though it doesn't sound like anywhere I would want to live. It's a funny list so far, considering a definition for the word *squat* comes right after directions on how to get the bus to pull over when you have to take a crap.

I'm picturing some sort of squalid apartment building or abandoned factory, so I'm pretty surprised when we pull up in front of an enormous home with a brick walkway and overgrown lawn. I guess I was expecting some kind of industrial zone, but the neighborhood is as suburban as the one I live in. Only after we pass through the gap in the eight-foot-high hedges on either side of the walkway do I start to notice anything out of the ordinary. Hanging from a branch in one of the hedges is a wind chime made entirely of twisted forks. In one window, Tibetan prayer flags hang in place of curtains, and in another there are strings of red glass beads. Jesse knocks, and when no one answers, he turns the handle and lets himself in.

We all follow close behind. The first room we pass might have been a living room. The only furniture left is a long, low coffee table pushed up against one wall and ten or so mismatched cushions spread out on the floor. There's an upright piano, an amplifier, and a couple mike stands set up on one side of the room. An enormous banner painted on canvas hangs over this setup and reads, "Dance Like No One Is Watching".

The place isn't filthy, but it's not exactly clean either. A few abandoned plates and bowls are stacked in the living room with the remnants of what looks like soup molding inside. The carpet is curling up along one wall and sprinkled with patches of bread crumbs. There's still no sign of inhabitants as we walk down the hallway towards the back of the house. The walls of the hallway are covered with intricate finger-painted art resembling tribal designs. I'm admiring these when I slam into the back of Lyle. He turns around and gives me a glare as I blush and apologize. He's still not really warming up to me.

There's a warm, yeasty smell floating in from somewhere in front of us. "Hi," I hear Jesse greeting someone. We all push forward into the kitchen. The bread baker is a short guy in his twenties with curly brown hair and wire-rim glasses. He's wearing camouflage pants and is shirtless except for a dingy white apron.

"Welcome to the Shire," he says and smiles warmly. "I'm Mark."

Everyone introduces themselves, and we sit down on benches around a long wooden table. Mark talks at us for a while, explaining the workings of the house and the various roles that the five current full-time residents play. He makes bread and hummus every day, or as needed, and is also responsible for cleaning the bathrooms. I raise an eyebrow, thinking back to the state of the living room. The bread smells incredible, and I try to ignore the fact that he keeps wiping his nose with the back of his hand.

"I call it Alien Garlic Bread," he says. "Because it's out of this world." He laughs hardest at this until he snorts. Then without any segue, he adds, "If you guys want to crash here tonight, we're having a tempeh stir-fry and vegan chocolate cake." My stomach lets out an audible groan.

Mark snorts again and says, "I guess that's a yes, huh, man?"

***

After we set up our sleeping bags on the floor of an unused bedroom, I wander around back, where there's a swimming pool that's been filled in with dirt and turned into a garden. Aside from a few withered and blackened tomato vines, most of the rows are covered with hay. I turn my head at the faint sound of strumming and see a guy, at least a few years older than I am, hanging his legs off the second-floor balcony, a battered guitar in his lap. "Hey, man," he calls. I give a little wave in return. "Did you just roll in with those guys in the bus?"

I nod.

"Cool," he says. "I'm Dylan."

"Andrew," I say.

"Yeah," he says like he already knows or isn't listening. "Is, um, Emily, is she like with anyone?"

"What?"

"Like that short anarchist guy? Are they like together?"

"Um, I'm not really sure. I haven't really been with these guys for all that long."

"Yeah," he says and blows his stringy bangs out of his eyes. "Sorry about that." He picks up his guitar and goes inside. I keep walking around the side of the house, but I stop when I hear voices. It's Emily and Lyle, and neither of them sounds happy.

"I know you don't believe me," Emily is saying, "But I didn't know he would be here."

"And now you want to leave?" Lyle says, sounding exasperated. "And I'm supposed to explain what exactly to everyone else? What's the big deal? It's only one night."

There's a long pause during which I slowly creep backwards to avoid getting caught eavesdropping.

We eat our tempeh stir-fry and vegan chocolate cake with spoons and knives. The squat had a visitor last month who turned all their forks into wind chimes like the one I saw walking in. Mark's been living there the longest, almost four years. He said no one bothers them because the place was such an eyesore before they moved in. They've actually improved the property values just by keeping the lawn and the bushes tidy. Mark says the owner is a real estate company in Cleveland, but Bess, one of the other housemates, insists it's an actual person whose aunt lived there with a bunch of cats until she died about ten years ago. Apparently the power company will give you service without proof of legitimate residency as long as you're willing to pay the bill. Another useful fact for my life-after-high-school list.

Besides Dylan and Mark, the three other housemates are women, so it's not hard to figure out that it's Dylan whom Emily has some problem with. Every time he speaks, she winces. She barely touches her food during dinner, but with the crowd around the table, her silence goes unnoticed, except by me and probably Lyle. Dylan offers to play music after dinner, so everyone grabs a seat in the living room except for Emily, who disappears, muttering something about a walk.

Dylan plays some covers that are okay and then some of his own stuff, which is pretty drippy—a lot of love songs with obvious rhymes. G and I play spades until my eyelids feel like they're wearing lead aprons. When I roll out my Spidey sack and climb in, Emily still hasn't come back.

In the middle of the night I get up to pee, carefully stepping around the sleeping bodies. It's too dark to tell who's there and who isn't. Stumbling a little bit down the hallway, I catch my wounded big toe on a loop of carpet and curse softly as pain knifes my foot. I slap the tile wall to the right of the bathroom door until my hand finds the switch. The compact fluorescent bulb is naked and gives off a greenish glow as it hums to life. Something rustles the shower curtain, and I freeze as my heart jumps into my throat. The pressure in my bladder is gone, and I contemplate just turning around and going back to bed. It's probably just a cat. I reach forward and shake the curtain to see if I can scare out the offending feline. Instead I see a hand.

"Drew!" It's Emily. My brain manages to register this before my throat releases the girly horror-movie scream that was about to pass my lips.

"Jesus! You scared the shit out of me." Her nose is red and her cheeks are tear-streaked. She's sitting cross-legged at one end of the giant claw-foot tub. "What are you doing in the tub?"

She sighs and wipes at her cheeks with the back of her hand. "Oh, I came back really late from my walk. You guys were all asleep, and I didn't want wake anyone fumbling around for my stuff." She looks at me, a faint smile on her lips. It occurs to me that I'm standing in front of her in my boxers and a T-shirt. Why is she smiling? Am I hanging out the front of my shorts? I try to casually adjust things to avoid that possibility and sit down on the toilet seat in front of her.

"So you couldn't find a couch or anything?"

"I felt safer in here."

"Right. In case there's an earthquake?" I joke.

She gives me a sad half-smile. "Yeah, something like that."

I'm not sure what to say to that. I'm not sure if she wants me to ask what she means. I sit there on the toilet, lightly tapping my fingernails against the porcelain cover. There's something blank and defeated about her sadness. It's something I recognize, maybe even relate to. I put my hand on her arm, but it's not enough. I want to be closer to her. "Well, I'm awake now. Mind if I join you?" I say it like I'm joking, but when Emily smiles for real and scoots to one side, I shrug my shoulders and step into the tub. "Kinda cold," I note as I lean up against the wall of the tub. "Not so great for sleeping. You should come back in." Emily looks like she's considering it, but then shakes her head with that same sad smile. "Well, we can't have you getting cold now can we?" I want to cheer her up. I want to be the one who makes her smile again. Which I guess is why I do what I do next. I reach over and turn on the water.

"Jesus, Drew. What are you doing?"

For a minute I'm afraid I'm the big jerk here. The water is cold and soaks my boxers and the bottom of my T-shirt. "Warming up?" I suggest and look hopefully at Emily.

It works. She laughs and flicks some of the water at my face with her fingertips. "You're crazy!" The water is getting warm now. I pull the stopper on the drain and the tub begins to fill. Emily pulls off her sweater and her thick wool socks. I stand up and hop out of the tub, glad that my boxers are a dark color.

"Where are you going?" she asks.

"Surprise." I open the wooden cabinet above the toilet, hoping what I want is in there. Bingo. I dump the contents of a plastic container of lavender bubble bath into the tub and step back in. Soon we are up to our chins in big fluffy white bubbles. We make bubble beards and bubble mustaches and smack the bubbles between our palms like little kids. Every time the water cools off we drain a little and add more from the tap.

"So you and Dylan know each other, huh?" I say all casual. As if I haven't been thinking of a way to bring it up for the last twenty minutes.

"It's obvious, isn't it?"

I nod because it's better than admitting to being an eavesdropper.

"Yeah," she goes on, "it's total bullshit that he's even here. I'm the one who told him about it. And he said it sounded like a bunch of dumb hippie freeloaders."

"Mmm." I know better than to share my thoughts about the cleanliness of the place. "So you guys were together once?"

"Yeah." She holds up some bubbles in the palm of her hand and blows them toward my face. "Back when I believed in monogamy." She says it like she's forty years old, and I would laugh if she didn't look so sad and so serious. She's staring at her knees, which rise up out of the bubbles like two cloud-piercing mountain peaks. "I actually thought I loved him." For just a moment I can see it in her face—how much she did love him and how hurt she is. "He totally knew it too. And he used it to manipulate the crap out of me. Don't ever fall in love, Drew, if you can help it."

"Seriously?" I say.

She shakes her head. "No. You're right. Love is a good thing. A really good thing. Just don't ever fall in love with a self-centered musician."

"Okay," I agree, hiding my smile with the back of a soap-bubbled hand. What about a dreadlocked Hula-Hooper with a slight flair for the dramatic?

"He would say he was going to be somewhere and then purposely not go. I'd show up looking for him, and when he wasn't there, I'd confront him later and he'd act like I misheard him, like I was the one being all crazy. And then other times he'd be so loving and amazing and he'd tell me how amazing I was. It was back and forth like that, and it made me feel completely psycho sometimes. I don't know if I'll ever love anyone ever again."

"What about Lyle?"

"Yeah," she says, and sighs as if this is an answer we both understand. "Sorry, Drew. I'm sure you don't want to hear all this crap."

"No, I do. I really do." Maybe I'm a bit too insistent, because she looks at me funny and then holds up her fingers to show me.

"Pruned," she says. She reaches over to show me and gently ruffles my hair. I feel a flicker of annoyance at being pet, like a dog or a younger brother.

"Yeah, we should probably get out before we get hypothermia or something," I say. But neither of us moves.

"Thanks, Drew," Emily says, and it sounds pretty sincere.

"Anytime."

"Anytime I want a bath?" she jokes.

"Uh-huh." I want to add more, but I don't. She can take it however she wants. We both stand up in the tub, soaking and covered with bubbles. There's one threadbare towel hanging on the rack.

"Here," Emily says and throws it to me. "You go first. Dry off, and I'll meet you in there. Can't sleep in here now that you soaked my bed." She turns around, and I strip down and towel off as best I can. I wrap the bath mat around my waist and leave my soaking clothes hanging over the edge of the tub. Thankfully I'm using my backpack as a pillow, so I find my extra boxers easily and slip back into my sleeping bag. A few minutes later I see Emily's silhouette as she slips quietly into the room. I lie there for a while thinking about how much has changed in the last thirty-six hours. A girl touched my knee. I took a bath with a girl. Not just any girl; a hot girl I actually like. Or at least I think I do. Is it wrong to want her to feel about me the way she felt about Dylan, even if it made her crazy? Maybe it's the bathwater; the wrinkling and pruning of my fingers stretching my skin. I feel closer to the world in a good way, on the inside looking out instead of the other way around.

ON THE ROAD AGAIN

Jesse guesses it's about four hours to Cleveland from where we are, and from there we'll keep heading south. The festival they keep talking about isn't for another couple weeks, but Jesse seems to get a little antsy whenever they have a bad show. It's the only time I see him look anxious at all. So we leave Buffalo the next morning after oatmeal and more Alien Garlic Bread, which truly is incredible, though not the greatest combination for taste or breath.

I feel like I've been away from home for months instead of days, and I have to keep reminding myself that it's only Sunday and that Mom expects I'm arriving home sometime tomorrow. This thought is like a book that keeps falling from its shelf. Rather than look at it, I simply put it back on the shelf and keep moving on.

The two shows in Cleveland and the next day in Louisville barely yield half of what the Freegans made in Rochester. I'm beginning to understand why Lyle was interested in staying another night. Having a draw, like an artist's open house or a street fair, makes a huge difference in the number of people who turn out and are willing to cough up a couple bucks for entertainment.

We're hanging out around the van between shows in Louisville, and I keep looking at my watch as if the time passing is going to change what I know I need to do. I know Mom is out there somewhere, pacing the house, waiting for me to call and say I'm coming home. It's two o'clock, and then it's ten after, and then two thirty. Finally, at quarter of three, I stand up suddenly and announce that I need to find a pay phone.

"Do you want company?" G asks.

"Sure," I say. This phone call will be harder, much harder, and not only because Mom is going to be livid when she realizes I'm not on my way back to Glens Falls. She's going to want answers, answers that are only starting to take shape in my own head.

There's a pay phone about a block and a half from the van, but the receiver is missing the cover, belching out a mess of multicolored wire. We wander around for a bit until we find a useable one near the public library. G takes a few polite steps away and pulls a set of juggling balls out of her pocket. I take a deep breath and make the collect call.

"Hi, Mom," I say after she agrees to accept the charges.

"Hello, Andrew. I hope you're calling to tell me what time your bus gets in." There is a long moment of silence that follows this declaration. In that moment I realize that up until right now I wasn't sure how this conversation was going to go. I wasn't sure if I was going to let her convince me that it was time to come home. A hot shower and a homemade dinner does sound pretty good. But not good enough.

"Mom, I'm really sorry if this upsets you, but I'm not ready to come home. I really like these people and I'm having a good time. And as weird as this sounds, I think I'm learning something too." I say this last part softly so G can't hear. I don't know why I bother, it's not like that part even registers with Mom.

"I don't believe this," she hisses. "Andrew, we had an agreement. You said you would be home today."

"Actually, *you* said I would be home today."

"What about school? The quarter closes in less than three weeks."

"I don't think I was going to pass this quarter anyways."

"I can't condone this behavior, Andrew."

"I'm not asking you to, Mom. Look, I know it's not ideal. You don't know exactly where I am or who I'm with but—"

"Do not minimize that!" For the first time Mom's voice breaks, and I can hear that she's crying. "You do not know what it's like to have you out there, god knows where, with god knows who, doing god knows what. You do not know what that's like as a parent, so don't pretend you do!"

"I'm sorry." I pause for a minute. "I'll try and do a better job of checking in."

"That would be helpful," Mom says. Her voice is still tight. "You're going to miss your grandmother's funeral," she adds.

"Yeah, I kind of figured that. I guess I'm hoping she would understand."

My mother sighs loudly. "She probably would." I know it takes a lot for Mom to say that, and I appreciate that she's not using Mima's funeral to guilt me into coming home. So I decide to pick on Dad a little to make her feel better.

"So Dad's back from his vacation?"

"Apparently."

"He left me a jerky message."

"He's worried about you too," Mom says. Now I definitely need to get off the phone. My running away is not supposed to team the two of them up against me.

"I gotta go, Mom. We're leaving soon, so I gotta go."

"Andrew, where are you?"

"Uh, Louisville."

"And where are you going exactly?"

"I'm not really sure, Mom. South."

"South? Where do you sleep?"

"In the van. It's really pretty comfortable. Listen, I really gotta go. I'll call you soon." As I hang up I can hear her saying that she loves me. I walk over to where G is bouncing one of the juggling balls up and down on her foot, Hacky-Sack style.

"Hey," she says. "How'd that go?"

"Eh, okay, I guess. She's not happy that I'm staying."

G shrugs. "Why are you staying?"

The question catches me off guard. "I don't know. I'm having a good time, and I thought it was okay with you guys. I mean if it's not, just let me know," I stutter a bit.

"Sorry, I didn't mean to freak you out. We're happy to have you hang out with us. I just wanted to be sure you weren't staying because of Emily."

"Well, it's not," I reply shortly.

"Sorry, my bad," G says. We walk together for a while without saying anything.

"Why do you care anyway?" I ask. "I mean, what if it was part of the reason for me staying? Would that be the worst thing in the world?"

"No. And it still wouldn't be any of my business. I just wouldn't want to see you get hurt."

"Why do you say that? What do you have against Emily, anyways?"

"Well, for one thing, she's a dry drunk."

"A what?"

"A dry drunk," G repeats. "Look, none of us drink, right? But I'm straight edge. I made a conscious choice to stay away from drugs and alcohol. I don't want it around me; I don't want it in my life. When we hooked up with Emily in Burlington, she was a mess. She had some boyfriend problem; she was drinking and probably other stuff too. Lyle helped her clean up her act, and she latched on to us and the whole straight edge thing too."

"So what's wrong with that?"

"Look, I'm glad that Emily isn't drinking and that she's doing better and whatever. But if you're drinking to get away from something, you can't just decide to stop and not deal with the stuff that made you drink in the first place. You're like a ticking time bomb. Something's going to set you off one day and you'll be right back where you started from. She's a drunk, just one who happens not to be drinking right now."

"Like your dad?"

"Like a lot of people," G says.

"Maybe she's really changed," I offer.

"Maybe. I wish I could believe in change like that. I wish I'd seen more of it. But what I have seen is that Emily likes attention and drama. A lot of attention and a lot of drama. And your arrival has neatly provided both."

"What do you mean?"

G looks at me like I'm purposely being dense. "You're like Emily's little project, you know?"

"Oh great."

"But seriously, she like gets off on introducing you to her hippie vegan pseudo anarchist ideas. And you think she's hot, and don't even try to deny it because I've seen you staring at her. She is cute. But she knows it, and that's not so cute. She's already got Lyle wrapped around her little finger, and she's using you to stir up the drama."

"So you're saying she doesn't like me for me," I joke nervously.

"Heck, no. I mean *yes*, she probably does like you for you. I'm just saying that's not her only motivation, and I'd hate to see you get hurt, or like throw away some other part of your life just to follow her around the country."

"What makes you think my life is so great, anyway? Maybe I should be throwing it away."

For the first time in the short time that I've known her, G looks pissed. "Whatever," she says shortly. "I'm not going to go there."

"Go where?"

"Explain everything you've probably got when you're acting like a spoiled douchebag." She stomps away from me, and my jaw drops.

I walk after her because I don't have anywhere else to go. Should I be apologizing for something? Before I can stop her to ask, G turns around. Her face is still red. "I'm sorry," she says. "I hope you will stay with us for as long as you want." She pauses. "Even if it's just for Emily."

"I thought lesbians weren't supposed to say douchebag," I say. She rolls her eyes, but she smiles a small, tense smile. I don't know how I can make G understand that when I'm with Emily, even when she's rambling on about her old boyfriends,

135

I feel useful, not used. "Thanks for looking out for me. I'll think about that, really I will. I guess it probably sounds kind of pathetic and desperate to you. But I don't think I really care what her motivations are."

"And if it doesn't work out, you can always go home," G says.

"Yeah, I know." I say this maybe a little too quickly. G cringes, but she doesn't say anything more.

THE MEATOLYZER

The next morning Tim nudges me awake with his foot. He puts a finger to his lips and gestures toward the van door, which he opens without making a sound. I shake the sleep out of my head, pull on my clothes, and follow him outside.

"Secret mission," he says when we're well enough away from the van. "Sausage, egg, and cheese."

"Gross man. I'm not eating that out of a dumpster."

He shakes his head. His trademark spiky hairdo is flattened from sleeping, and his boxers billow out the top of his pants. "No need, brother. My treat. In exchange for your silence." We walk a couple blocks from the Louisville Walmart parking lot, where we slept for the night, and there are the golden arches. The trademark smell of grease fills the air. "You know, Mc-Donald's manufactures those smells. They actually have to add the chemical smell to the food so all the food smells exactly the same no matter where you are in the country."

I wave my hand at Tim to get him to shut up. "Just let me enjoy it, okay?" And I do enjoy it. We sit and silently scarf down two egg, sausage, and cheese biscuits each, some hash browns, and ice-cold Coca-Cola. It's kind of disgusting how much I enjoy it. Afterwards we're both just slumped there in the booth in a self-induced salt and fat coma. "So I take it you're not really a vegan?" I say.

"Nah." Tim shakes his head. "I mean, I see their point at all. It's better to eat less meat, lower impact and all that. And I don't mind eating veggie when I'm on the road with these guys. But I just can't give it up altogether, especially not pork product, man. I love me some bacon and sausage." He smacks his lips, and we both sit there silent again for a while. I watch as a very pregnant woman balances a tray in one hand while holding the hand of a squirming toddler in the other. "I guess we should head back," Tim finally says after the breakfast club of octogenarians clears out of the table behind us.

"Yeah, I guess so. What are you going to tell everyone about where we went?"

"Dunno. I figured we'd hit the Stop and Shop dumpster next door on our way back and come back with provisions."

"Okay," I say, and haul myself up and out of the booth.

The supermarket dumpster turns out to be a real jackpot. Tim hoists himself up inside and tosses back promising-looking bags for me to pick through. The first such bag yields several bottles of Fresh and Fruity all-natural smoothies. They are due to expire today, but they're still cold from the cooler. I pull these out and set them on the ground. The next bag doesn't have anything useable, or if it did, it it's now coated in an exploded container of cheese dip. A third bag produces several crushed boxes of Rice and Spice mix. The cardboard is ripped, but inside the plastic packages are intact. It's turning out to be a pretty good haul when we're interrupted by a guy with big chops and a gruff voice poking his head out of the store. "Hey, what do you think you're doing?" he shouts.

"Liberating you from the excesses of capitalism, man," Tim says. It wouldn't have been my first response, and the guy with the chops doesn't seem to know what to make of it either.

"You can't be in there. That's private property."

Tim sighs like the guy has uncovered the obvious, but he makes his way to the edge of the dumpster like he's going to get out. "There's no law against going through the trash," he says. "Your store was throwing this out. It's not like we're stealing or anything."

The guy squints at us, like he's trying to put it all together. "We got plenty of stuff inside," he says. "Why don't y'all just come in and buy something here? Can't have you in the dumpster though. Can't imagine we've got insurance on that."

Tim hops down with another big sigh. "Thanks anyway, man." The guy doesn't say anything when we collect the stuff I've already set aside, but he watches to make sure we leave and waits until we're out of the parking lot before he disappears back into the store.

"So, Andrew," Tim draws my name into a deep breath in my face. "Do I smell like sausage?"

I recoil at his warm breath in my face. "No, mostly you smell like dumpster."

"Good, because I wouldn't want Emily to give me the meatolyzer." We both snicker as Tim describes a make-believe device that would flag and capture vegetarians when they fell off the wagon. When we get back to the van everyone's excited about the juice and the other stuff we got. No one even asks why we were up and out early.

***

Once we get going it's a long day of driving from Louisville to Nashville and then on to Memphis. We stop the van so the Freegans can perform in Nashville, but they barely bring in enough to cover a tank of gas. Lyle wants to try another spot, but he's outvoted by everyone else who would rather move on to Memphis. It's another three and a half hours on the road, and by the time we pull into Memphis everyone is ready to get out of the van for a while. It's too late to set up for a show, so we decide to split up again and scout the area. This time I'm with Jesse. We wander the streets in the main tourist area until we end up at the Beale Street Landing on the banks of the Mississippi River.

"Have you ever seen it before?" I ask Jesse.

He nods. "I've been across a couple times on road trips. But you know, it's funny. I don't think I ever got out of the car and really stood next to it. That's something different, you know?"

"Yeah, it's browner than I thought it would be." The water flowing past us is a deep coffee color. Jesse doesn't seem to be in any real rush to leave, so we just stand there for a while, taking in the sunset and the crisp air next to the riverbank. "Do you think you'll go back to school?" I ask him after a while.

"No, too much money," he says.

"So what do you think you'll do?" Going to college has always been a part of any future I ever discussed with my parents.

"I'm not sure," Jesse says. "My grams had to sell my dad's house, and pretty much everything inside it, when he died to pay off what he owed in college loans and back taxes. But there's some land she was able to hang on to. I might try and see what

I could grow on it. You know, a small operation—organic and all that. It's just an idea. I really like the idea of being able to support myself, live off what I can grow and all that."

"Do you know how to do that stuff?"

"A little bit." Jesse smiles. "Actually a buddy of mine from school has an older brother with a small place not too far from here in Arkansas. It's not exactly on the way, but I was thinking we might swing by and pay him a visit. See if we can work on the farm in exchange for food for a couple days. I'd like to see what he's got going for crops and livestock."

"That sounds cool," I say.

Jesse laughs quietly and looks down at his shoes. "You're a pretty open-minded guy, Andrew."

"What do you mean?"

"I mean I don't know too many sixteen-year-old guys who would think becoming a farmer or traveling around in a van with a bunch of hippies is cool."

I think about this for a while as we walk back to the van. I've been called a lot of things before: emo, goth, gay, lazy, an underachiever, apathetic, but never open-minded. Emily said it too. I decide I kind of like it. *I'm open-minded.* I try it on in my mind like a hat or a new piece of clothing. It seems to fit. I try and imagine telling this to Mom and Dad. *I ran away and learned that I'm really open-minded.* I can see their faces; Dad looking confused and Mom just disappointed. *It's not enough. Even I know that on some level.*

Everyone's back at the van but Lyle. He and Tim apparently got separated when Tim stopped to record some street musicians. "We're going to have to be on top of our game to make some money around here," he says. "Those guys were good." Emily and G found a spot called Court Square they like for performing the next day. Emily has the camp stove out and is boiling water for some spaghetti. I'm rooting through the plastic bags, looking for a box of pasta, when the phone rings. It's such an unfamiliar noise that we all stop and stare at one another.

"I thought your phone was dead," G says.

"It is," I say. "That's not my ring." Everyone starts rummaging through the clothes, bags, and books on the van floor to find the source of the mechanical ringtone. Emily finds it first: a phone buried underneath a pile of dirty socks and long underwear. She shrugs her shoulders and flips it open.

"Hello? Who? No, I'm sorry, there's no Carter here. Up with People? Lady, I think you have the wrong number."

Suddenly a very pale Lyle is standing behind her. He grabs the phone from her hand and walks away from the van, but not before we hear him say, "Hi, Mom. No, sorry, that was some stupid kid on the trip."

No one says anything, but we're all trying hard to go about our business quietly and simultaneously look like we're not trying to eavesdrop. I see Jesse and G exchange a look, and I wonder if they knew more about Lyle than they've been letting on. After a few minutes Lyle is back with a tense, confrontational look on his face. "What was that all about?" Emily asks. "Since when do you have a cell phone? And who on Earth is Carter Delisle?"

"That's what my parents call me," Lyle answers gruffly.

"I thought you didn't speak to your parents," Emily says.

"Wait a minute, wait a minute," Tim interrupts. "You guys are both from Burlington right?" Emily nods, but Lyle doesn't say anything. "And you're a Delisle? Like *the* Delisles?

Like the ones who own Delisle Paper and like half the forest in Northern Vermont."

Lyle's face has gone from ghost white to beet red. "It's not *me*," he stresses. "It's my mother's family, and I don't have anything to do with them anymore."

"Except when they call you on your secret cell phone," Emily snipes.

"Take it easy, Emily," Jesse says softly.

"Don't tell me what to do. Maybe you don't care that he's been lying to us. But I do. What the hell is Up with People anyways?"

"They're like student ambassadors around the world," I offer. "They visit people in other countries and share their culture and stuff. We had some kids from Nigeria and Ghana visit our school at the beginning of the year."

"So your parents think you're some kind of student ambassador?" Emily's voice is bitter. "That's rich! I can't believe you said you ran away. Do your parents send you care packages too?"

The whole thing is awful. Lyle looks mortified, and I can't even look at him or G, because it's a little sickening how much Lyle's life sounds like an echo of mine.

"I only told them that so they wouldn't send the police after me or some private detective. As long as I check in every few weeks, they don't care. They don't really care where I am anyway as long as I'm out of their hair."

Emily shakes her head. "Boo hoo, sounds like a sad story. Poor neglected rich boy."

"Hey," Jesse interrupts again. "I think that's enough." It's the only time I've ever heard Jesse raise his voice, and the effect is immediate. Emily stomps off, and Lyle goes after her. I take over the spaghetti, but I'm so distracted that I add too much pasta and forget to stir. The result is an enormous starchy lump that I try to disguise with globs of tomato sauce and garlic powder.

"Not much of a chef, are you, Andrew?" G says as she attacks her pasta with a fork and knife.

That night it's my turn to sleep up in the pop-up. I'm a little nervous to be sharing the space with Tim because, one, it's the closest I've ever slept to another guy, and, two, his flatulence can be pretty overwhelming. But he assures me that spaghetti doesn't really have that effect on his digestive system, and within about five minutes he's breathing slow and deep. I can't fall asleep right away. I watch out the small screen window, trying to tell myself that I'm not waiting for Emily to come back and that I'm not hoping that she's alone.

HOT SPRINGS

Eventually I must have fallen asleep, because when I wake up, it's morning and they're both asleep, albeit on opposite sides of the van floor. I try to go back to sleep, but after a few tosses and turns I realize it's futile. The creaking van door does exactly what I hoped it would; awakens Emily and no one else. She smiles and creeps out after me. We walk without speaking down to the river. Emily sits down on the browning grass, and I plop down next to her and start pulling apart clovers. I'm staring at her out of the corner of my eye. I love the way the baby hairs just above her ears form tiny golden ringlets.

"Do *you* think I overreacted about Lyle?" she asks.

It feels like a test question. Is the right answer the obvious one, the one that will influence the best outcome for me, or is it the one that makes me look like a good guy? "I don't know," I say truthfully.

"I'm kind of sensitive about people lying to me," she says and looks off mysteriously. I think about what G said about Emily and her love of drama. I don't take the bait.

"If it makes a difference, I don't think he intended the lie for you specifically."

Her face falls a little. "Yeah," she admits, "you're probably right.

"G thinks—" I start to say.

"G hates me," Emily interrupts.

I'm quiet, which I don't want her to take for agreement. "I don't think she *hates* you."

Emily shrugs. "She doesn't like me." I don't say anything. Emily starts to pull at the grass in front of her. "What about you, Drew? Have you ever had your heart broken?"

"Nope. Not even close."

"Lucky."

"Um, sort of. In a monastic kind of way."

Emily laughs. She throws back her head, and I have a sudden urge to kiss her throat. "You're good, Drew. You're a good person. I need more good people in my life." A fearful look crosses Emily's face for just an instant and then it's gone. She stands up and pitches a handful of grass into the muddy river. I wait a minute before reluctantly getting up. We walk back to the van together, and she catches my hand and swings it like we're little kids at the zoo. Her palm is soft and warm. My heart is warm too. Emily thinks I'm a good person. Can't really remember the last time someone said that to me. Mima probably. I swallow hard at the lump in my throat.

After breakfast, Jesse outlines a plan to head for Hot Springs, Arkansas, where there's a bluegrass festival going on all week. He's hoping to make enough money to get across Texas, which he describes as an inhospitable place for people like the Freegans. He notes Austin as a possible exception. Still, it's a big state, and everyone agrees it would be good to have some funds socked away before making the crossing. Shirley has proved herself a more than reliable ride, if a little on the thirsty side when it comes to miles per gallon.

Mostly it's G and Tim and Jesse who do the talking. Lyle and Emily are silently sullen, and I'm still along for the ride. There are no strong objections when Jesse mentions the possibility of visiting his friend's farm after the bluegrass festival is over. So we've got a plan, at least for the next week or so. I'm kind of hoping for some opportunity to take a shower.

Before we leave Memphis I find a pay phone in the park down by the river and call Mom again. It's awful. She cries and tells me she hasn't been sleeping, and I try and tell her not to worry. She brings up school again and tells me that all my teachers have been asking about me. Which, with the exception of Ms. Tuttle, I kind of doubt. I've left enough schools to recognize that semi-relieved look teachers give you when you tell them you're leaving, and they realize they'll have one less paper to grade and one less kid to worry about. It's really hard to get off the phone. She keeps stalling in a way that makes me feel incredibly guilty. I wish I could put into words why I can't come home yet, so she would know that it's mostly not about her. But I would have to know those words first.

Back at the van, the air is still heavy with Lyle and Emily's drama. I pick up my book again. I'm rereading the letter that McCandless writes to the old man he befriends, the one where he tells him how important it is to lead a life of adventure and new horizons. And even though it strikes me as kind of an unfair thing to tell someone in their eighties, I feel for the first time like McCandless and I might actually have something in common. Jesse is driving and Tim is riding up front, trying to get Shirley's ancient stereo system to hook up to his video camera so he can play us the street musicians he recorded in Memphis. G and I are playing Spit in the back. Lyle is pretending to read, and Emily is throwing stony glances in his direction. Tim gives up on the stereo and pulls out a dusty shoebox from underneath the passenger seat. "Okay, people, enough drama. It's random CD time!" he announces. G passes up the boom box they use for performances, and Tim makes a big show of closing his eyes and pulling a disc at random from the box.

"They were Jesse's dad's," G says. "None of the CDs are labeled, and there's a lot of classic rock and bad eighties hair bands, so consider yourself warned." But the CD that Tim picks out turns out to be a totally innocuous classic: Paul Simon's *Graceland*. Soon we're all bobbing our heads to "Boy in the Bubble." By the time "Graceland" comes on, we're all humming quietly. "You Can Call Me Al" has us all singing the chorus at the top of our lungs. If anyone thinks that the lyrics to "Diamonds on the Soles of Her Shoes" are particularly appropriate to this morning's squabble, no one says anything. And for a while all the tension between Lyle and Emily seems to slip out the window on the moving musical breeze.

The CD is over, and it's agreed that we should wait for a while before playing another one since they need the stereo for the show, and batteries aren't cheap. Emily scooches over to where G and I are playing cards and pretends to be interested in the game for a while. Eventually she lies down with her head on my thigh and starts reading the arts section of a Memphis newspaper. G looks up from her cards to give me a raised eyebrow, which I ignore. "How about a little space here, Emily," G says as she goes to deal the next hand.

"I don't hear anyone else complaining," Emily says as she moves over half a millimeter to the right. Eventually she sits up and starts stretching her head and neck from one side to the other. "I slept like crap last night," she remarks to no one in particular. "I must have slept funny because my neck kills," she adds. At this point I'm sufficiently distracted, and G manages to throw down her last cards and win the game before I can stop her.

"Sucker," she says to punctuate her win.

"Andrew, will you rub my neck?" Emily asks.

"Sure," I say, ignoring the little cough that G gives and the tightening of the muscles along Lyle's jaw.

I've never rubbed anyone's neck before, much less the neck of a girl that I find incredibly attractive. I focus all my attention on moving my hands and rippling my fingers in a way that I imagine would feel good. I must be good at it, though because Emily is sighing and almost moaning as I work on the knots around her neck and spine. Lyle is reading even more intently than before, and I just keep telling myself I'm only the masseuse here and this really isn't my problem. Maybe if I were a bigger person I would try harder to ignore Emily's attentions, but I'm not.

Emily's neck beneath all that hair is surprisingly dainty. For just a minute I have a flash of Margaret's neck from back in English class. Compared to Emily, Margaret's neck seems tame, even boring. Would Alex think Emily was hot? He definitely wouldn't approve of her dreads. Did I even speak to any girls the entire time I was at St. Mary's? What was wrong with me? And what's different now? This is the scarier question.

What's Wrong With Me. It was another list I had in the divorce diary, except it's blank. I remember being asked to write it down, as a pathetically obvious attempt to dig out my insecurities, but not being able to think of something. I remember the counselor lady, an overweight woman with tightly curled brown hair, pointing out how great it was that I didn't have anything to write down here. As if it was proof of anything besides the fact that I couldn't think hard enough to write something down.

When we arrive in Hot Springs, Emily grabs her backpack and announces to all of us that she's going off to have some alone time. Lyle mumbles something about wanting to find a hardware store and wanders off solo as well.

"I thought I saw signs for a YMCA on the way in. Anyone want to try and grab a shower?" Jesse says.

"YES!" I shout, and G and Tim both look at me and crack up. The four of us drive in circles for a little bit, asking directions, and eventually make our way to the Hot Springs YMCA. This is not the YMCA I remember from my childhood swim lessons. There's no peeling paint or hair stuck in the rubber mats on the locker room floor. This is a brand-new facility, and after the desk clerk looks us over a few times and checks with her supervisor, we are allowed into the locker rooms to shower and clean up.

If it weren't for Tim's singing I could stay under the hot water for hours. As it is, my fingers are pruned when I finally emerge from the stall. I use the soap provided in the dispenser to wash everything, even though I'm not sure it's meant for hair. I wish I had clean clothes to put on over my clean body, but this will have to do for now. Jesse mentions something about going in on a load of laundry together if we can find one of those places with an industrial-sized washer and dryer.

We head back to the center of town in case Lyle and Emily have returned, but there's no sign of either of them, so we leave the van and decide to scout out the local dumpsters for some variety in our dinner. Downtown Hot Springs is actually kind of cool. It feels a little like an old mining town from one of those Western movies, except with a bit of Southern flavor. I read on one of the tourist signs that Native Americans used the naturally heated water as a gathering place for years before Europeans came along. The old bathhouse buildings line one side of the street, and on the other are restaurants and little galleries. I think of Mom and how she would like it here. I consider for a moment buying a postcard and sending it to her before I remember that I have no money.

Dad would like it here too, with all the old buildings. Our last family vacation was in third grade, when we went to Washington, DC. They had a couple fights over whether or not I was old enough to see the Holocaust Museum and which was more important for me to see, the Lincoln Memorial or the Vietnam Wall. But mostly it was good. I remember eating ice cream and walking in that huge park they call the mall. I remember holding both their hands.

We duck into an alley behind a really good-smelling barbeque restaurant in search of dumpster treasure. We're just pulling up the lid when the restaurant's proprietor, a heavyset black man with a belly bulging out and around his apron strings, sticks his head into the alley.

"Hey," he calls, "What you doing in my dumpster?" his English is accented in a way I don't recognize.

"Sorry, man," Jesse says and lets the lid fall back down.

The man studies us for a minute, taking in our wet hair and our dirty clothes. "You want some dinner?" he asks. "I got a dishwasher didn't show up tonight. You wash some pots, and I'll feed all of you." The smells from the kitchen grow stronger and more irresistible the longer he stands in the doorway. We follow him into the back of the restaurant. "I'm Gene," he says. "This is my place." We're standing in front of a huge metal machine with plastic racks and a metal tray on either side. "You know how to use a Hobart?" he asks.

Everyone nods except for me. Gene looks at me for a minute. "You come scrub pots. Everyone else back here. Aprons are on the wall, hairnets are in the back. You finish all these."—he gestures at the stacks of plates and silverware that have clearly been piling up all day—"and I feed you really good stuff. Deal?"

"Deal," says Jesse, and he sticks out his hand to shake. Gene has the meaty hands of someone who wields a big butcher knife for a living, and his arms are crisscrossed with small pink oven burns. I follow him to another part of the kitchen, where a huge sink sits piled with pots and greasy trays. He hands me a pair of elbow-length rubber gloves and shows me where the dish soap and scrubbers are.

"You do this before?" he asks. I've narrowed his accent down to somewhere Caribbean.

"Nope."

"You let these big rice pots soak," he advises. "Then they clean out nicely. These other trays, they greasy but they clean up easy."

"Okay," I say, making a mental addition to my list of useful knowledge for the rest of my life. Who knows, there might be a lot more washing of pots and pans at the rate I'm going.

He pauses for a minute. "You a long way from home, huh?" I smile and nod, not sure if he means geographically or just the fact that I'm in the back of a restaurant about to tackle a sink full of dirty pots and pans. Either way, he's right. "Me too," he says. "Me too."

He's right about the rice pots. They're the worst, especially at the bottom, where burned rice is caked on in an inch-thick layer. The trays are greasy with barbeque sauce and chicken fat, but most of that slides off easily into the sink. Once they're done I walk them across to the Hobart, where G and Jesse run them through to fully sanitize them. They have definitely worked one of these machines before; the trays fly in and out with precision timing, and the machine rarely sits still. Tim moves at his usual meandering pace unloading the clean dishes and finding their spots on the shelves one at a time. When I finally get burned rice out of the bottom of the last pot, the front of my jeans is soaked with dishwater and my back aches from bending over. There's something satisfying about looking at an empty sink, and something completely disheartening when Gene comes around the corner with another pile of dirty trays.

He laughs when he sees my face. "No, no my friend. You're done for tonight. These are from tomorrow's prep anyway. They need to soak. We leave them here. Come out with the others and have some dinner." Out in the restaurant Jesse, G, and Tim are sitting in front of platters of steaming food. Old road signs cover the walls, and brightly painted wooden animal sculptures perch above the red leather booths. The waiters and hostess are still busy bussing the last of the tables, but there are no customers left inside and the lights in the front window have been dimmed down. I swallow a big mouthful of saliva generated by the food in front of me. There's a huge bowl of red beans and rice, another steaming bowl of some kind of dark greens, a platter of barbeque chicken, and a tower of fluffy yellow corn bread.

We eat without speaking for the first few minutes until Gene looks concerned at our silence. "Something no good?" he asks.

Jesse shakes his head vehemently and swallows a huge mouthful. "No, man, no. Everything is incredible. Sorry, we're all so focused on eating we got all quiet. But it's amazing, really. Thank you!" We all nod and grunt our agreements.

"No need to thank me," Gene says. "You guys help me out tonight. Without all of you, we'd be here late doing dishes." He looks critically at G and Jesse, who have heaping piles of everything but the chicken on their plates. "You vegetarians?" he asks. "You should have said. My wife, she's vegetarian. I make her a smoked tofu she can't get enough of, man. You should have said."

"It's okay," G says. "Rice and beans are my favorite."

"Listen," Gene says as we're finishing up. "That guy who no-showed tonight? I fire him anyway. I like you guys. You come back tomorrow night, get me through until I can find someone else. I make you my famous smoked tofu, okay?" I'd agree to anything if it meant I got to eat like this again, and it seems like as good a plan as any we've got. Gene sends us out the door with bursting bellies, a bag full of corn bread for breakfast, and our promise to return the next night. My eyelids are fluttering as I stagger along behind Jesse and G, eager for even the hard van floor, as long as I get to lie down.

***

Emily is hanging out back in the van, but there's no sign of Lyle. She eats a couple pieces of corn bread and then pulls me aside to tell me something. "Listen," she says in a hushed tone. "I think I found a way into one of the bathhouses. You want to go for a swim?" Every ounce of my body wants to lie down in the van and shut my eyes. Well, almost every ounce. Over her shoulder I see G. She doesn't look up or try and get my attention. Which I decide to accept as her unenthusiastic acceptance of my continued interest in Emily.

"All right," I say. The smell of Emily—patchouli and cinnamon—when she's whispering in my ear is invigorating enough.

"I knew you'd be up for it, Drew," she says and squeezes my shoulder. She has no idea.

HOT WATER

The marble steps and columns in front of the Buckstaff Bath-house make it look more like a courthouse or an art museum than a spa. Through the tall front windows I see elegantly dressed people mingling, drinks in their hands. "It's some kind of private party," Emily says. "But they're only upstairs. The baths and locker rooms and everything are in the base-ment." I follow her around back, where there's a less formal entrance guarded by a tall, skinny guy in his early twenties wearing a baggy and unimpressive security uniform. In place of a gun he has a dinky-looking pair of plastic handcuffs and a wooden baton. He looks extremely excited to see Emily and significantly less so to see me.

"Hey, girl," he says with a pronounced Southern drawl. "I thought I told you not to bring anyone with you."

"I know," Emily says in a cutesy voice I hardly recognize. "But he's my younger brother, and he caught me sneaking out and threatened to tell our daddy if I didn't bring him with me." She throws her arm around my shoulders and I shake it off, acting the part to perfection. *Younger brother? What the hell?* My face is red with embarrassment as Emily walks over to Curtis—his name is stitched on the front of his starched, blue-collared shirt—and taps his chest with her forefinger. "You're still going to let me go for a swim like you promised, right?"

Curtis hesitates, but even I can tell it's for show. "All right, but don't take too long. I could get in big trouble for this, you know?" Emily stands on her tiptoes and kisses him on the cheek.

"You're the best!" she says and grabs my hand before I can act on my impulse to get the heck out of there. I can't believe she just passed me off as her younger brother. It's not so much that I care about Curtis. It's just that what I've seen hits a little too close to home. Is this what I look like to G and Jesse and those guys? I pull my hand away from Emily as soon as we're inside the bathhouse.

The bathhouse is a long room with a low ceiling covered in decorative tile. The baths are long, shallow swimming pools made of white stucco. The overhead lights are off, and the only light in the room comes from the glowing blue-green lights in the bathwater, which cast ripples of aquamarine light all over the walls and ceiling. I follow Emily wordlessly down the narrow passing space between the bath and the wall, trying to hold on to my resentment over the Curtis issue. There's a red button in the wall that she presses, and immediately the rushing sounds of Jacuzzi jets fill the air and the enormous pools start frothing. "You're coming in, right?" Emily asks. I give a little shrug. "Are you mad about something?" She cocks her head to the side.

"I just don't like the way you handled that guy out there," I say without too much conviction.

Emily snorts and laughs. "Who? Curtis?" Then she looks at me again, this time with a little disbelief. "Drew, are you serious?" She takes a step closer and stares at me. I look over her head at the bubbling water, anywhere but at her gray eyes, her adorable upturned nose and her soft, pink lips. I shift awkwardly from one foot to the other. "Drew, are you jealous?" I roll my eyes, but I still can't look at her. I want to retort that no, I'm not. But the words are stuck like chunky peanut butter in the back of my throat.

Because the truth is that yeah, I'm jealous, of Curtis and of Lyle and anybody else who gets her attention. It's not like I want Emily all to myself. It's that I want us to have something exclusive, something I don't have to share with Lyle, or Curtis or G or anybody. The wanting is there, tugging at the bottom of my gut. I can't remember ever wanting something so intense from another person. As if she's reading my mind, Emily takes another step towards me. I take a tiny step backward against the cold, clammy wall. She puts her hand on my belt and hooks one finger over the waistband of my jeans. She tugs ever so slightly with that one finger, tugs me toward her. I still can't look down at her face. I'm afraid she'll start laughing and make this whole moment a joke. But then she reaches up and puts her other hand on the back of my neck and guides my face down towards her slightly parted lips.

Emily tastes like she smells, sweet and earthy. She teases my tongue with hers and tugs a little on my bottom lip before she lets go. I'm staring down at her, stunned, wondering if that just really happened and when exactly it's going to happen again. I put my hands up to her face and kiss her again. This time a little more aggressively. I feel her lips turn up into a smile, and she laughs into my mouth. "Come on, Drew," she says. "Let's go for a swim."

Emily pulls away, leaves her clothes in a heap on the floor, and slides over the stucco side into the nearest pool. I'm glad it's pretty dark. I'm glad she can't see my immediate and dramatic reaction to her kisses. I dunk my head into the warm water as soon as I can, trying to stay calm amid all the lustful thoughts from my overstimulated brain and body. When I come up for air she is lying on the far side of the pool, her head resting against the edge. The curves of her breasts are just at water level. I stay where I am. She sighs loudly, "This water feels incredible, doesn't it?"

"Uh-huh"

"You know, they don't use chlorine in here or anything. Just natural salts and minerals. It's supposed to be incredible for your skin."

"Oh yeah?" I swim over closer and find a dark spot near where she's lying and let my head rest behind me. My body floats out in front of me and I close my eyes, still careful to keep my lower half below the surface of the water. Every so often I open my eyes and glance over, but Emily's eyes are always closed. After about ten minutes of this I leave my eyes closed completely and don't open them until I hear a splash next to me and Emily is gone. I see her swinging dreads retreating into the darkness. She comes back wrapped in a plush white towel and throws a second one at me. I grab it before it hits the water.

"We shouldn't push our luck," she says. "I don't want Curtis to get in trouble." I am totally capable of ignoring the reference to Curtis at this point. Curtis who? I'm the one who was naked in the pool with her. I'm the one she was kissing just minutes ago. I pull my clothes on and use the towel to dry off my head. Curtis must be making the rounds, because when we emerge from the bathhouse he's gone. Emily scratches the word *Thanks* into the concrete with a piece of quartz from the landscaping around the bathhouse.

We're walking back towards the van, and I'm not saying much because I'm trying to think of a way to kiss her again before we get back. Finally, when we're almost a block away, I just grab her hand and pull her close to me. She kisses back, but this time there's reluctance. She puts her hands up to my hands, which are on either side of her face, and pulls them down. "We can't be like this in front of everyone," she says.

"I know. Because of Lyle, right?"

"It's not just Lyle, although yeah, I don't want to hurt him. Being a couple or whatever doesn't work in this kind of situation. Besides I don't believe in that kind of commitment anyway. You know?"

I nod but then realize that I don't know. "No, I don't know. What do you mean?"

"I mean I don't believe we're really meant to be monogamous creatures. Humans, I mean. I don't really think we're cut out for monogamy. I don't think it's natural."

"Oh," I say. I must sound disappointed, because Emily stops walking, turns, and brushes my hair from my eyes. She looks at me critically, smiles, and then kisses me again. When she kisses me I don't care about monogamy or Lyle, or Curtis, or any of it. I just don't want her to stop.

"You're good at that," she says. "But can I tell you something?"

"Sure."

"You shouldn't put your hands on someone's face when you're kissing them. It's a controlling gesture, like muzzling a dog. It's very patriarchal."

"Okay," I say. "Duly noted."

UP AND DOWN

In spite of what she says, I'm still a little disappointed when Emily curls up on the opposite side of the van from me. And the next morning, when she barely meets my gaze and then goes off with Tim to do some dumpster recon, I'm practically depressed. I don't even realize it's all over my face until G asks me if I've talked to my mom recently.

"No," I say, sounding sour, I'm sure.

"Well you're sure acting salty about something," she says. "Something happen with you and Emily last night?" She actually doesn't sound all that judgmental, and there's part of me that would love to get her opinion on the whole thing. But I also already feel like I know what she's going to say, and mostly it's a big "I told you so."

"No," I lie. "I just kind of woke up thinking about my grandmother and how messed-up the whole thing is." I feel bad lying about Mima. It's not an outright lie, but it's certainly not what's on my mind this morning.

"Sorry," G says. There's not much else she can say. "There's a free concert happening over in the park in about an hour. It's a kickoff for the bluegrass festival. You want to check it out?"

"Sure," I say.

We make our way over to the park without talking much. I'm thinking about Emily and how incredible it was to kiss her. But weirdly I don't feel happy right now. I should be happier, right? But what I mostly feel is scared that it might never happen again.

I look at my watch. Right now I'd probably be changing for gym or staring out the window in Ms. Tuttle's class while she begs and pleads with us to acknowledge Shakespeare's greatness. I never really got why anyone would want to be a teacher. It's like a half-step away from being a prison guard. But now I really don't get it. School is the biggest scam ever and completely inapplicable to everything about real life that I've seen so far, except maybe for some stuff in books.

The park is already filling up with people when we arrive. Mothers with sticky little kids are spreading out blankets, and a lot of older people are showing up with lawn chairs. There's a bandstand in the middle, and a trio of musicians is tuning up and tapping their microphones. There's a man on guitar, another on banjo, and a woman with a big stand-up bass. G and I stake out a spot underneath a big spreading oak that's just beginning to brown. After about twenty minutes the music starts. It's not really anything I'd choose to listen to on my own, but it's undeniably catchy, and pretty soon I'm tapping along and admiring the soulful voice of the female bass player. All the songs sound vaguely familiar. I'm sure they're classics in this part of the country, because a lot of the audience members are singing or humming along. A few kids are dancing up front the way that little kids dance; just bending their knees a lot and running in circles.

After about half an hour they finish their set, and after a few announcements advertising their performances during the festival, they are replaced by a foursome of young guys in tall cowboy hats and jeans. These guys play a faster, more countrified version of the music we just heard, and it really gets the audience going. There's a lot of hooting and calling out to the band for special requests. The music is so fast that the fingers of the banjo player and guitarist are a whirling blur and the lead singer's lips seem to be moving a beat ahead of the sound that's reaching my ears. I stare up into the trees and let the sound wash over me.

Suddenly everything goes dark as a pair of hands covers my eyes from behind. "Guess who?" Just the smell of her makes my heart move up toward my throat and my crotch twitch.

"Hillary Clinton," I say. She snorts and giggles and shakes my head to indicate no.

"Lady Gaga," I guess again, and again she shakes my head. I reach up and pull her hands away. My head is just underneath her chin. I expect her to pull away, but instead she scooches forward with one leg on either side of me, and I lean back so my head is resting against her chest. I can feel the movements of her chest with every breath, and the collar of her soft flannel shirt is tickling my cheek.

***

The Freegans perform their show that afternoon, and afterwards we all show up at Gene's to wash dishes and get fed. The smoked tofu is pretty good, but I still prefer chicken. There's something about the way tofu is always pretending to be some other food—that and the texture gets to me. But Emily loves it;

she sits next to me at dinner and is practically bouncing out her seat with joy. She begs Gene to give her the recipe, and he tells her she can help him make it the following night.

As we walk back to the van, Lyle, who's been pretty quiet all day, coughs a little before speaking. "I just wanted to say, I'm sorry for lying to you guys about my family. It was a dumb thing to do, and I'm sorry."

I really want to dislike Lyle. He's been pretty cold and snobby towards me from the start, but even I can't ignore the humble and heartfelt nature of this apology. "Don't worry about it, man," Jesse says.

"Water under the bridge," Tim adds poetically.

"It's not important to me," G says. I don't say anything. I never asked Lyle about his family, and he never offered any information. Emily is also quiet, though her expression is sort of sad and pensive. Selfishly, I hope she doesn't forgive him.

The next day, when we're setting up for the show, Lyle approaches me with fifty feet of nylon rope coiled around his shoulders. "It seems like you're going to be with us for a while," he says.

"Yeah?" I say, thinking he's about to be confrontational.

"Well, I just thought you might like to learn the knots we use to hang this stuff. You know, in case you wanted to help out ever." He seems flustered, and I can tell it's not exactly how he meant it to come out. "I mean, you asked me once if you could help out, and I didn't really have time to show you then, but if you wanted to learn now. I mean, I could show you now if you want."

"Sure," I say and follow him over to the light post where he and G have been hanging their trapeze. He shows me how they use a smaller rope with a rock tied around one end to bring the rest of the rope up over the streetlight, or tree branch, or whatever they're hanging from. He shows me how to join the smaller rope to the thicker piece using a sheet bend and how to tie the whole thing off using a clove hitch followed by a series of half hitches. I'm a good pupil, following directions diligently and waiting until he's done talking to ask questions. It helps that learning how to tie a knot seems infinitely more useful than learning to structure a five-paragraph essay. As if to reward me for my attention, he shows me a few more knots: a bowline and a monkey's fist, which makes this little ball of rope.

"It's not that useful," Lyle says. "But it looks cool. And if you didn't have a rock, you could use it to weight the end of your rope."

The monkey's fist *is* cool, and I sit down with a piece of rope to practice. I'm trying to ignore the part of me that's thinking about how that was a pretty decent interaction with Lyle, and maybe he's not so bad when he's not feeling threatened. Even harder to ignore is the voice that's saying maybe I should forget about Emily for a while if it's going to cause all this drama among the Freegans. Even though it's been a few days since that night at the Hot Springs, if I think about it I can still conjure up the softness of Emily's mouth. That's all it really takes to get me to forget about Lyle and his feelings.

Ignoring other people's feelings seems to come pretty easily to me, though it's not a trait I like to admit to. I was eleven or twelve the first and only time I saw my dad cry. It was one of my weekend visits in the city. I could never sleep that well in Dad's apartment. I guess some people find the city noises to be soothing, but the orange streetlight glow and rumbling of car engines that pervaded the apartment made me feel like

I was sleeping in the middle of the day. I slept lightly, waking again and again throughout the night. It was during one of those nighttime wakings that I found my father sitting at his kitchen table, his head in his hands, his shoulders shaking. At first I thought he was laughing. In my day/night confusion I remember thinking he had beat me to the Sunday comics—being annoyed because it was the only part of the paper I really liked. When I realized what I was witnessing I stepped back and stood in the doorway, just watching. Instead of trying to comfort him or even asking him what was wrong, I found myself thinking about the book I had just read about a kid with cancer. I was really impressed with all the stuff his parents did to try and make his life better. I wondered how my parents would act if I had cancer, and I stood there in the threshold, half-pretending that Dad had just gotten some terrible news about my condition. I went back to bed before he could see me watching him.

**

Our days in Hot Springs fall into a kind of rhythm. We're all on our own after breakfast until around noon, when we meet up at the van and prepare for the first show. I get a map of the parks and trails at the visitor's center and usually head to one and find a spot to read or go for a walk. It's the kind of thing I never would have done at home, but here it just feels right. I've gotten to the point in the book where it's just the gritty details of his starvation leading up to his death. It's not like I don't know what happens, but sometimes I think if I read closely enough I can change the outcome. Something about the book is bothering me lately. I think it's his journal entries—the parts where Krakauer quotes his writing directly. McCandless writes in the third person, something that never bothered me when I read the book before. But this time it strikes me as contrived, especially for someone so intent on the importance of having experiences. How can you really experience something if you're always observing it from the outside? Maybe it just hits a little too close to home.

A lot of my mood depends on how Emily's treating me that day. I give her plenty of opportunities to spend time with me alone, but she always manages to worm out of it—or to invite Tim to come with us. Just when I'm ready to write her off completely, she'll plunk herself down in my lap or wrap an arm around my waist. Beyond those occasional touches there's been nothing else physical between us. I'm beginning to wonder if I imagined that whole night in the bathhouse. I certainly imagine it enough when I'm drifting off to sleep at night.

There are darker things that come to me at night too. I dream of Mima—which is usually a good thing. I remember how safe and secure I felt when I was at her house; how I trusted her to take care of me. That's not the dark part. The dark part is that when I wake up I think about Emily and my parents in equal but very separate parts. I pretty much wrote Dad off a while ago. But I wonder when I stopped trusting Mom and when, and if, I'll ever be able to trust Emily.

JUST LIKE IN THE MOVIES

It's after one of these strange dream sleeps that I come up with a plan to take Emily out on the closest thing to a date that our situation allows. I know it's kind of a test I'm setting up, even though I'm not willing to fully admit it. The biggest hurdle is getting her to agree to go. I wait all day until I'm sure it will just be the two of us alone. When I ask her if she wants to join me for a secret mission that night, I'm surprised at how easily she agrees, given the way she's been avoiding time alone with me. My plan is almost thwarted by another free concert in the park, but luckily it's Lyle who asks if anyone wants to go. They're back on speaking terms, but things are still a bit tense.

So everyone else heads over to the park after we finish at Gene's, and Emily and I go our own way. "So what's this all about?" she asks as I lead her down an alley between an art gallery and a restaurant.

"Secret mission," I say, and I hold my finger up to my lips. The forced silence is good. I don't want to talk about what we're doing or even think too much about it. I just want to know how she's going to react. The alley leads us behind another set of buildings. There's a big blue dumpster, and naturally Emily assumes that's why we're here. She lifts the lid, but its only occupants are the flies that come buzzing out. She raises an eyebrow in my direction.

I push on an unmarked door next to the dumpster and boldly take her hand in mine. We're in a dark room. I wait a minute for my eyes to adjust. Then the bright green sign for coming attractions illuminates the faces and open seats in the darkened theater. I grin as I hear her let out a tiny gasp of excitement. I pull Emily behind me into two seats at the end of a row and turn nervously to see her reaction.

"Oh my gosh," she gushes. "This is perfect. How did you know about that door?"

"I was scouting the dumpster a couple days ago and someone had left the door open just a crack," I whisper. "So I rigged it so it would stay open, just a crack."

"Awesome."

"Yeah, sorry I couldn't get us some popcorn too."

"Oh, I can handle that," Emily says. Before I can ask, she's out of her seat and moving quietly through the darkened theater. A preview for some action movie that came out last month in New York is flashing across the screen. She comes back a few minutes later with a bag of warm, buttery popcorn and a two courtesy cups of water.

"Don't tell me Curtis works here too?"

Emily snorts and laughs, attracting a glare from the people in front of us. "No, dummy, I just got all teary and told them I dropped mine inside. Works every time."

I timed it so we would enter during the darkness of the previews, but not miss any of the movie. My movie choice seems perfect given Emily's self-proclaimed cheesy taste in cinema.

It's a romantic comedy about a guy who dies but prearranges to have his girlfriend receive a series of letters designed to help her move on with her life. I'm not really paying attention to the plot. I'm too busy paying attention to Emily. Little things, like the way her breath catches during the really sappy parts or her fingers, which have drifted over to my knee and are absent-mindedly rubbing the ribs of my corduroy pants.

When the lights come up, I see her face is red and tear-streaked. For a second I wonder if this was a terrible idea and she hates me for picking such a cornball movie. But then she sighs loudly and says, "That was wonderful. Totally cathartic. I'm like a new person!" The middle-aged woman sitting in front of us turns around and smiles at her.

Outside the movie theater, she wraps her arms around me in a huge friendly hug. It's not exactly what I had in mind, but it's a start. "You picked that out for me, didn't you?" she asks as we walk back towards the van.

"Yeah."

"You remembered what I said about movies?"

"Yup."

"Oh, Drew," she sighs. "What am I going to do with you?" I have some answers, but none of them are anything I dare say out loud. "Oh, look at the moon!" Emily shouts before I can try any of my terrible one-liners.

***

I study the moon that night through the camper window. I'm not sure what I expected to learn about Emily's feelings or my own. I had a good time. I like being with her. But I already knew that. My eyelids are heavy, but I'm reluctant to fall asleep—afraid my dreams will reveal something I don't really want to know.

***

Jesse and G spend some time scratching their heads and staring at a local events calendar taped to the pharmacy window before determining that it's time to move on. Jesse wants to spend at least a week at this farm he keeps talking about before making the final push to the festival in New Mexico. On our last night in Hot Springs Gene promises to cook us a feast of "his food," as he calls it. It turns out he's from Haiti. He made a boat crossing about fifteen years ago and ended up in Florida before making his way north to meet up with some cousins who were living here in Hot Springs.

Gene outdoes himself on the feast. In addition to a huge platter of rice and beans, he makes a vegetable stew with okra and corn and a grilled fish dish wrapped in plantain leaves, as well as a pile of fried plantain chips. We stuff ourselves, knowing the next hot meal might be a ways off.

"I wish I could afford to hire you all," he says, looking down at his meaty palms as we get ready to leave.

"You've done more than enough for us," Jesse says. "Thanks to you, we've been able to save our money, and we'll have more than enough to make it across Texas."

"To New Mexico," Gene adds. We've told him about the festival. "And then where will you go?"

"Who knows?" Jesse says and grins. "Wherever the wind takes us."

"It's no good forever," Gene says. "All this moving around. Eventually you find your home. You find your way back home."

172

I feel like he's looking right at me when he says this, but it's just for a second. "You find your way back here to my place any time," he adds, this time addressing the group, and gives one of his enormous grins. As we're leaving he makes Emily a present of his smoked tofu recipe written on the inside of a cardboard cornmeal box. She promises to guard it with her life.

G stays behind for a few more minutes, talking to Gene. I'm far enough away that I can't hear what they're saying. When she catches up to us she's wiping her eyes and shaking her head like she's trying to get rid of something.

"What was that about?" I ask.

"I just told him I admire him for what he's done; starting over from nothing in a completely new place."

"Yeah," Emily adds, "Gene is a really wonderful decent human being," she says. "So are you, Drew." I pull her arm and her body closer to mine in kind of a hug. I look back at G, expecting her to be rolling her eyes or looking angry, but she seems as confused as I am by the comparison.

ON THE FARM

We follow route 270 out of Hot Springs through the beautiful and sparsely populated Ouachita National Forest. Every so often there's a gas station and a cluster of buildings selling tired-looking T-shirts and commemorative rocks. We stop for lunch by a branch of the Arkansas River and feast on Gene's leftovers. The stream is running low, and for a while we hang out and explore, skipping stones and jumping from rock to rock. Lyle starts a game of follow the leader, so we all shed our shoes and roll up our pant legs. The water is breathtakingly cold, and I linger on each dry rock, gripping with my toes and willing the warm stone to transmit some heat through the soles of my feet. G is right in front of me and Emily is following behind. Every so often I slow down so that Emily and I will end up together on an impossibly small rock. Every time it happens she giggles and grips the back of my shirt, pressing her body into my back. It's bliss. I'm not even paying attention to where we're going. I'm just following G, who's following the leader.

I talk to Mom again, and she sounds a little less desperate this time. She tells me she's been reading a book on raising the strong-willed teenager. I tell her this probably isn't a bad idea, and I mean it. Something is different for me, so why shouldn't things change for her too? I tell her about finding the divorce diary and she even laughs and asks me if there were any answers in there. I tell her no, only more questions. This strikes me as a very adult answer. I think we're both a little sad to get off the phone. As soon as I hang up I want to tell someone about the conversation. I survey the scene at the gas station: Emily is stretching, Tim has his headphones on, and Lyle is reading his book while Jesse pumps the gas. G must be in the bathroom. As I look at them I realize how alone they are in the world, even as they're together, they are alone.

***

Outside of Mansfield, too tiny to really be called a town, Jesse finds a small dirt track and turns down it by a wooden sign that reads "Rock Ridge Organic Farm." The first three words are painted green and, as though that color ran out, the last word is orange. We bump down the road at about five miles an hour. The ridge between the tire tracks is grown high with grass and wildflowers. I hope Shirley can go in reverse, because I seriously doubt we're going to find anything down here— including a way to turn around.

Just as I'm rehearsing the opening scenes of *Deliverance* in my mind, the road opens up into a farm field bordered by a split-rail fence. There's a beat-up-looking trailer parked in the middle of the field, and chickens surround it, pecking diligently at the ground. On the other side of the road is a similar field, but this one has sheep in it and a couple of people pulling bales of hay off an old pickup truck. At the bottom of the hill is a good-sized red barn—the kind you'd find in a picture book—and a small farmhouse with a partially completed addition covered in building paper. "Uh, do these people know we're coming?" I ask as the van grinds to a halt.

"I hope so." Jesse grins impishly. The people who were up in the sheep pasture are walking down the hill towards us, and a beautiful woman holding an enormous bowl of green and purple cabbages appears in the doorway.

"Hi," she says warmly. "You must be Jonah's friends. Jeremiah said you guys might be stopping through. I'm Skye." Skye has a wide forehead framed by dark blonde hair. Her eyes are a penetrating blue. She looks to be in her early thirties, but she's one of those people who could be twenty-five or forty-five. Before anyone can respond or introduce themselves, the man from the field hops the last of the split-rail fences and walks over to where we're standing. He has an enormous, bushy brown beard, and he's trailed by a teenage girl wearing an odd combination of tight jeans and knee-high rubber boots. I try to smile at her, but she doesn't meet my glance. She seems to be taking the whole group in with interest. "These are Jonah's friends from Burlington," Skye calls over our heads.

"I'm Jesse," Jesse says with a little wave. "Jonah said he'd let you know I might be coming through. We'd love to hang out for a couple days and get a sense of your operation here. I mean, if that's cool. We're willing to help out however we can."

"Jeremiah," says the man with the beard. "You met Skye, and this is our daughter, Littlefern." The girl in the tight jeans coughs and narrows her eyes at Jeremiah. "Sorry, I mean Lindsay." We all give little waves or handshakes and call out our names. Skye and Jeremiah do that intense eye contact thing that I've almost gotten used to from Jesse. After introductions,

Jeremiah points us in the direction of an unused pasture where we can set up our tents. "We're glad to have you hang out for a couple days. Jonah mentioned you were interested in learning about small agro."

"Well, *I* am," Jesse says. "These guys are just humoring me for a couple days."

"Well, as long as they don't mind pitching in, we're happy to share what we have here with you." We all answer in one way or another that we're happy to help out, do whatever is needed. Out of the corner of my eye I see Lindsay roll her eyes. She walks away from the group and starts pulling at the tall grass around one of the fence poles and waving it at a nearby sheep.

Jesse backs Shirley up into the open field and pulls five olive green pup tents out from underneath the back seat. They're all labeled with rubbery yellow peeling letters that say *Camp Nawaka*. "Boy Scout camp went out of business near home and had a big yard sale," he explains. There are five tents and six of us. We all look awkwardly at them arranged in the grass like overstuffed sausages.

G grabs one first. "Come on, Em, you and I will share," she says and stakes out a prime spot underneath one of the browning alder trees. The tents go up easily and smell like sunbaked rubber on the inside. There's just enough room for two sleeping bags or one sleeping bag and a backpack. If I can't share a tent with Emily, at least it will be nice to have a little space of my own for a couple nights.

Once the tents are set up, Lindsay wanders over. She's changed into a clean T-shirt as tight as her too-tight jeans. It's white and says the word *Pink* in sparkly green letters across her chest. "Jeremiah said I should see if you guys want to hike up the ridge," she offers. She throws a couple cloth bags at us. "There's an old orchard. It's pretty overgrown, but we can usually still get some apples."

We traipse along after her across the fields. "Watch out for Gus," she adds as we pass through the sheep pasture, pointing to a ram with a particularly menacing-looking set of horns. "He's wicked aggressive when he's horny." Gus follows us as we make our way through his territory, but he keeps at a safe distance. I walk quickly to avoid finding out what a two-hundred-pound, aggressive-looking sheep can do when he's horny, and I find myself walking next to Lindsay.

"So how come you're not in school today?"

She looks at me like I'm a complete moron. "It's Saturday."

"Right," I say. "Yeah, I guess I've kind of lost track of the days lately."

She eyes me up and down. "How come you're not in school like ever?"

"How do you know I'm not eighteen?"

"You're not."

"Yeah, I'm not. I guess I'm on a little hiatus from school." As soon as I say it, I wish I could have said break instead. "I guess I'm just trying to figure some things out."

"Oh," says Lindsay, rolling her eyes for the umpteenth time. "Wel,l you'll fit in great here. Everyone who shows up here is trying to figure something out. Jeremiah and Skye don't even care if I go to school or not. I mean, I'd have to study something, but they don't care if I want to stay home and be homeschooled or whatever."

"But you don't want to?" I ask.

"Are you kidding me? There's absolutely nothing to do

here and no one around for miles. It's boring enough here on the weekends. I'm glad to go to school on Monday morning just to get away from the chickens and the sheep shit."

"It's pretty here," I offer.

"Yeah, pretty freaking dull." We walk in silence for a while and then stop to wait for the others to catch up. Tim is lagging behind, as usual, and Gus starts trotting after him.

"He likes me!" Tim shouts as Gus nudges him with the top of his head.

"That's because he hasn't smelled you yet," Lyle shouts back.

The ram hits him again in the back of his upper thigh. This time Tim stutter-steps forward. "Hey," he calls out, a bit surprised. "That was hard."

"Walk faster," Lindsay calls out. Tim looks back nervously at Gus and starts taking big strides across the field. The ram is fixated on him, but not moving. Now he starts trotting after Tim, his head lowered

"Here comes your boyfriend," Lyle shouts out.

"Shit!" Tim shrieks and starts running for the fence, but Gus is steadily gaining on him. He hops over the split rails just before Gus delivers a bruising blow to the wooden post and collapses in the long grass, panting.

"I don't know why you're being so picky," Lyle says, grinning. "I think he's kind of cute."

"Wrong species, wrong gender," Tim says, his chest still heaving.

"Hey you're the one who's always complaining about not getting any. Beggars can't be choosers." Tim glowers at him from the ground.

"What about your parents? They don't care that you're not in school?" Lindsay asks me.

"No, they care. I just didn't really give them a choice about it." This sounds tougher than I intend it to.

"You ran away?" For the first time Lindsay sounds a little bit impressed.

"I mean, I plan on going back eventually." *Why is it so easy to say it to her?*

"How long have you been with these guys?" she asks.

"Why do you say it like that?"

"I don't know. You just seem different than them."

"A couple weeks."

"Wow. Skye and Jeremiah are pretty laid-back, but they would completely lose their shit if I disappeared for a couple weeks." She reaches over and playfully punches me in the arm.

"How old are you?" I ask, wondering if she's flirting with me.

"How old do you think I am?"

Hmm. I know there's a trick in here. I can't remember if you're supposed to guess older or younger. "Fourteen?"

She rolls her eyes like I'm wildly off. "Almost fifteen. How old are you?"

"Sixteen."

She shrugs. "Pretty much the same."

At the top of the hill the woods open up into an overgrown field filled with small bushes and miniature birch trees. The rows of apple trees with their twisting and gnarled branches are still clearly defined among them. Most of the apples are rotting or gnawed at our feet, but there are a few small ones left on the trees. Lindsay says if we pick enough Skye will make an apple crisp, and that's reason enough for me to start climbing. The sun is sitting low in the sky, and after I've filled my bag more than halfway I find a place up in one of the trees where I can lean back against the trunk and prop my feet up on a branch. It's a perfect spot. Emily is scrambling around in one of the trees, her dreads swinging wildly as she reaches for an apple. Her long skirt rides up around her thighs as she straddles a particularly large branch. I close my eyes, and the voices of the others fade into the background. Soon all I can hear is my own breathing, slow and steady. And oddly it seems like I can feel the tree breathing too, moving against my back like we're somehow connected.

I think about Jesse and what he said about fending for yourself and growing your own food. My stomach rumbles at the thought of warm apple crisp. Is happiness really that simple? I feel pretty good right here right now, and the only thing I'm observing or paying attention to is myself.

Something tugs on my shoelaces. I open my eyes and see G smiling up at me. "Having a moment?"

"It's nice right here. Come on up."

She drops her bag of apples and scrambles up beside me. She leans back in a little crook right next to me and lays her legs across my lap. She drums her fingers quietly on her leg. Her fingernails are gnawed down to nothing. "You're right," she says, surveying the surroundings. "It is pretty nice up here." She tips her head back so it rests against the tree. "Andrew, what are you going to do when this is all over?"

"Eat apple crisp," I say, even though I'm pretty sure that's not what she means.

"Seriously."

"Seriously? I don't know. Go back to school, I guess. Go back to my old life." It's the second time I've said it in an hour, and it's starting to sound more and more like a plan. *But not yet,* I want to tell her, *not yet.* I wonder if G thinks I'm wimping out by running back to my suburban lifestyle instead of heading off like Gene into uncharted waters. I know I'll be different somehow, and hopefully everything else will be different too.

G sighs. "I think you should be writing some of this down."

"Some of what down?"

"This! You know, this moment and this tree and this farm and everything. And what you think about it. Because once you get back into your life, you're going to wonder what it all meant."

"Did Ms. Tuttle send you?"

"Who?"

"Never mind," I say. I know she's right, but I'm not going to give her the satisfaction of being my Yoda. I swing down from the tree and pick up my bag of apples. "What about you, G, are you writing this all down?"

"This?" she says. "This *is* my life. Nothing confusing about that." It's meant to be a joke, but I hear a tiny bit of sadness in her voice. She must hear it too, because she screams out "Geronimoooo," jumps out of the tree, and tackles me in the grass.

That night during dinner I get up from the table and go the bathroom. Next to the composting toilet is a warped mirror framed by chunks of broken pottery. I stare at myself in the mirror, and I'm honestly a little surprised by what I see. My eyes seem brighter, and there are a few more freckles on my nose. My hair has grown out a little bit. It's almost as shaggy as

Jesse's. I touch the back of my head where I always pat down an annoying cowlick, but it's all grown in. Jesse's green-and-black-checked lumberjack shirt is the same one I've been wearing for days. It's become like my St. Mary's uniform. I think about what Lindsay said and wonder what she sees that sets me apart from the Freegans and if that's a good or a bad thing.

KILLING CHICKENS

The next morning G wakes me up by shaking my tent on her way to pee. "Wake up, sleepyhead. It's time to earn our keep." I cross paths with a frazzled-looking Tim staggering out of the woods. There's a long red scratch across his left cheek.

"What happened to you?" I ask.

"Freakin' nature," he says. "I found a great crap spot and then, right as I'm squeezing one out, something snaps behind me. I jumped up so fast I practically took a dump in my pants, and I got this," he gestures at the scratch on his face. "I hate camping," he says in a low voice. "I'm sleeping in the van tonight." I laugh and walk past him to find a place to conduct my own bit of morning business. Afterwards I put on the cleaner of my two filthy T-shirts and walk over to the farmhouse, where Skye has laid out some homemade bread and jam.

Lindsay is perched on a wooden stool, licking the jam off her bread. It's a little bit sexy, but mostly kind of gross. Jesse and Jeremiah appear deep in conversation over a seed catalog. Emily, G, and Tim wander in after a while and help themselves to some bread. After everyone has eaten, Jeremiah outlines the plan for the day. Skye is going to work on getting their restaurant orders ready to deliver in Fort Smith. They mostly supply places in Hot Springs, but there are a few places in Fort Smith that order greens and root vegetables from them. Jeremiah is going to kill chickens.

"Normally, I'd wait another month or so. But it's a lot of work for just the three of us, and since you guys are here, I thought I'd take advantage of the extra hands," he explains. "We'll have a fried chicken feast tonight, and we'll put away the rest for winter." He turns and looks at Jesse. "I imagine you would rather see what Skye's doing today, since it's more of the business end. The rest of you can pick whatever you have the stomach for."

"I'll kill chickens," Tim volunteers. "I've had enough plants and trees for one day," he whispers.

"Me too," I say, because it seems like the more interesting of the two options.

"I would rather work in the gardens," Emily says primly. G and Lyle don't seem to have a preference, so Jeremiah sends Lyle off with Skye, and G comes with us. Jeremiah heads off to the barn to gather a few things and says he'll meet us up by the chicken trailer in a few minutes. When we arrive at the chicken trailer, Emily is there. Her head is bowed toward the ground and her arms are slightly extended with her palms up.

"Did you change your mind?" I ask.

"No," she says. "But I wanted to say good-bye to them and thank them for their life and spirit."

"Oh," I say. I'm hoping she finishes before Jeremiah gets there. After another minute she drops her hands and raises her head.

"I think they're ready to go now," she says with a completely straight face. She walks over and squeezes my hand before heading back down the hill to catch up with Skye and the others. I watch her go; her too-big jeans are held up around her skinny hips with a paisley-patterned men's tie. I've been practicing a conversation in my head for several days now—a conversation in which I try to make it clear, without sounding too pathetic and desperate, how much I want to kiss her again.

Jeremiah backs his old pickup into the pasture, and we help him unload the supplies piled in the flatbed. We set up a couple of folding tables and roll out an enormous wooden stump with two nails protruding from the top. The stains and bits of feather left on the stump leave no question about what it's for.

Jeremiah gets a fire going and organizes the equipment as he explains the process to us. "Catching the birds can actually be the tricky part," he says. "But once you have one, you need to tie up its legs and swing it around a few times over your head. That will make it sleepy. Then one of you needs to hang on to the legs and one of you needs to swing the axe." He stops and looks critically at us and then down at our footwear. "On second thought, I brought a sledgehammer too. I think I'd rather have you guys swing that. That way one person can just rest the axe on the chicken's neck and the other person brings down the sledgehammer on top of the axe. It would hurt a lot if you missed and hit yourself with a hammer but it probably wouldn't mean as much bloodshed."

"I call feet," G says.

"I want to swing the hammer," Tim says.

"I guess that leaves me holding the axe."

"Classic," says G, and she smirks at me.

Jeremiah nods. "Okay, whatever you want. Once it stops moving—and it will move around a bit—you need to bring it over here to the water." He points at an enormous stainless steel pot of water that is beginning to bubble over a large propane stove. "We dunk the birds for a minute or so to loosen the feathers and then we string them up over here to let the blood drain and pluck them. Once they're bare you can bring them over to me at that other table, and I'll gut and quarter them. They're pretty much ready to go in the freezer or the frying pan after that."

I look over inside the plastic fence surrounding the chicken trailer. The birds are busy pecking at the ground and at each other. A few curious ones have come over to inspect our setup. It's hard to imagine them as the pale pink pieces of meat stuffed neatly on Styrofoam trays that I've seen in my refrigerator.

Jeremiah is right about catching the birds. Part of it is my own timidity. I've been eating all kinds of meat my whole life, but I still don't really want to pick the ones to die, so I sort of halfheartedly chase them around in circles. Tim gets the first bird and lets out a cowboy-style "Yahoo!" as he swings it over his head.

I look away when Tim brings the sledgehammer down on top of the axe, but the smell of fresh blood fills the air immediately—a warm, metallic smell like rain hitting a summer pavement. By the fifth bird my sneakers and the bottoms of my jeans are spattered with chicken blood, bile, and tiny feathers. The pile of heads next to the stump grows, and my stomach turns over a little less each time one hits the ground. We do five at a time and then pluck them before moving on to the next group. Some of the feathers are hard to get out and if the bird gets cold sometimes we have to dunk it twice. When the feathers come out, they leave a small pucker in the skin that contracts and closes up. With the feathers are gone, the birds look more and more like meat. It's a lot of reality, and for the first hour I'm pretty queasy about the whole thing. But when I think about eating fried chicken that night, the feeling goes away. I watch sidelong as Jeremiah instructs Tim on how to gut the birds; first slitting them up the middle without puncturing any of the noxious organs and then pulling out the entrails whole. After that they're quartered. I'm interested, but not so interested that I want to be invited to participate.

Sometime in the early afternoon Skye comes up with sandwiches and a huge pitcher of iced tea, which I gulp down greedily. I didn't think that after seeing so much blood I would have the stomach to eat, but I devour the food in front of me. "Come on down when you're done," Skye tells us. "I'll get the big tub going for all your clothes." We kill, de-feather, and gut the last bird by midafternoon, but it takes a couple more hours to get everything cleaned up.

"Strip," Skye orders me when I find her tending the fire beneath a huge metal washtub outside the farmhouse. I'm so excited about the prospect of clean clothes that I shamelessly shed everything but my boxers and toss it into the bubbling tub. "Emily said you didn't have a lot of extra stuff, so I left you a towel and a few things of Jeremiah's outside the shower. Why don't you go wash up before we start cooking supper?"

I knock lightly on the wood next to the faded green paisley curtain that stands in for a bathroom door. "Drew?" Emily calls. "Is that you? You can come in." Emily's face is flushed and pink from the shower, and she's wearing only a blue towel that's lost most of its pile. She's rubbing some sort of beige cream into her face. "Isn't this stuff amazing?" Emily gushes. "Skye makes it. It's like an exfoliating cream or something. She told me to try it after my shower." I sit down on the closed toilet next to her and give a big sniff. It smells a bit like oranges and a bit like almonds. She puts one foot up on my knee and continues rubbing the lotion into her calf. "Man I forgot how tiring working on a farm is. My back is killing me. Maybe you can give me one of those killer massages later."

"Uh-huh," I say. I'm staring at the foot on my knee, trying really hard not to look up at the gap where the towel doesn't quite come together. Emily is preoccupied with her lotion, and if she notices my interest in her towel, she doesn't say anything. She moves on to the other leg and keeps talking. "Skye and Jeremiah are really amazing people. It's too bad about Lindsay though."

"What do you mean?"

"I mean she totally rejects everything they've worked so hard to create here."

"Well, isn't that kind of normal? I mean just because her parents are kinda cool and hippies doesn't mean she's going to want to be like them any more than you and I want to be like our parents."

Emily sighs. "And she's a total skank."

"Whoa, really? You think so?"

"You should watch out, Drew. You should have heard the way she was talking about you today out in the fields. It was like she'd never seen a guy before."

"Maybe she's just never seen such a fine specimen," I joke, but Emily ignores me.

"And I was all, like, I'm trying to pick kale here and just be in the moment and she's just going on and on about you and asking me about you. It got really annoying." I wait for details without saying anything. But Emily just shakes her head and goes back to her lotion. When she's done, she puts the ceramic lid back on the container, sighs again, and sits down squarely on my lap. I adjust my head a little so her wet mop of dreads isn't right in my face. But Emily takes my arms and wraps them around her, pulling me in close again. "I used to love this," she says.

"What?" I say quietly.

"Being wrapped up in a towel and held." So I hold her and we don't say anything else for five or maybe ten minutes. It's only closeness; there's nothing really sexual about it. "I'm getting cold," she finally says and turns to plant a small, chaste kiss on my lips. "I think that's the stuff Skye left for you." Pointing to a pile of clothes and a towel in the corner, she leaves me sitting on the toilet with a cold damp space where her warm body just was.

JEREMIAH'S MEAD

When Skye brings the chicken out on a big silver sheet pan, brown and glistening from the hot oil, all my memories of blood and soggy feathers fly out the window. I was nervous about the rest of the Freegans, but they all assured me that they were willing to eat meat if they knew where it came from, who raised it and killed it. Everyone except for Emily. "I'll try," she had said primly. "I'm just not sure my body still produces the enzymes to digest meat." G snorted and rolled her eyes.

Emily puts the smallest drumstick on her plate and gnaws at it gingerly. Everyone else dives in with gusto. Watching vegetarians eat meat is truly something to behold. Jesse, Tim, and G are stuffing it in as fast as they can, barely bothering to wipe the smears of chicken grease from around their mouths.

Jeremiah offers us all wine after dinner. It's mead, actually, he tells us proudly, that he made himself from honey harvested from their bees. The Freegans all nod appreciatively, but of course no one asks for any. It seems like Jeremiah really wants us to try some. So without thinking too much about it, I thrust my cup forward and say I'll try it. I've tried beer before, but I never really got the appeal. Every once in a while, when I'm really bored on a Friday night, I'll drink some of Mom's red wine and enjoy the spins while I watch stupid stuff on YouTube.

This stuff is strong. It's sweet too, and it warms my whole body. Before I can refuse Jeremiah is refilling my cup to the brim. I smile and shrug. I've never been drunk before, so I guess I don't really see it coming. It's weird. I feel super focused on whoever is talking or right across the table from me. But at the same time I start to lose awareness of what's going on to my left and right. Everything in my peripherals gets kind of fuzzy. And yet I can't help staring intently at the person talking. I think I'm listening, except I'm not really sure what Jeremiah is saying. These little thoughts keep floating through my mind like subtitles in a foreign movie. They say things like "I'm really warm." Or "I feel comfy."

Lindsay is sitting next to me, and when I turn to look at her I notice that tonight she's wearing makeup. Just a little bit, but her lips are pink and shiny. Her teeth don't look so crooked anymore. I smile at her. I'm smiling at everyone. Jeremiah is talking about their goats and which ones they're going to breed, and which ones they're going to eat this winter, and how much hay they need to put away to keep them fed and comfortable.

"I love hay," I blurt out. "It reminds me of hayrides."

G and Jesse are looking at me like I've said something really funny, and Emily just looks annoyed. Jeremiah nods like he totally gets me and starts talking about the hay they've harvested that year. I feel a hand on my arm, and I look over at Lindsay.

"I could show you the hayloft later, if you want," she says. This time I notice her eyes, which are green and sparkly. They're lined with a little bit of purple eyeliner. It's smudged in the corners.

"Okay," I say. Because this sounds like a great idea. Suddenly there is a loud screeching sound of wood drawn quickly across wood and my chair is jerked backwards.

"Andrew and I will do the dishes," Emily announces. She's standing behind my chair with the collar of my shirt crumpled in a tight fist at the nape of my neck. I shake off her grip and nod good-naturedly. I don't get that Emily's annoyed until we're back in the kitchen and she's practically throwing wet plates at me to dry. Each plate is handmade and weighs about four pounds.

"Slow down," I say. "I don't want to drop anything."

"Yeah," she says acidly, "you don't want to upset our hosts or anything. Not until after you screw their daughter anyway."

"What? What are you talking about?"

"Oh please. Don't think you were being subtle or anything. That girl practically had her hand down your pants at dinner, and you're trying to pretend like nothing was going to happen. You don't even know her. You don't even care about her. You're just going to use her and toss her aside. This is what alcohol does to people, Andrew. It takes really good sweet people and makes them do stupid insensitive asshole-ish things!"

I reach over in front of Emily and the mountain of bubbles about to overflow the sink and turn off the water. The super-focused power of the alcohol turns all my attentions on her, but instead of my brain going a million miles an hour with what-ifs and random thoughts, I just stare at her, my mind a buzzing blank space. I stare at her face, at the soft roots of her hair. She's got a red spot on the top of one cheek that might turn into a zit. She's jealous, and somehow it's because of me. "I'm sorry," I say. "I've never been drunk before."

Emily sighs loudly. She's studying me carefully, searching for any hint of insincerity. She's worried about getting hurt. This thought hits me like an anvil in a Road Runner cartoon. She must care about me if she thinks I could hurt her, right? The conversation coming from the dining room is loud. I can hear Jesse and Jeremiah arguing about wind power versus solar power. "You could have really hurt that girl," she says, but her tone is generous, like she's already forgiven me for what I didn't do. She turns back to the sink and plunges her hands into the soapy water. I'm fixated on her neck. And I guess it's the mead, because I've never been this bold before in my entire life. But before I can stop to consider whether it's a good idea, I pull the dreadlocks off the side of her neck and kiss her right below the ear. I leave my lips there for a second before I pull my mouth slowly away.

The noise that comes out of her mouth is somewhere between a sigh and a moan. I jerk back, thinking she's going to slam me over the head with a cast iron pan. Instead she turns and grabs the front of my shirt with her soapy hands and pushes me backwards into the wall beside the stove. She's kissing me, but this time is different than before. This time she's kissing me like she's lost something between the back of my tongue and my tonsils. She's pulling hard on my lips with her lips and she's running one hand through my hair and pulling on the back of my head so hard it almost hurts. But I'm not complaining. It feels incredible. And when I'm not thinking about the way she's grinding her legs into my legs, I'm half-wondering what I did exactly to provoke this reaction and how I'm going to get her to do it again and again for the rest of my life. Emily grabs my hands and shoves them up against her breasts.

She's kneading my hands into kneading her breasts. It's kind of like I'm feeling her up, and it's kind of like she's feeling herself up. It's a little weird but for whatever reason it seems to work for Emily because she's still moaning like she did when I first kissed her neck.

The sound of more chairs scraping backwards breaks the spell. She pulls away from me, and we're both panting and a little bewildered. Everyone brings in the rest of their dishes but Emily and I are quiet. Everyone must know what was just going on, but no one says anything. Even G has no snarky comments to offer. Lindsay lingers in the kitchen for a little while, putting away the dry plates and rearranging things on the counter. But when it's clear she's not going to get any kind of attention or conversation from either of us, she leaves to join the others in the living room.

Jesse is tuning his guitar, and when I glance around the corner I see Jeremiah hunched over a banjo and Tim with his recording equipment out. Skye has a pair of spoons in her lap, and Lindsay is curled up on the couch with a book. When she sees me, she looks up hopefully, but I avoid her eyes and scurry back into the kitchen.

The sounds of the music take the place of any conversation between me and Emily. I'm super aware of every movement she makes and any little noise or cough that escapes her lips. Dishes have never been so clean. A kitchen has never been so expertly scoured. When we're finally done, we stand and stare at one another. *Please don't let this be it.* She takes my hand. "Come on," she says. "Let's go back to your tent."

We sneak out the kitchen side door and run through the yard and down the road toward the tents. We stop every fifty feet or so and mash our faces together. I don't make the mistake of grabbing her face again, but I grab her everywhere else, pulling her back towards me, wrapping her arms around my neck and shoulders. My chin is wet from our dripping kisses. I feel like I'm going to explode.

We practically dive into the tent, shoving my backpack and clothes to the side. Hopefully she doesn't notice how much it smells like my feet in there. Emily pulls her shirt over her head and I take that as an okay to do the same. It's dark inside the tent, but there's no mistaking the soft feel of her nipples when they brush my chest. I reach up and cup one of her breasts in my hand. But Emily isn't really much for the soft touch. She grabs my hand and mashes it against her chest again. She's got her other hand at the back of my neck and she's sucking voraciously at my face again. This is all pretty straightforward, and so far my complete and total lack of sexual experience hasn't interfered with either one of us having a good time, but I'm a little nervous about what comes next. It turns out, at least with Emily, not too much more information is needed. She grabs my hand and thrusts it between her legs, writhing and moaning without me doing much more than wiggling my fingers so they don't break between the viselike grip of her thighs. She does this for a while. She's still kissing me with the same ferocity, but every time I try and move her hand below my belt line she quickly moves it away again. So I give up on that end of things. Finally she gives a long, almost bovine, moaning sigh and rolls away onto her back.

I'm quiet. I'm not sure if it's over, and I have no idea what to say. The steamy air in the tent cools quickly. Emily reaches down for my sleeping bag and pulls it up around us. She drapes an arm across my chest, and I snuggle her in close. I'm trying to think of something to say, some way to explain what it means to me to be close to her like this. But before I can completely compose my thoughts, I realize she's snoring.

I take care of things on my end and eventually fall asleep myself.

THE OTHER OFFER

When I wake up the next morning the walls of the tent are covered with condensation, threatening me with a clammy canvas touch. I don't shy away or move a muscle, because in the night Emily flung an arm across my bare chest. It was the first thing I was aware of when I opened my eyes, the weight of that arm just below my nipples. I stare at that arm, a girl's arm touching any part of my skin. It seems like a miracle. I lie there, staring at the arm and the back of Emily's head, which is twisted away from me, until I think my bladder might explode. I sadly lift the arm, which flops almost lifelessly on its owner, and sit up.

"Gotta pee," I say. Emily murmurs something incomprehensible, which I take for agreement that yes, it would be best if I didn't pee right here in the tent.

The sky is an early morning gray, the kind that could turn deep blue by midmorning. The grass is still soaking wet and cold against my feet. I take a minute to roll up the bottom of my pants so they don't get soaked before finding an agreeable tree to water. Leaning against a peeling birch, I realize that my head is pounding. Every step I take sends a thud through my sinuses. After rummaging around in the van for a sweatshirt,

I head into the farmhouse to see if anyone else is awake. Skye is up and making coffee. She hands me a steaming mug without a word and before I can protest that I'm not really a coffee drinker. "Will this help my head?" I ask.

She smiles. "Jeremiah's mead is strong stuff. Especially if you're not used to it. Coffee will take the edge off."

I sit down at the table and interlock my fingers around the heavy earthen mug. It's got a blue-green glaze on it that reminds me of the color of the ocean. "Are you the only one up?" I ask.

Skye shakes her head. "Jeremiah's still sleeping, but I think I heard Lindsay get into the shower a little while ago. We're trying to conserve the water in the rain barrels for eating and washing dishes, but try telling a teenager she can't shower every day and you've practically got a revolution on your hands." She rolls her eyes.

I shrug and smile. I know we both know that I'm a teenager too. But it's nice that for right now, I'm some other kind of teenager, the kind you can tell your problems to. I'm staring at my mug, feeling pleased with myself. The coffee is hot and bitter, but I force myself to drink it without grimacing and without asking for sugar. I look up to ask Skye about the plan for the day, but she's left the room.

I turn around when I hear footsteps, but this time it's Lindsay, wearing ripped jeans and a faded gray T-shirt advertising some kind of agricultural fair. Her dirty blonde hair is wet, and she's running a big plastic comb through it, sending splatters of water on to the floor. There are still traces of last night's purple eyeliner around her eyes. She pours herself a cup of coffee and dumps three heaping spoonfuls of sugar in it. She slurps when she sips. "I could show you the hayloft now if you still want to," she offers.

"Sure," I say. "Why not?"

She shoves her sockless feet into a pair of knee-high rubber boots that are sitting by the door and hands a similar pair to me. "Here, wear Jeremiah's."

"Do you always call your parents by their first names?"

"I don't know, sometimes."

The boots are caked with mud on the outside but surprisingly warm and comfortable to slip on. I follow Lindsay into the barn, where she climbs the narrow spiral stairs to the hayloft without spilling a drop of her coffee. Once we're up there, she sits down on a bale of hay and I choose one opposite her. "So this is it," she says.

"It's nice." There's a skylight above us, and the sun is high enough to send in a shaft of buttery light flecked with dust and chaff from the hay. Lindsay takes another slurp of her coffee and sets the mug down beside her. She leans forward, elbows on her knees, and looks at me.

"You can have sex with me if you want." Blood rushes to my face and pounds in my ears. When I don't immediately respond she continues. "I mean, I won't tell your girlfriend if that's what you're worried about."

"She's not my girlfriend."

"Well, whatever she is, she's definitely the jealous type."

I'm wondering if I have to answer the original question or if Lindsay will just let it go and assume I'm not interested. I'm more interested in the way she said it than anything else. Kind of the same way she offered me a pair of her father's boots.

"So do you want to?" she asks.

"We probably shouldn't," I say. *There's a lot of daylight right now*, is what I'm thinking. I'm picturing the two of us fumbling around in this hayloft, and it just seems awkward and uncomfortable and maybe a little bit awful. "I mean, I'm staying with your parents," I say as if to align myself with the other adults.

Lindsay rolls her eyes. "Not like they'd care. They're the ones who gave me the condoms anyway."

"Yeah," I say, although this idea is a little shocking to me. I try to imagine the headmistress giving me condoms. "But they probably didn't mean for you to use them with someone you just met."

Lindsay sighs like I'm totally missing the point. "There's nothing wrong with having sex."

"Is that what Skye and Jeremiah say?" I smile like I'm making a joke here. Like the conversation isn't that serious. Like she hasn't just seriously offered to have sex with me.

"Basically, and that it's like an act of divine love and deep emotional intimacy or some bullshit like that," she adds.

"Yeah, see that's the part I don't think we'd really be getting."

"Whatever," Lindsay shrugs. "They were like two years older than I am now when they had me. You can't tell me they were out for divine love and deep emotional intimacy when they were sixteen. Besides, I just want to see what all the fuss is about. But if you don't want to, that's cool." She looks down at the hay beside her and starts pulling individual strands out from beneath the twine.

Then I say something that I mean to be snarky. At least I think I do. "I think I'll hold out for deep emotional intimacy. You know, just in case it's worth it."

"Do you love her?" Lindsay asks.

"Who?"

"Emily, duh."

"Oh," I pause. "I don't know." What would I have said last night in the tent?

"Do you want a blow job?"

YES! I think. "Um, now?" *Idiot, idiot, of course she means now.* "I probably shouldn't um, wouldn't be a good, to do that I mean." I stammer out some poorly assembled words of rejection. *Idiot. How can I say no? What the hell is wrong with me? Maybe Annaliese Gerber isn't the curse. Maybe I've been the curse all along and I just didn't know it.*

Lindsay sighs again. "All right, well, I told Skye I'd collect the eggs for breakfast so I should probably go do that."

"Okay," I say.

"Yeah, it is okay." She looks annoyed. "Can you take my mug back to the kitchen?"

Finally, a simple question to which I can give a simple answer. I nod and take the empty coffee mug from her hand. I follow her down the metal stairs, the adrenaline shaking my hands, wondering with each step if I've made a huge mistake. But I don't think so.

THE GEMINIDS

For the rest of the week, I spend my days carefully avoiding being caught alone with Lindsay or Lyle, and my nights sweating up the Boy Scout tent with Emily. I learn how far apart to space beets and broccoli, how to cold-water wash greens and arugula, and what it feels like to fall asleep with someone's soft breath against my earlobe. All additions to my list, which I decorate with tiny sketches of the different vegetables we plant and harvest. There's not much to do on the farm at night. Some nights Jesse and Jeremiah play music, and one night we play team charades, an activity Lindsay declares unbelievably dorky before she joins in. Most of the time I stare across the group at Emily, waiting for her to yawn so we can both make excuses and head back to our tent. I try and tell myself that the physical part is as amazing as I want it to be, but it's pretty much always the same. After the third night I finish myself off keeping one hand cupped around Emily's breast. I think she pretends to sleep through it.

On the morning of our last day, we help Skye put together the orders for Hot Springs. Once we load everything into the walk-in, there's not much to do except pack up our tents. The afternoon air is cool and crisp, and a warm sun hangs low in the sky even though it's only two o'clock. Emily and I wander back up to the apple orchard. After we pass Gus's sheep pasture, Emily takes my hand, loosely interlocking her fingers with mine. The sun warms my face, and I take deep breaths as if happiness were something I could store up and hold on to. I show her my spot in the apple tree, and we climb back up and lie across the branches, our legs overlapping. I close my eyes and try to feel the tree breathing again. It's so quiet. I'm aware of the crinkling of every dried-up wrinkly leaf that twists and rubs against the bark.

"Drew," Emily says, breaking the silence. "You really like me, don't you?"

"Well, yeah," I say without opening my eyes.

"Why?"

"What do you mean, why?" There's a scary quality to this question and answer, and I don't want to be the curse in my own life anymore.

"Never mind," Emily says quickly. But there's a space that's opened up between us. A space for me to say just the right thing. And I know I have the right thing to say, because it's truly what I feel.

"Because you're strong. And you're fun, and funny. Because you care about things and believe in things, even if they're not the things I believe in. And that makes you beautiful, so amazingly beautiful. And you *are*, beautiful I mean. Like physically." I can't open my eyes. I'm afraid to see how she'll react to all this. When I finally work up the courage to open my eyes, Emily is looking away. She's biting her lower lip and staring down at the grass. She wipes her eyes with her sleeve and finally looks at me.

"Wow," she says. "I think I love you too." It's a whisper. I almost don't hear it, but I can't ask her to repeat it. My heart is beating so hard in my chest. I reach over to take her hand; it's the only part of her I can reach from where I'm sitting. But she curls her fingers up so I'm wrapping my fingers around her fist instead. I'm so happy, I feel like my heart might explode against my ribs. When I close my eyes I imagine the two of us traveling the world together, backpacking in Europe, hiking mountains in Alaska, or lying on a deserted beach on some warm tropical island.

Emily clears her throat to say something else, and I give her what I imagine is an impassioned look. I'm ready for whatever other declarations she has to make. "We should head back," she says. "I know Jesse wants to leave before it gets dark."

It's not quite what I imagined she would say, and she only meets my smile with a little half-grin, but it doesn't matter. I was here and I heard her say it. She loves me. That's not something you just throw out there and then take back a minute later. I wonder if this makes her my girlfriend. I at least know Emily well enough not to ask. I hold her hand tightly even though her fingers don't quite return the pressure, and I give her big dopey grins all the way back through the fields.

While packing up to leave the farm, I look fondly at the grass that's been rolled flat in a perfect rectangle where the tent just stood. *I'll always have a soft spot in my heart for this field*, I think as I roll up the Boy Scout tent.

Tim leans over my shoulder to see what I'm staring at. "I'm just glad I won't have to listen to Emily moaning and grunting anymore," he says, as though reading my mind. My face turns bright red. Tim claps a hand on my shoulder. "Sorry, man, I'm all in favor of getting some nooky, but you two are loud. And I mean loud!"

It never occurred to me that everyone could hear us, but how could they not with the tents spaced just a few feet apart?

Nostalgia aside, I will be glad to head towards a bit of civilization. I owe Mom a phone call; there's no way around it. And she's going to rip me a new one for being out of touch for almost a week. It's almost finals time back at St. Mary's, and then it will be Christmas break. Even if I went back today, there's no way I'd pass the quarter. I hope she's been reading her book about the strong-willed teenager. Maybe she'll be a little less crazy when I finally talk to her.

I haul my tent and my backpack over to the edge of the field where G and Jesse are packing the van. G is stacking everything on top of the back and middle seats, leaving the way back next to the door free of stuff. "Why are you doing it like that?" I ask.

"The Geminids are tonight," she says.

"Geminids?"

"Yeah, it's a meteor shower. We're going to be on the road, and I don't want to miss it. I figured if I sit back here, I'll catch less light from oncoming traffic, and I might have a shot at actually seeing something."

"Cool. Can I fit too? I've never seen a meteor shower before."

G shrugs. "Fine with me, if you think it's okay with everyone else."

"Yeah, why wouldn't it be? Never mind, actually. Don't answer that," I add quickly before she can say anything.

Our good-byes with Skye and Jeremiah are prolonged and kind of sweet. Skye gives us a big bag of granola that's still warm from the pan she baked it in. They both seem interested in Burdock and talk loosely about going next year. Lindsay barely looks up from her book. "Good luck, hippies," she calls from the sofa. We all wave back awkwardly. Despite her apparent indifference to our leaving, I imagine her life is about to get quieter and more boring once we're gone.

We pile into Shirley. Jesse has to shut me and G into the back. It's tight quarters, but it's also kind of cozy wedged between the trunk door and the piles of bags and tents. We can hear everyone else but we can't see them. "Holler if you gotta pee," Jesse says from the driver's seat. If Emily is annoyed by my seat choice, she doesn't say anything, so I figure I'm in the clear. It's already getting dusky by the time we finish our good-byes, and Shirley bumps back down the long, grassy driveway.

Being out of the van for a week has been nicer than I realized. After the first hour my back is cramped and my butt feels like I'm sitting on golf balls. There's not much room to shift positions in the little cave we've created for ourselves. I stare at the sky, waiting for it to erupt in the silver confetti that G has described.

"We probably won't see anything until after midnight," G says when she sees me looking up. "Wanna play cards?" We play an endless game of war that evolves into Spit, which evolves into rummy. I try to read for a while, but it's too dark even with the lights on the highway. It's all right, though. There are things about the book that are irking me in ways they never did before. McCandless was kind of an asexual guy—something his few close friends attest to in the book, and something I used to find kind of comforting. Not all cool guys get girls. But the closer I get to Emily, and all the Freegans, the more unnatural his celibacy seems to me. Not just his celibacy, but his complete lack of closeness to anybody except these people whose lives he passed through. It's like he could only get close to people he knew he was going to leave.

Jesse gives a little hoot when we cross into Oklahoma and then again when we reach Texas. After that it's pretty quiet until we stop for a bathroom break around Wichita Falls. Everyone stumbles in and out of the gas station, bathroom trying to go without fully waking up. Lyle offers to drive, but Jesse insists he's fine and says he'd rather just keep going and try to make New Mexico by dawn. No one really argues. We're all happy to crawl back into the van and pass out again.

The next time I wake up, the road is dark, but the sky is bright with starlight. G is awake, her face pressed against the side of the van, her dark eyes reflecting the tiny pinpricks of light. "What are you looking at?" I whisper.

"Cassiopeia."

"Cassio wah?"

"Cassiopeia, right there, looks like a *W*." She jabs at the window with her thumb towards a zigzag line of stars. "She was a queen who was really vain. She was jealous of her own daughter so she farmed her out to marry some sea monster. Then the head of all the gods put her in the sky upside down to punish her for her vanity."

"She's upside down?"

"Yeah, I guess so. It's kind of hard to see."

"I can never see what people are talking about when they point out those things."

"Constellations?"

"Yeah."

"It doesn't matter," G says. "You can make up your own. Like that one right there. See the four bright stars that kind of make a boot shape? I'm going to call that Andrew's Boot. Now you have to tell me the story of how it got there."

"Seriously?"

"Seriously. Make it good."

"Okay," I pause and think for a minute. "Okay, once there was this kid named Andrew, and everyone thought they knew who he was. His teachers thought he was a good student who was just unmotivated. His parents thought he didn't mind that they were divorced, and his mom thought it didn't matter that he switched schools every three years. Most of the kids at his school thought he was gay or a goth or a snob, and he just went along with all of it. Then one day he cracked and went off on a road trip with a crew of total hippie freaks." I stop for a moment and check that G is still smiling. She is. "And his mom got so mad after she didn't hear from him for a week that she threw all of his stuff out onto the curb, and one of his shoes bounced really high into the sky and it stuck. The end."

"Not bad," G says.

"Not bad? Just not bad?"

"You really think your mom is still mad at this point?" she asks.

"I think she's going to kill me."

"Maybe," G says. "Maybe she's just really worried at this point, about where you are and when you're coming home."

"I thought this was *my* story," I said somewhat sulkily.

"Okay, well, I didn't really like the ending. I wanted to know what was going to happen to Andrew. Like what happens when he finally goes back to his real life?"

It's too late at night for this comment to annoy me. "Hmmm," I say, "He's going to be different."

G leans forward. "Yeah?"

"Yeah."

"Like how?"

"Like he's going to know what he wants."

"Wow," G says, like I've said something really profound. "That's a tall order."

"Most of the time," I amend it.

"That's probably more like it," she says.

"Thanks." I flick one of the playing cards at her, and she bats it away with the back of her hand. I could say more. Like how surprised I am that it isn't that hard. That I want Emily and apple crisp and somewhere warm to lie down at night. And out here those things are enough. Back home, I'm not so sure. "Okay, your turn." I stare up into the sky, trying to think of a good one for G. "There. See those three stars right in a row?"

"You mean Orion's Belt?"

"Not anymore. From now on that's known as G's Trapeze." I wait for a moment. "You have to tell me the story of how it got there."

"I'm thinking," she says. "Okay, but this is kind of a long one."

"Okay," I say. "Let me check my calendar. Nope, nothing doing for the next few hours. Take your time."

"Wiseass." She pauses a moment longer. "Okay, G's first trapeze was in her backyard at home. It was part of a swing set in her backyard. It had green and yellow wooden bars, and it was the nicest thing in their not-so-nice neighborhood. It was better than the one at the park that was missing rungs and only had one swing that hung uneven. Her dad bought it when he won at the track. He put it together one fall afternoon while she and her sisters ran circles around him, waiting for it to be finished. He drank cans of Miller Lite and when he finished one, he would crumple it up and throw it at the girls, who would squeal and run away."

"Your dad threw beer cans at you?"

"Yeah, and that was when he was being nice. Anyway, it didn't last long. That winter he lost a lot. He lost at the track and on the boxing matches. So he took it down so they could burn it in the fireplace because they couldn't afford to pay for heat. That was before they burned the girls' schoolbooks and made them lie about losing them to their teachers. And instead of throwing beer cans he threw the furniture and the lamps. But even then it wasn't that bad, as long as she wasn't drinking. Once she started, that's when things got really ugly.

"G and her sisters basically took care of themselves. They started hiding the food so they would have something to bring to school for lunch. Nobody checked that to see that there wasn't anything between the slices of bread. Their clothes were clean enough to escape the teacher's notice. Who knows how long it could have lasted?

"It would have lasted except for the fire. She was the last one up. She was supposed to put the screen in front of the fire like she'd been told a hundred times. But she fell asleep. And when she woke up the carpet was sparkling with orange embers. She didn't do anything, even when the embers curled into yellow flames. She didn't do anything because for once it was warm in the living room. She just watched the flames devour the carpet, and as they moved hungrily toward the couch, that was when she realized that it might be getting out of hand. But it was too late."

"Did they die?" I whisper in the darkness.

"No. Everyone made it out. But her older sister, not the oldest one, the middle one, her blanket caught on fire as they were crawling out of the house. She wouldn't let it go and it burned her arm and her shoulder. I think the oldest knew what happened. She knew why the fire had started. She never said anything, but G never went back. Somehow, when the family moved from the shelter to the apartment found by their church, G didn't go with them. She went to live with her Uncle Paul and her Aunt Ginger until she was too much for them to handle. And after that it was the state—foster home after foster home. No one ever came to visit, and she never asked if she could go home. It was like *she* died in the fire."

I don't say anything. I'm not an idiot. I can tell that this is a true story.

"So the next time she saw a trapeze it was many years later. She had always been fearless, but on the trapeze she was even more so. When she's up on the ropes twisting in the air, she has nothing to lose and nothing to prove. But when she's up there she always thinks of the first one, the one that burned. So that's why it burns in the sky." She's quiet for a moment. "The end, I guess."

"Wow," I say after a few minutes of saying nothing. "I'm sorry." As soon as I say it, I wish I hadn't. It's not what I meant. "I mean thank you."

"Thank you for what?" G says suspiciously.

"Thank you for thinking enough of me to tell me that story."

"It's just a story," she says, even though we both know it's not. Suddenly a pinpoint of bright light flashes across the sky. It's followed by several more that are smaller, more like white ash. "Did you see that?" G says excitedly.

"Yeah, was that it?"

"It's starting."

We watch the meteor shower in silence. It really is like a shower, like the sky is raining light. I remember the fireworks shows that I used to go to with my parents on the Fourth of July. I lie back in the van the way I used to lie back on our picnic blanket—my head in Mom's lap, the salty smell of the corned beef sandwiches Dad would make in the warm summer air. I watch the silver confetti burst in the night sky. In the hum of Shirley's engine I can hear music, but I guess it's only in my head; the reeling twangs of a banjo and the sharp twangs of a fiddle. An echo following me down the highway from Hot Springs. It's lonely music, traveling music, like something the Joads would have listened to around the fire at night. But it doesn't make me feel lonely. Instead I feel like I could reach out and touch everyone everywhere. G squeezes my foot when there's a really good eruption of light. I think about the story she just told, about the sparks of light in the carpet and trapeze in the sky. I think I know why she called me a douchebag back in Louisville. And I *am* sorry.

THE SMURTS

Just before dawn, we pull into a rest area outside of Amarillo, Texas, and we all stagger out to use the bathroom. I don't remember the end of the meteor shower, or falling asleep, but both seem like they happened a while ago. Jesse needs to sleep and no one else feels like driving, so we pull out the sleeping bags and curl up in our various spots on the van floor. G and Lyle take the pop-up. Jesse and Tim have the front seats, which leaves me and Emily in the back.

Emily snuggles up to me, her back to my front. I think it's called spooning. She pulls my arm around her, and I shake my head a little to avoid being suffocated by her dreadlocks. She still smells sweet, like Skye's homemade orange and almond lotion. It's moments like these that make me seriously rethink the offhand comments I make about going home.

It's only a few hours before the warmth and brightness of the daylight make sleeping impossible. I walk unsteadily out of the van and splash some water on my face in the rest stop bathroom. Coming out of the bathroom I run into Jesse, who is heading for the convenience store to buy some milk for our granola. "I doubt they'll have any soy milk, but Emily can eat it plain," he says. I fall in beside him, ignoring the stares from the family with three small children piling out of the minivan parked next to Shirley.

I scrub a couple dollars from Jesse and leave a message on Mom's machine when I know she'll be at work. It's a total chicken move, I know, but this way Mom will know I'm alive, and I won't have to explain to her for the thousandth time why I'm not on a bus heading back to New York. The message I leave is long and rambling. I tell her stuff about the farm and killing chickens and digging up my food out of the dirt—stuff I didn't even plan on telling her. I don't say anything about when I'll be back. Better not to get her hopes up.

After I leave a message I feel a lot better. Skye's granola is amazing, and once we're back on the road I'm free to sit back and watch the rolling hills of Texas turn into the dry desert country of New Mexico. Jesse tells me the place we're going is just north of Roswell on Route 70. I find it on the map and watch as the tiny desert towns flash by outside the van windows. Everything is beige and brown and dusty green. The buildings aren't more than two stories, and down every side road it's possible to see where civilization ends and the desert takes over.

We stop by the side of the road for lunch by a washed-out creek bed, but there isn't much food left in our supplies. Emily makes some pasta, but all we have for sauce is some olive oil and garlic powder. It's pretty gross, actually, but I manage to choke it down with a few more bites of the last of Skye's granola for dessert. Jesse surveys our supplies. "We'll have to stop in the next big town and do some serious scrounging," he says. "We've got a little cash for groceries, but I'd rather save it for gas. And I don't want to show up completely empty-handed."

"Clovis looks like it might have something," I say, poking at the slightly larger letters on the map. Jesse looks over my shoulder.

"Yeah, we'll try there."

In Clovis we find a local supermarket called Callahan's with a bountiful dumpster. With the memory of pasta and garlic powder fresh in my mind—and on my breath—I have no qualms about jumping right in with everyone else and sorting through the bags. We score some slightly browning bananas, bags of precut lettuce, bags of carrot sticks, several containers of yoghurt, some individual-sized Jell-O pudding cups, and a whole bunch of Halloween-colored Oreo cookies. Tim tears into a package of these and stuffs several orange-and-black cookies in his mouth before anyone can say anything.

"Those are made with horse hooves," Emily announces.

"That's a myth, actually," Lyle says quietly.

Either way, Tim is undeterred. "Mmm, horse hooves are my favorite." He rubs his belly and sprays Oreo crumbs. Emily mostly looks annoyed at Lyle. When she turns away, I grab a stack of Oreos from Tim and shove them into my mouth. They're hardly even stale, and the sugar explodes on my tongue. The final coup from this particular dumpster is the unearthing of four slightly squished premade pies from the bakery section: two cherry, one pecan, and one apple. Jesse suggests that we put these aside to share at Burdock. We pick through for a while longer, but aside from a few more bags of carrots nothing else is uncovered. It seemed like a good haul, but when all the food is laid out in front of us there's not that much to make a meal out of.

Jesse looks at his watch. "Should we try one more? I'd like to make it there before dark."

"We could drive around and see if there's a Super K or a Walmart on the way out of town," G suggests.

"Yeah," Jesse agrees. "Strong concerns? Major objections?" No one has any, so we pile back into the van and head west, looking for the nearest big-box establishment. Before going on the road with the Freegans I never realized how many small towns have Super Kmarts or Super Walmart. It's kind of sad when you drive down Main Street and half the storefronts are boarded up. At the end of Main Street there's usually a traffic light and then a few fast-food restaurants and a big chain store, sometimes even two.

For right now, though, I'm glad to see the familiar markings of a Super Kmart since it means I might have more than yoghurt and lettuce for dinner. The first thing we pull out of the Kmart dumpster is a big box of macaroni and cheese packages that an overzealous employee nearly shredded with a box cutter. Each of the individual boxes is slashed open with a sharp cut down the middle. The pasta and artificial cheese packets are in perfect condition, so we pull these out and place them next to the van. In the back corner of the dumpster I find a bag that's impossibly heavy and start tugging on the top. Tim looks at the bag stuffed in the corner and shakes his head. "If it's that heavy, it's probably not worth it man. It's probably some kind of industrial garbage."

"I don't know. I have a good feeling about it."

Tim shrugs his shoulders and helps me free the bag, tugging on the bottom while I lift from above. "Dude," he says, "if this turns out to be an exploding bag of dirty diapers, I'm going to kill you."

"Whatever it is, it's metal," I say, pointing to the way the bag is bulging in distinctly can-like formations. We wrestle the bag over the top of the dumpster and onto the ground, where Jesse pulls it apart. It's filled with unmarked canned goods.

"Sweet," Jesse says. "Mystery cans."

"Where did the labels go?"

"They peel them off so people like us won't be as tempted to go rooting through their trash."

"That's lame."

"Yeah, speaking of which, we should get going," G says. "We've been out here for a while."

"So, the worst that can happen is they tell us to move along, right?" I ask a little nervously.

"It depends if they really feel like being dicks or not," Lyle says. "Technically this is abandoned property, and there's nothing illegal about going through the trash. But the dumpster itself is private property. A lot of people, especially in small towns, have ended up with a night in jail on trespassing charges. It's not really worth fighting it. They usually let you go the next day. It just kind of depends how uptight the locals are."

I hop over the side of the dumpster and wipe my hands on my jeans. "Let's not find out."

"Hang on a minute," Tim says. "I think I just found something cool."

"Edible?" Jesse asks.

"No, wearable. Dude, check these out." Tim hops over the side of the dumpster, wearing a thin cotton T-shirt with a bright blue cartoon character on it and orange bubble letters. It's about a size too small for him, and over his clothes it's skin-tight.

"What are the Smurts?" Emily asks.

Tim looks down at his chest. "Not the Smurts, the Smurfs. You know, the little blue guys—Happy Smurf and Handy Smurf, Grumpy Smurf and Smurfette. There's a whole bag of these shirts in there."

"No," G says, "it definitely says Smurts."

"That's must be why they're in the dumpster," Jesse says. "It's probably a misprint."

"I'm keeping these," Tim says happily. "They'll probably be collector's items one day. Of course, you all can have one." He pulls a T-shirt out of the bag for each of us and throws it at us. They're all children's size large, which explains why they look so tiny on Tim. "You'll thank me one day," he says assuredly.

THE LABOR OF THE BEES

The turnoff for the Dusty Bottoms Family Campground is the only thing around for a mile in each direction, with the exception of a small, seemingly misplaced coffee shop just opposite the end of the dirt road that leads to the campground. The coffee shop appears to have been dropped there by aliens. On its roof is a full-sized plastic black-and-white-patterned cow with the name of the shop spray-painted on its side: Steamers. Outside the coffee shop is a bench where two white guys wearing snuggy caps and skinny jeans are drinking out of reusable steel mugs. On the other side of the door is a bike rack where a dozen bikes are squished together like junkyard art.

We turn down the road for the campground, and Steamers passes from view. "It's the off-season," Jesse explains from the front seat. "So we basically have the place to ourselves. During the summer they do a pretty good business with people coming to see Roswell and the national parks and stuff." As we bump down the dusty dirt road, we pass all different kinds of camp setups on either side of the van. There are a few traditional tents and a couple camper vans like Shirley, but most of the sites feature a homemade version of shelter: a few tarps and tentpoles assembled to keep the sun and the rain at bay, some picnic tables, and a lot of trash bags and duct tape.

"Not everyone here is straight edge," Jesse says. "But there's a chem-free section where we can camp. It definitely tends to be a little quieter over there at night." I look over at Emily, who's staring out the window blankly.

Jesse pulls Shirley into a small cul-de-sac where a few cars are parked and a number of picnic tables have been pushed together. A large white tent has been erected over the picnic tables, which are set up like a kitchen. When I get out of the van I can see that some people are working on food preparation and off to one side there's some kind of meeting going on. "Have you been here before?" I ask Tim as we're walking over to the tent.

"Nah, not here," he says. "They used to have it in Vermont. That's how Jesse got involved. But then a few years ago Rippy, the guy who organizes it, and his partner Danielle moved out west, and so the whole thing just kind of moved with them. That's Danielle," Tim says, pointing out a woman in front of us with a brightly flowered shirt. As we get closer I realize that the bright flowers are actually painted directly on her skin; each breast has an enormous orange sunflower centered on the nipple. She's bending over a giant bowl of pasta salad, mixing it with her bare arms. Each time she bends over, her flowered breasts undulate in the direction of the pasta salad. When she sees us coming, she looks up and smiles.

"Jesse!" she exclaims. "You made it!" Her smile lights up her whole face. Jesse introduces us around, and she gives us all the full attention of her bright eyes and that same warm smile. I try not to stare at her flowered nipples. "Rippy's in the middle of a thing," she says, gesturing over to the meeting and the tall skinny guy wearing a jester's hat who appears to be facilitating. "But you guys can sign up for meal prep and cleanup and then set up your spot. I'm sure he'll be done by then. He'll be really excited to see you guys. Wow, all the way from where?"

"New York," Jesse says. "What's going on over there?"

"Honey," Danielle says. "Some people think we shouldn't have it here."

Jesse nods like he understands. But I must look confused, because Danielle looks right at me and says, "Some people think it exploits the labor of the bees."

"I'm sure Rippy will sort it all out," Jesse says.

"Yeah," Danielle says and smiles knowingly. "I'm sure he will."

I'm not so sure though. I can't hear what she's saying, but a short girl with frizzy red hair is pumping one fist in the air while holding a plastic bear full of honey in the other. She looks pretty serious.

On one table underneath the tent is a series of clipboards where we all sign up for cooking and cleaning shifts. Next to that table are two poster-sized pads of paper set up on easels. One says *Today* and the other says *Tomorrow*. Perfect for me. Someone named Rosie led a cactus identification hike this afternoon, and someone else called Tanner led a workshop on making your own medicine from common household items. Dinner is scheduled for 6:30, and afterwards there's going to be bonfire at the big fire circle, wherever that is.

Tomorrow morning only has one thing scheduled, an edible plant walk with Adrian, but Jesse says it will probably fill up as more people arrive tonight. "A lot of stuff just happens last-minute," he says. There are several workshops set up for the afternoon, including one called "Passive Resistance to Police Brutality" that sounds interesting.

"What's the Bike Derby?" I ask.

"Sweet," Jesse says. "When's that?"

"Tomorrow night. What is it?"

"It's kind of wild. I don't know if I should tell you or just let you wait and find out for yourself." I shrug, trying to pretend like I don't care, but I must look annoyed because Jesse laughs and claps me on the back. "It's kind of like gladiators on bikes. Everyone gets these junky bikes and rides them around in circles, trying to bash other people's bikes. The last one riding wins."

"Are you guys going to perform this year?" Danielle is standing behind me and Jesse, one hand on his shoulder and the other, gripping a wooden spoon, on mine. "Christmas Eve Carnival on Sunday night."

"Jesus Christ! Christmas Eve is Sunday night?" I blurt out.

Danielle smiles sweetly. "It's weird to be away from family, huh? I remember my first holiday away. Even though I always fought with my parents about gift-giving and the capitalist consumer-driven nature of the whole thing, when it came down to it, I really missed them. Now I barely notice. It's so warm here anyway, it hardly feels like Christmas."

"Yeah, I guess so. I guess I lost track of time."

Danielle smiles sympathetically. "I know how that is. Hey, listen, you guys. Dinner's not for a little while. Why don't you go get set up? We'll ring the gong when it's time for grub." She gestures at a tin plate hanging from one of the metal tent poles overhead.

I don't feel like getting back in the van, so G, Emily, and I walk behind as Jesse pilots Shirley down the sandy, rutted road. We pass two guys and a girl in anarchist attire similar to Lyle's, and I'm reminded by their smell that everyone here is definitely not chem-free. They give us a friendly wave and a squinty-eyed smile. I smile back, but Emily tightens her grip on my arm.

We pass another campsite where a girl is beating on a ceramic drum while a guy tries to coax a brownish paste into a toddler's mouth. "Reminds me of home," Emily says in a way that's only partly nostalgic. "Bird and Darryl used to make their own baby food for the twins. The stuff was pretty gross though."

We find a campsite that's not too far from a water spigot with a few stunted oak trees for shade. I have a feeling we'll be grateful for these when the sun is overhead around noon. Emily doesn't even bother putting her stuff in G's tent. This time she just tosses her bag in with mine without any other comment. I try to avoid looking at Tim when she does it, but he doesn't say anything this time.

We've got a little time to kill before dinner, so I open up the divorce diary to the last list I made. Figures, it was a Christmas list. Two columns again: things I wanted and things I got. Nothing on the two lists matches. Even though I don't really remember writing the list, I remember being annoyed at Mom and Dad for getting me a bike instead of the Xbox I really wanted.

This Christmas I wanted some friends, and I can honestly say I have some. They're not really what I had in mind back at St. Mary's, but that doesn't matter. I wanted a girl to pay attention to me, and I wanted a hand job from someone other than myself. Well, I kind of have that. She did say that she loved me, or she thought she loved me. Emily is sitting on the other side of the campground, clacking away on her knitting needles. I try and catch her eye but she doesn't see me. I feel a wave of annoyance at the variability of her attention.

The gong sounds for dinner, and we grab our plates and forks and head back to the center of the campground. Back at the kitchen tent a buffet station has been laid out and piled high with food. There's the pasta salad that Danielle was working on earlier and some unidentified patties that G informs me are something called "nature-burger."

"It's not bad if you cover it with ketchup and mustard," she says. I just take one of everything. I'm hungry and the food is hot, which is pretty much a winning combination.

Emily snuggles next to me on one side of a picnic bench. Danielle, who's now wearing a shirt but definitely no bra, sits down next to me on the other side. Jesse, Tim, and G sit across from us. I catch sight of Lyle finding a spot with some of the other anarchist outfits, and the other benches around us fill up with unfamiliar faces. Normally I'm pretty psyched whenever Emily pays attention to me, but I'm trying to eat, and something about the way she's stroking my arm and nuzzling my shoulder is kind of claustrophobic. The conversation goes on around us, but clearly the PDA seems a little out of place to everyone else as well.

Everyone dives into their food while Rippy stands up and makes a speech welcoming us all to Burdock. As he's wrapping up the logistical information about cooking and cleaning crews, Emily leans over and whispers in my ear, "Tonight's the night."

Before I can ask her what she means, Jesse proposes that

we all go for a soak in the hot springs after dinner. "It's pretty amazing under the stars," he adds. "You guys all in?"

Emily is looking right at me. It feels like everyone is looking right at me. "Uh, yeah," I say. "Definitely." I don't think anyone else notices, but Emily slides slightly away from me on the bench and eats her dinner quietly. I'm pleased with my response; glad that I'm doing things instead of just watching them happen and annoyed that Emily doesn't seem to approve.

After dinner we head back to the campsite to grab towels and swimsuits for anyone who wants or has one. When we go to leave for the hot springs Emily has disappeared. "Maybe she went ahead?" Jesse suggests. He's wearing a flashlight headlamp style, which gives him the appearance of a hippie miner.

"She'll catch up if she wants to," says G.

"Let's go," I say. And I can tell that my agreement is the deciding factor. It's a small choice, but it's the first one I've made in a while—especially where the Freegans are involved. I want to go to the hot springs. I want to be here, exactly where I am. The hair on my arms stands up, and the air I'm sucking in tastes fresh. The trail to the hot springs is in back of the kitchen tent and winds its way through a narrow gully surrounded by six-foot sandstone walls on either side. I guess it would be a little creepy if you don't like tunnels or elevators, but it makes the trail easy to follow. I fall in with Tim, who's lagging a little behind the rest of the group. "Getting tired?" I ask.

"Yeah, you know how it is. This time of day is pretty rough after my meds wear off."

"I've never heard of anybody having no adrenaline."

"It's actually called Addison's disease," Tim says. "It was weird. Before they diagnosed it my parents thought I was just the laziest kid on Earth. When they found out I actually had a disease, they didn't even believe it for a while. The doctor finally convinced them, and explained it to them, and I think they felt really guilty. My parents are like really traditional Chinese when it comes to my older brother and sister. I mean, really uptight about going to the right college, doing Chinese language school, and getting good grades and all that. But ever since they found out about the Addison's, it's like I can do whatever I want. They're the ones who bought me the video camera and paid for this expensive arts camp when I was in high school. I know they knew about me partying and stuff, but they never said anything. It's cool, I guess, but it made things kind of strange between my brother and sister and me."

"Do you think they resent you for it?"

"I don't know if they resent me exactly. But it's like I have a totally different set of parents than they do. I mean, I get away with stuff they would never even think of trying. I mean, they're Quang and Jin right? Good Chinese names. We all had American names too, but I was the only one who ever told them to call me by mine. I mean, at school is one thing. But I made my parents call me Tim at home too."

"What's your Chinese name?"

"Chan Wu."

"Does anyone call you that?"

"Just my grandparents. Everywhere else I'm Tim."

"You seem like a Tim to me. Not that it matters what I think."

"Yeah, I feel like a Tim. I just wonder if I'll regret it someday."

"You could always go back to Chan Wu," I suggest.

"I don't think so," Tim says pensively. "I don't think you always can go back."

The path in front of us opens up to clearing where there are two natural stone pits, each about ten feet across. Steam is rising off them, giving the night a mystical quality. There are a few wooden benches on one side scattered with clothes and towels. A few heads are all that's visible of the other hot spring's soakers, and it's too dark to tell if Emily is among them. The desert air has dropped down to a cool fifty or sixty degrees, and as I strip down to my boxers I shudder a bit to keep warm. The water is warm, hot even, hotter than the pools in Arkansas, and as I ease my way in I feel my skin relax and every muscle in my body soften. The water has a sharp but not totally unpleasant smell to it.

"Aahhhhhh," Jesse lets out a huge sigh. "Man, this makes it all worth it. Every damn day in the van, every show where we make two dollars in change, every spaghetti-and-no-sauce dinner. I mean, this is it, man. This is the upside of living exactly the way you want to. Moments like these!"

"Amen." I recognize Danielle's sweet and mellow voice from the other side of the pool. She swims over to Jesse and nestles in beside him. I lean back, find a notch to rest my head in, and let my body float up to the surface of the water. The challenge is to hover just below the surface where I can stay warm. A streak of light brushes across the sky.

"Hey," I cry out and sit up, looking for G.

"I saw it," she says from somewhere nearby. "Leftovers from last night. We'll probably see more tonight since there's so little light pollution out here." The stars alone are a magnificent show, like someone splatter-painted the night sky with silver. There's so much light and so little depth perception. It's dizzying; like staring at a window screen and through it at the same time. I reach my hand out of the water, half-expecting to come away with a fistful of the tiny silver dots in my hand.

"Dude, are you all right?" It's Tim. I quickly submerge my hand into the water.

"Uh-huh." I'm better than all right. I let my mind drift back to New York. I think about Alex and people at school. It's probably snowing there or just about to. They're probably all getting ready for Christmas—going to the mall, making massive amounts of food. It's not that different to imagine what people are doing without me. The same things they would have been doing anyway.

Jesse's right: this moment does make a lot of things worth it. But Jesse's not me, and neither is G or Lyle. Or Emily. I wonder guiltily if there was something she needed. I'm sure I can make it up to her, find out what's wrong, and everything will be okay. I let these thoughts and the warm water soothe the kernels of worry in my mind.

When we finally get out my muscles are relaxed and my skin is tingly. I'm curious about Jesse and Danielle, who seem to be sharing a towel in a rather intimate way. As we walk back towards the campground I lag behind and ask G about it.

"Danielle? Yeah, they always screw around. She's got a thing for younger guys."

"I thought she was with Rippy."

"She is. But I guess they have an open relationship or whatever."

"So he doesn't mind?"

"I don't think so. It's pretty much all out in the open.

They're with each other, you know. But they can be with other people too. I don't know. Whatever, straight people are weird."

"Hey," I say, feigning offense.

"Especially you, Andrew. You're the weirdest of the weird."

"Thanks," I say, and I mean it.

Back at the campground there's a huge bonfire going and a whole bunch of people sitting around, listening to two guys and a girl play guitar and sing. I look around the circle hopefully, but there's no sign of Emily. I sit with G and Tim, Jesse and Danielle for a while, listening to the music. Pretty soon the warmth of the fire and the soft music begin to take their toll, and I can feel my head nodding forward on my neck like a broken doll's.

"Hey," G says, shaking my shoulder. "I'm heading back to the tents. You should come with me before you fall asleep and roll into the fire."

I'm too tired to argue, so I let her guide me back to our campsite. I'm thinking Emily must be there, but the inside of my tent is empty and our sleeping bags are still tightly in their rolls. I manage to unroll them and set them up the way we have been, so one is like a bottom sheet and the other's like a blanket. I fall asleep almost immediately.

When I wake up, I'm still alone. There's no sign that Emily has been there. What there is, is a pit in my stomach and the feeling that I've made a terrible mistake.

PART THREE

THE
FUTURE
SIMPLE

CHRISTMAS DAY

The immediate view from the hospital window is of the parking lot. But beyond that the first streaks of daylight are beginning to illuminate the sandstone shapes of the desert with reds and pinks. I stand up from the plastic chair that has been my bed for the night and stretch my hands over my head, hoping to crack my back. Nothing. I go over to the window and stare out past the parking lot to the strip of stores on the main drag next to the Roswell Hospital. A check-cashing store blinks with neon lights. Someone is emptying the trash cans at the twenty-four-hour gas station next door; otherwise, everything is gray and quiet.

I look back at the bed where G is lying motionless. There is a tube coming out of her nose and an IV coming out of her arm. The right side of her face is starting to yellow and bruise, and her right leg is supported by a series of ropes and pulleys that resemble a medieval torture device. The only sounds coming from the bed are the beeps of a heart monitor and an occasional loud, snorty breath that makes me look expectantly over to see if she wakes up, even though the nurses told me she would sleep for a while.

All of these things, the colors of her bruises and the sounds of the machine, are vivid and very real. Even as G snores, I am awake in a horrible, jittery overtired way. I am here, and I'm prepared for whatever comes next, I think.

"We gave her enough painkiller for a small pony," the short, pudgy, redheaded nurse I like best told me. Her nametag says *Dolly*. "A femur's a really bad break. Your friend is probably in shock. She'll wake up when she's ready."

There's a tray of food at the end of G's bed, delivered at some point in the night, but I feel too guilty to touch any of it. Eventually, the gross taste in my mouth is enough to push me to drink the red Gatorade in the pink plastic cup.

My backpack is on the floor next to the chair where I spent the night, but most of its contents are still back at the campground in my tent. I paw through it, even though I know there's no food. My dead cell phone, *Into the Wild*, a semi-clean T-shirt, a few miscellaneous flyers from our travels, including a menu from Adelaide's, and this notebook. This notebook with its stupid meaningless lists and no answers. G told me I should be writing things down, and I ignored her because I thought the point was to just keep moving and experience every new thing in the moment. It's the sight of her with those tubes coming out of her nose that makes me realize what happens when you keep moving forward without paying attention to where you're going.

I pick up the battered copy of *Into the Wild*—the back cover's come off somewhere in my travels—and walk it down the hall to the family waiting room where there's a shelf with a few other paperback orphans. I leave it there and walk away. I already know what he knows, and I didn't have to read Tolstoy or starve myself to death in the Alaskan bush to figure it out.

It's still early, but I know pretty soon there will be a

police officer here to interview me about what happened. I didn't even try to lie to the nurses about my age, and they told me that since I was a minor, they would have to call DSS and the local police. The thing is, I'm not even really sure what happened.

At the bottom of my bag is a capless blue ballpoint pen. I brush a few crumbs of granola and ink off the tip and find that it writes. The last time I wrote in here, I was back in Hot Springs, Arkansas, adding to my list of useful facts for life after high school—maybe even thinking that it was different than the lists that were in the divorce diary. But it wasn't. It was missing the guts, the feelings, the parts worth caring about. Now I have to write about the hard things, the things that are going to allow me to go home a different person than I was a few weeks ago. Because if I don't, then it's just like G said, I'll still be wondering what I'm coming to.

It's a little before six now. I don't know what time the police show up, but I figure since it's Christmas morning, I've got at least a few hours to sort out the last few days. That will be a decent start, and it will at least keep everyone from getting arrested. I'm sure one of the first things they'll do is call Mom, and I definitely need to get my story straight before that happens. G shifts a little in the hospital bed. The beeping sound of her monitor speeds up momentarily and then slows back down. The sound is unnerving. It's like she's reminding me to get my head out of my ass and start writing. I smile and reach over to pat her hand, avoiding the purple part where the IV is inserted. "Okay, okay," I say softly to the beeping machines and the sleeping G. I turn to a fresh page and pick up the pen.

WHAT HAPPENED WAS

I didn't really start to get worried about Emily until she didn't turn up for lunch. She had missed breakfast too, but I just figured she was off having some alone time, like she had done all the time when we were in Hot Springs. After breakfast I went with Jesse, Rippy, and a few other people on an edible plant walk. At first I tried really hard to remember all the names of the different plants this guy Adrian was telling us about, but after a while it started to blend together, and I just enjoyed the hike and the warm sunshine on my face. After the hike I dashed back to the campsite, fully expecting Emily to be there or at least to find some sign that she had been by. But there was nothing. When the gong sounded for lunch I rushed over, but she never turned up. I had signed up for a cleanup crew after lunch and made a point of asking everyone on the crew if they had seen Emily. No one had.

After lunch G waited for me to go to a workshop on nonviolent direct action. I was interested, even though I thought the workshop title sounded like a contradiction in terms. But after the lunch crew was finished, I was too distracted by Emily's disappearance to focus on much else.

"She's been acting a little weird since we got here," G said.

"You think so?" I was kind of annoyed at her for being the one to notice.

"Sometimes big groups of people are harder," G said vaguely. But there was a lot in that statement that wasn't said. For people who attract a lot of drama. For people who are trying through sheer willpower not to use. For people who are insecure like Emily. I knew what she meant. I knew all those things. But I was kind of annoyed that she wasn't giving Emily more credit. And I was kind of annoyed that she knew Emily as well, if not better, than I did. Did that mean I cared a lot more than I thought I did? Do I still?

I spent the afternoon wandering around the campground, asking people if they had seen her. I was starting to imagine her dehydrated and wasted in the desert or withering away in some cave, weakened by a scorpion's sting or being devoured by wild hyenas.

Finally I ran into the girl I had seen on the first day with the drum and the toddler. The toddler was wearing a very soggy cloth diaper and playing in the mud puddle underneath a water spigot. She had been up early with her son and seen Emily heading down the trail that led to the hot springs. She didn't know the time, but she guessed it was six or six-thirty. I had already walked over to the hot springs once that afternoon and seen no sign of Emily, but because I didn't have any better leads I walked back that way. There were a few people in the pools, but no Emily. It was comforting to know that someone had seen her at least once that day.

Right before the dinner gong rang she turned up at the campsite. Her face was sunburned and her eyes were bright.

"Drew," she said when she saw me. "I've had the most incredible day!" She wrapped her arms around my neck and started swaying like we were dancing. She smelled like pine trees.

"Where the hell have you been?" I said harshly.

But she answered like she hadn't even noticed. "It was incredible," she said dreamily. "I walked up to the ridge last night, and I just sat there, looking at the stars and thinking about everything, you know? And nothing at all. I tried to clear my head of all the polluting thoughts and toxic feelings I was having. And I just sat there, and then before I knew it the sun was coming up. So I came down to grab a little bit of food, but you guys were all still sleeping so I hiked back up there and just sat some more, and thought about things and waited."

"Waited for what?"

"For guidance, I guess. For my spirit animal to tell me what to do."

If I hadn't been so annoyed I probably would have laughed at this last part, but a quick glance at Emily's face told me she was completely serious. I bit the inside of my cheek before I responded. "So did you figure it out?"

"I think so," she said. But she didn't elaborate, and I didn't ask. We walked towards dinner together in silence. I was trying to come up with a way to say what I'd been feeling all day, how worried I'd been. But mostly, I realized, I was mad at her selfishness, and I didn't know where that conversational road would take us. When we were almost at dinner I grabbed her arm harder than I meant to and blurted out, "I was really worried about you." Those were the words I said, but in my mind it sounded like, "I'm really pissed at you."

She looked at me strangely. "That's sweet of you, Drew."

It reminded me of the way you would talk to an old person, or someone who was speaking English for the first time and doing a really bad job.

Emily sat with us at dinner but barely picked at her food. She kept sighing and staring off dreamily in the direction of the ridgeline. I could tell she was dying for someone to ask about her day, but no one took the bait. Finally Danielle took the bait. "How was your day, Emily?"

Emily shook her head. "You have no idea. This place is magical."

I expected Danielle or someone to snicker, but no one did. "It's pretty special," Danielle agreed. "But it's also pretty remote. If you're going to wander off, you should probably tell someone where you're going. Some people were kind of worried about you." Emily smiled and nodded but didn't respond.

"Soooo," said Tim. "The Bike Derby is after dinner, huh? Do you think anyone would mind if I recorded it?"

"I don't think so," Danielle said. "They would probably be pretty psyched. Some people have been working on their bikes all week." I thought about the pile of junked bicycles I had seen parked up by Steamers on the way in. Rippy came over to our table and stood behind Danielle. He was shirtless but still wearing the velvet jester's hat he'd had on the first day. He put his hands on Danielle's shoulders and began kneading her neck. "Everyone ready for Derby?" he asked without ever really looking down at the table. "I could use some help getting the fire going."

"I'll help," Jesse offered.

"Me too," I said. As soon as the words were out of my mouth I thought I saw a ripple of annoyance cross Emily's forehead.

Before I finished my food Emily got up from the table, took her plate, and relocated herself to a stump outside the tent.

"I think that's your cue," G said in between mouthfuls of squash stew.

"Whatever," I said, trying to sound more irritated than I felt. It was still my turn to be annoyed.

Jesse scraped the last spoonfuls out of his bowl and stood up. "You still coming, Andrew?"

I took one last look at Emily pouting outside the tent and made my decision. "Yeah, I'm in."

***

I lift my fingers up from the notebook paper and shift the pen from one hand to the other. I flex my hand wide open; my fingers are out of practice for this kind of thing. It's cloudy, and the day is still gray. G is sleeping, and the green bleep of the monitors goes on steady and certain.

A nurse comes in to check on G. This one is younger than Dolly but more severe-looking. Her brown hair is turning prematurely gray and is pulled back in a ponytail. She checks something on one of G's charts and plumps her pillow. I wince, waiting for her eyes to open and glare at the nurse, but G just moans slightly and settles back in to sleep. The nurse pauses at the end of the bed and eyeballs the untouched food tray. "You don't want any of this?"

"I wasn't . . . I didn't want to . . ." I mumble a half-response.

"She's not going to eat it," the nurse says, not unkindly. "They'll just come and clear it, and it will go to waste. If you're hungry, you should eat. I've got two boys about your age, and they're always hungry," she adds. She's barely out of the room before I pounce on the tray. It's not much; some applesauce, a banana, and a piece of cold turkey covered in congealed gravy. At first I hesitate on the turkey, but my hunger is stronger than my squeamishness. It's not that bad, and I wash it all down with some cold water from the fountain in the hallway.

I want to run down the hall after the nurse and ask her about her two boys, their names and how they're doing in school. But what I really want to ask is how she would feel if they ever ran away. I'm rereading what I just wrote about Emily, and there's a knowing that's creeping into my gut, one cold finger at a time. No matter what the circumstances, there are serious consequences when someone you love just walks out of your life.

The blinking digital display beside G's bed tells me it's a little before seven. I try and lean back in the chair to nap, but every time I do my brain, way more awake than my body, takes over. *What if I hadn't gone to make the fire that night? What if I'd tried harder to talk to Emily and find out what was bothering her? She was so selfish, but so was I. I'm not sure if it's an addition problem or a subtraction problem, but either way I don't think anyone ends up with very much.* I look over at G. She's going to be okay. I know she won't hold me responsible. *But what if I am?*

***

Rippy and Jesse and I hauled brush for the bonfire for an hour or so until the pile of wood was almost over our heads. Each time I thought we were almost done, one of them found another spectacular log that just had to go on top. It was becoming competitive when finally Rippy said he had to go get ready for the derby. Jesse and I cleared an area in front of the woodpile where people would ride around, and I helped him haul over two trash cans full of food scraps that Danielle had been saving since people arrived. This was for the audience to throw at the bikers as they circled around each other. "Some people bring their own stuff they grabbed out of dumpsters: rotten fruit, veggies, whatever. It just has to be biodegradable," Jesse explained.

I was getting pretty amped up for the derby and had more or less forgotten about Emily and her pouting at dinner. Besides, it wasn't like she hadn't been moody before, and I figured everything would sort itself out later. I went back to the campsite and found G, Tim, and Lyle digging through a duffel bag of costumes that had been stuffed under the seat. The van was like a never-ending Mary Poppins bag of weird items. "Where have you been hiding this stuff?" I asked.

"Special occasions," G said. She was wearing a dress over her clothes that looked like something a 1950s candy striper in a hospital would wear. Tim had on a paper Burger King crown and a very wrinkled silk smoking jacket. Lyle still had his usual anarchist garb on, but he had added an enormous blue polka-dotted bow tie and a pair of those nose, mustache, and glasses that all go together. G pulled out a shiny navy blue graduation gown and handed it to me. "Here, this is fitting somehow." She eyed me as I pulled the robe over my head. It was designed for someone much shorter, and my arms and legs stuck out beneath it. "You're still missing something." She bent over and rooted around in the bag until she pulled out a neon green trucker-style cap that said, "Virginia is for Lovers" in airbrushed ink. "Perfect," she said and plunked it down sideways on my head.

The four of us walked over to the bonfire together feeling pretty proud of our outfits. We definitely weren't the only ones dressed up. It was kind of like a reverse prom, like everyone had dug through their stuff and found the oddest clothes and costume bits to parade around in, but the atmosphere was still the same as a middle school dance with everyone checking each other out. There's definitely an art to looking weird and cool simultaneously. I looked enviously at one guy who sported a light brown suede suit with a yellow bow tie and no shirt. He had slicked his hair back and wore a pair of mirrored sunglasses that would have matched my hat nicely.

After everyone had milled around for a while Danielle brought out two big vats of punch, one labeled *Alchy* and the other *Non-Alchy*. I went for the one without booze; it seemed like the evening was going to get bizarre enough as it was. As I ladled some into my mug I noticed Danielle scanning nervously around the circle. "Did Emily find you?" she asked.

"No," I said. "Was she looking for me?"

"Yeah," Danielle said. I remember she looked like she wanted to say more. I remember she looked worried.

Rippy came out as the Master of Ceremonies, wearing his jester's hat and a pair of pants made completely of four-inch squares of different fabrics. Instead of a shirt his upper body was painted with streaks and swirls of color. "Ladies and gentlemen," he shouted into a small orange traffic cone turned megaphone. "Welcome to the fourth annual—"

"Fifth!" a few people in the crowd shouted out.

"Right, sorry. I lose track of time sometimes," he continued despite a few snickers. "The fifth annual Burdock Bike Derby!" Cheers and shouts went up from the crowd. Some people were beating homemade drums. It had been hard to tell how many people were actually at Burdock. Not everyone showed up for every meal, but everyone had come out for Bike Derby. It looked like a hundred fifty or two hundred people were there.

"All right then!" Rippy shouted into the cone. "Let the wild rumpus begin!"

He put down the cone, picked up a golf club, and straddled a bicycle designed for a kid half his size. It had a white banana seat with turquoise flowers. The U-shaped handle-bars had sparkly rubber turquoise grips, and one of them still had white and blue streamers hanging off the ends. Rippy rode the bike easily, though his knees came up to his nose every time he pedaled. He rode around the circle, one hand on the handlebars and one hand swinging the golf club. Other people on equally ridiculous bikes began to come out of the crowd and join him in the circle. Every time someone joined in a big cheer went up from their friends. The first few laps were clearly just for show. Each biker had some kind of light weapon: either a whiffle ball bat, a golf club like Rippy's, or just a big stick.

The circle was getting packed with riders when finally Rippy took a whack at someone's bike with his golf club. The crowd went wild, screaming and cheering. This was clearly also the cue for everyone to begin throwing food scraps at the riders. I winced as a girl with short, bleach-blonde hair took a ketchup-covered nature burger full on in the face.

"They can only hit the bikes with their weapons, not the people," Jesse explained. "The point is to disable the other rider's bike. The last person still pedaling wins." The crowd groaned as a guy with a purple Mohawk took out the blonde girl's front tire with a swing of his aluminum bat. She fell over and then pulled her bicycle carcass to the side of the ring. The crowd cheered for her as she good-naturedly took a bow. We watched as, one after another, the bikers took each other out, shoving sticks in spokes and whacking away at the metal frames. Rippy was clearly a crowd favorite, although he also took more than his fair share of food-scrap bombs.

After a while there were only three riders left circling each other: Rippy, the purple Mohawk guy, and a girl named Rosie with biceps bigger than my thighs. That's when Emily showed up and wrapped her arms around my neck, sinking her chin into my shoulder. "Drew, I need to talk to you now," she said, pressing her breasts into my back in a way that was totally distracting.

"Um, okay," I said. "What is it?"

"Alone. I need to talk to you alone."

There was something strange about her voice. It was muddled, almost slurred. I wasn't that psyched about leaving the derby before seeing the outcome. "Can it wait a minute?"

G was sitting next to me and sniffed sharply in Emily's direction. "You stink," she said. "Have you been drinking?"

Emily ignored her. "No, it can't wait a minute. I need to talk to you now," she insisted. Her closeness and the insistence in her voice had an almost hypnotic effect on me.

Where were you all day? I thought to myself as I grudgingly gave up my front-row seat at the derby. I turned back around in time to see Rippy take out the purple Mohawk guy with a swift stroke to the rear tire. Emily took my hand and pulled me away from the derby, back towards the kitchen tent and the trail that led to the hot springs. I let myself be led for a little while, but finally I jerked my hand away and stopped walking. "What?" I said. "What's so important that it can't wait?" Maybe if I'd known what she wanted to say, I wouldn't have been so abrupt. Maybe if the derby hadn't been so fun, I wouldn't have cared about going off with her. But I did.

"I want to be with you, Drew," she said simply.

"Okay. Well, here we are." I looked back towards the fading light of the bonfire, wondering if anyone had been crowned the winner.

"No, I mean I want to be *with you*. I want you to make love to me on top of this mountain." My jaw fell open. I couldn't have been more surprised if she'd told me we'd just won a dishwasher on *The Price Is Right*. I stared at her.

"*Have you?*" I finally said after a few more awkward moments of silence. "*Have you* been drinking?"

Her voice turned bitter. "I thought that's what you wanted. I thought that's why you were always shoving my hand *down there*."

Her description of my lame sexual fumblings sounded out of place after declaring that she wanted to make love to me on a mountain, but that wasn't the only thing that seemed out of sync. "No," I said. "I mean yes. I mean I wanted you to touch me." My face turned bright red. "I wanted you to *want* to touch me." I took a deep breath, "The way I wanted to touch you."

"Well that's what I'm saying."

But it wasn't and I knew it wasn't. And what I felt wasn't confusion or lust or even curiosity. What I felt was mad. "You know, ever since this whole thing began, whatever it is, it's been on your terms. When you wanted me I was there, and when you wanted to be alone I gave you time alone. So, so . . . " I stuttered, unsure of where I was going with this. "I don't really think it's me and my needs that you're thinking about."

Emily narrowed her eyes at me. "So I'm the one being selfish? I'm offering you the greatest gift a woman can offer a man, and you think I'm being selfish? You're really screwed-up, you know that, Drew?"

Oddly enough, the voice that I heard in my head in that moment wasn't my eighth-grade health teacher warning us about the dangers of teen pregnancy or genital rot. And it wasn't my mother alluding in a roundabout way to the existence of condoms underneath the bathroom sink or my father telling me to keep it my pants and not mess up my life. It was Lindsay. In that moment Emily reminded me of Lindsay, and I didn't want to have sex with her any more than I wanted to have sex with Lindsay. "I'd rather wait," I said. "Until you're sober and you're sure that's really what you want."

I don't know how I knew this. I figured I was about to go down in history as the lamest teenage guy ever. I could picture my own freak-show exhibit. *He refused sex from not one, but two girls!* I even liked Emily. And she liked me, thought I was a good person and supposedly even loved me. But somehow I knew I was right. I thought about Mima and how much I really missed her, because when I was with her I was really there, I was someone worth being and worth being with. I guess I thought Emily made me feel that way too, some of the time. I thought I was doing the right thing for both of us.

Emily's eyes were blazing, picking up a bit of the bonfire's glow. I crossed my arms over my chest to suggest that I wasn't backing down. But then I saw it. I saw it before I could say anything, before I could soften my posture and say something that would allow us both to back down and talk like people who actually cared about each other. I saw fear. Behind her anger, beneath her buzz, Emily was terrified. I opened my mouth to speak, but she spoke first. "Suit yourself," she said coldly and left me standing there alone in the night.

WHERE THERE WERE WILD THINGS

I stop writing and chew on the end of the pen. I've reached the last part of the story that I'm really sure of. I'm nervous about putting anything else down in writing because maybe it's true and maybe it's just how I imagine it happened. But once it's written down it's sure to have a kind of reality that doesn't exist when it's just in my head.

I never really liked the book *Where the Wild Things Are*, but it was one of my dad's favorites. I never really liked it because I never really liked Max. I always thought Max had it pretty good, and I couldn't understand why he felt the need to run off. If he hadn't been such a pain in the ass in the first place he wouldn't have been sent to bed without any supper. He wasn't beaten or abused or even yelled at, and still he stormed around like he was so mistreated and unhappy. I never thought he deserved to be angry.

Now that I'm thinking about Emily and how she treated me, I feel a little bit like Max. I wonder if I deserved to be angry. It's weird, and I don't really want to connect the two, but I'm also thinking about Mom and wondering if I deserved to be angry at her. It's all completely exhausting.

I put the pen back down to the paper, but the words aren't ready yet. And then, like she can read my mind, G opens her eyes. I sit straight up; the pen and notebook fall off my lap onto the floor. I'm wondering if I should ring for the nurse or something, but instead I wait to see if she'll stay awake or do anything else. I mean, G hasn't actually been in a coma for ten years or anything, and opening her eyes, while significant to me, probably doesn't represent a major medical breakthrough for the nursing staff.

Her eyelids flutter a little bit like Mima's used to do when she was falling asleep during *Jeopardy*. She hated to get caught falling asleep while watching TV. She said it made her feel like a *real* old person. So whenever she did, she would shout a random answer out at the TV as soon as her eyes opened again. It was pretty funny. The clue would be something like "gas that makes up 70 percent of the earth's atmosphere" and Mima would scream out, "What is Andrew Jackson!" "I thought I had that one," she would say. And I would nod, and we would keep on watching.

G is definitely waking up, though. Her eyes are open now and she's taking in the surroundings of her room, the blinking machines and the new daylight coming in through the long hanging blinds. I pick my notebook and pen up off the floor without taking my eyes from her face. She slowly licks her lips and makes a face like the taste in her mouth is pretty bad. There's a cup of ice water next to her bed that I grab and maneuver the straw towards her face so she can drink. She takes a small sip and licks her lips again. "Thanks for staying with me," she says. Her voice is a little scratchy. She lifts her head to look down at her leg suspended in the air and surrounded by white plaster.

"Hmm, that doesn't look good."

"Compound fracture," I tell her. "The bone came through your leg."

She turns a little pale and waves off the details with one hand. "Did they call your mom?"

"Not yet. At least I don't think so."

"They will. And they'll probably send a cop in too. Have you thought about what you're going to tell them?"

"Kind of," I say, and I pick up the notebook from the floor.

"That's good," G says. "I'm glad you're getting it all down, but that's not what you want to tell the cop when he shows up."

"Okay, what should I say?"

G is quiet for a minute. She looks out the window thoughtfully. "We were hiking. Just you and me. Let them think we're boyfriend-girlfriend or whatever. I mean, you don't have to come out and say it. They'll just assume it, and don't tell them otherwise. But it was just the two of us; that's the important part. I fell and hurt my leg and some people gave us a ride to the hospital."

"Why can't we tell them the truth?"

"They'll go straight to Burdock," G says. "As long as they fly under the radar, the cops around here don't really care what goes on there in the off-season. But we don't want to give them a reason to go sniffing around. I'm sure you noticed that not everything there was completely legal. Plus, you're underage. I don't want to get Jesse or Tim in trouble for transporting a minor across state lines."

"Okay, but how did you and I meet in the first place?"

"The same way we actually met; a bus station. We hit it off and decided to travel together for a while. A runaway story.

The cops won't look too closely at that. They don't really care that much as long as everything has a tidy ending."

"What about when my mom shows up? I don't know if she's going to go along with our story."

"Nancy might surprise you," G says.

"Hey, when did I tell you my mom's name?"

G shrugs and looks out the window again. "Will you see if there's a nurse around? I could use some more of whatever painkiller they're giving me."

I walk out in hall, dazed, thinking about the story G fed me and wondering if the police officer will buy it coming from me. I've never been a particularly good liar when it comes to massive deviations from the truth. Little things are easier, like calling a C-plus a B-minus or telling my mom I was studying with friends at the library when really I was sitting by myself.

The nurse sitting at the desk goes quickly down the hall to G's room with some pills in a paper cup. I take my time walking back. G hasn't asked me what happened yet—how she fell and broke her leg. I wonder if she knows the truth. I wonder if I know the truth.

When we pulled up to the hospital I didn't hesitate for a second. I knew what would happen. I knew that unless I gave a fake name, they would track me down and call my mom and I would be heading back on the first plane to Glens Falls. I knew all this, the same way I knew that Jesse and Tim weren't going to park the van and follow us in. They looked sad and they looked sorry, but they pulled away all the same. I didn't even get a chance to say good-bye. I guess I'll worry about that later. Tim at least is still in school. I could probably track him down someday if I really wanted to.

The point is, I chose it. I chose to care about G and even Mom. I chose to think about the kind of attention that really matters, and I decided to let Emily go, for now. Because if I've learned anything in the last few weeks it's that sometimes you do have to choose. After what happened, it seems like the right decision.

Back in the hospital room, the medicine is kicking in and G's eyelids are already beginning to quiver. Pretty soon she's out cold again. I take my notebook and my pen and pull a chair into the hall. What I have to write, I don't want to write with her lying right there next to me.

THE CARNIVAL

After my fight with Emily I went back to the Bike Derby, but it was over and people were drifting away from the fire. It was like I was in one of those teen movies where the main character races to get to the prom and arrives just as the janitor is sweeping up the last of the confetti.

Emily didn't make it back to the tent that night either, and when I woke up her backpack and her sleeping bag were gone. She wasn't at breakfast, but she turned up at lunch hanging all over one of the squinty-eyed anarchist guys. She sat sideways on the picnic table, rubbing his shoulders and picking little bites of food off his plate. I tried not to stare. She was laughing a lot and tossing her head around. The guy she was with looked more annoyed that she was eating his food than like he was enjoying his backrub.

G assessed the scene and gave a one-word opinion, "Classy." I didn't respond. In spite of the way she'd been acting, jealousy still burned like acid in the back of my throat.

I spent most of the afternoon alone. I didn't feel like going to any of the workshops or hanging around the hot springs. It was too hot to swim anyway. Burdock had lost a little bit of its shine; now it just seemed dusty and dirty. I walked up the road to Steamers on the off chance that they had a pay phone. Inside the shop a kid was wiping down some huge coffee urns. In the back I found a payphone but there was no dial tone and three pieces of hot pink gum stuck to the receiver. "No phone," I said conversationally to the kid cleaning up, hoping he might offer to let me use the shop's phone.

"Nope," he agreed without looking up.

By the time I got back to the campground it was time for my meal-prep shift. Danielle gave me the job of making "no bake" chocolate peanut butter cookies. She gave me a grease-stained recipe card and showed me where she had laid out all the ingredients. I wondered if everyone got this treatment or if she could tell by looking at me I was clueless in the kitchen. Regardless, it was good to do something to take my mind off Emily, and the cookies came out okay, as far as vegan no-bake cookies go.

Dinner was finished in a bit of a rush. Most people seemed to be hurrying to prepare for the Christmas Eve Carnival. Personally, I was doing my best to pretend it wasn't Christmas Eve so I wouldn't think about Mom all by herself. There wasn't much for me to do since I wasn't performing, so after dinner I took a slow walk around the campground, waiting for the night's events to begin.

I saw Emily. She was hanging out around a small fire with the guy I'd seen her with earlier and a few other people. I felt like a stalker, but I crept in closer to get a better look at what was going on. The sweet stink of marijuana hung in the air, and there was a bottle being passed around the circle. I winced as Emily took a big swig and handed it off to the person next to her. Suddenly she stood up and announced loudly that she had to pee. She headed right for the bush I was hiding in. I stumbled backwards, and a stick snapped loudly beneath my weight. For a second I thought our eyes met in the firelight, but then one of the guys said something about coyotes and everyone started laughing and howling loudly and I managed to escape unnoticed.

I trudged back to our campsite, but it was empty and a bit depressing to be there all alone. I'd never been alone to make a point before. It just seemed to happen by default. I didn't feel noble or righteous without Emily around. I just felt lonely. Eventually I found the rest of the Freegans near the bonfire site setting up for their show. They were rushing around, trying to get everything ready for their big performance. I knew it mattered a lot to them to put on a good show for Burdock. Emily's Hula Hoop and props were there, laid out like she was just about to show up and grab them.

"Seen Emily?" G asked as she bustled by with an armload of costumes.

"No," I lied without meeting her eyes.

"Can you help Lyle with the ropes?" she asked. "He's stressing out about finding somewhere to set up the tightrope."

"Sure," I said, glad to be given a task.

I found a very stressed-out-looking Lyle trying to rig a tightrope between two gnarled scrub oaks. The trees were brittle. Every time he found a place to tie off one end, the other would snap. He was sweating, and there was a big streak of dirt across his forehead. "Can you do the high ropes?" he asked before I'd had a chance to offer or say anything. He looked up at me, a little panicked. "I found a spot and they're all laid out. Someone just needs to tie them up. I showed you that, right?"

"Yeah," I said. "I can handle that."

"Just have G check it when you're done," he added.

"No problem."

Lyle had shown me the intricate set of ropes and knots that allowed the trapeze to swing freely and safely enough for them to perform their act. I hadn't done it in about a week, but he had been so determined to make me practice the knots that they came easily with muscle memory. I grabbed G as she passed by and she gave the whole thing a cursory look. "It's great," she said without really looking.

"Seriously," I said and grabbed her arm. "Make sure it's right; it's the first time I've done it alone."

"All right, all right." She stopped and looked over the knots I had tied. She grabbed the trapeze bar and gave it a few test swings. "It all looks right, Andrew—" She stopped midsentence. I turned to look at what had caught her attention. It was Emily. She was hopping on one foot, trying unsuccessfully to get the other into her striped tights. She was clearly in an altered state. One by one the other Freegans took notice. First Jesse, then Tim, and finally Lyle. They were all staring at her. I looked down at the ropes in my hand instead; the whole thing had the feeling of dry brush about to burst into flame.

Emily stumbled and sat down, finally getting her other leg through the opening of her striped tights. She looked up at the group. "What?" she said icily. Everyone except G looked away. Emily stood up, marched over to me, and threw her arms around my neck. I turned my head as she leaned in to kiss me and her open mouth fell on my neck, which she began licking and nuzzling. "I missed you, Drew," she said. "I'm sorry I was acting so crazy."

I was painfully aware of everyone around us and particularly G, who was shooting daggers in our direction. "Can we talk about it later?" I whispered into her ear.

"You're not performing like that," G said.

Emily let out a big sigh and turned to face her. She hung her arm around my shoulders like it was the two of us against G. "Lighten up," she said. "I'm fine."

"G's right," Lyle said. "You're wasted. You can't do the show like that, even if it is just the hoops. It's not what we're about."

"Oh really, Carter?" Emily said caustically. "Why don't *you* tell me what *we're* about then?"

I cringed and pulled away from her. Lyle shook his head. His cheeks turned red. "Everyone else is over it, Emily. Everyone except you." But still he walked away.

"So that's how it is, huh? I'm the bad guy? It's all of you against me?"

"Nobody's *against* you," I said.

"Yeah," G said. But her voice was a little less convincing. "We're not against you, but you need to find another way to deal with your shit."

Emily crossed her arms over her chest. "That's interesting coming from you," she said. "And just how do you deal with your shit, G?" Emily sputtered self-righteously. "By running from it? By being a freakin' dyke? You think that's going to keep you safe? What's your deal anyway? So what if you like girls, you never hook up with any of them. You're like a lesbian nun! What the fuck happened to you anyway? Were you like abused as a child or something?"

I winced. Emily was inches from G's face, her accusations hanging in the air.

G stuck her hand out Heisman-style and connected just below Emily's neck, shoving her backwards. Emily hit the ground hard. I started towards her, but only for a second. "My shit is none of your business," G said in a low, controlled voice. "It's none of your business because I don't run around like a drunken whore making it everyone's business."

Emily stood up and reached forward like she was going to push G back, but G batted her hands away easily. "Screw you," Emily shrieked at the top of her lungs. "Screw all of you!" She screamed again and ran from the fire circle. I watched her go. Even though I cared about her, I wanted to stay. I had a sinking, tearing feeling like I was living through my parents' divorce all over again. Like I had climbed up the ladder of a high diving board with no way to back down. I stared in the direction Emily ran off in. "Do what you need to do," G said to me.

"I want to stay," I said.

"Then stay."

***

There's a light rapping on the hospital door that brings me back to the present moment. A man in his mid-fifties with a thick brown mustache pokes his head in through the doorway. He smiles in a friendly enough way. "Are you Andrew? I'm Officer Hanley. The nurses paged me last night when you and your friend turned up." I look at his brown work pants and his faded blue denim shirt. "I'm technically off duty," he says, taking in my gaze. "But I'm the captain of our district, and I didn't want to hand this off to anyone else on Christmas Day."

"Sorry," I say.

"It's all right. My kids already tore through their presents, and my mother-in-law's here; she and I could use a few hours apart." He looks around the room at G hooked up to the machines, down at my small backpack, empty of its contents. "Do you think you and I could have a little conversation?" I nod. "How about we head down to the waiting room so we don't disturb your friend here?"

I follow Officer Hanley down to the waiting room and have to remind myself several times not to tell him the whole truth. He's the kind of guy you want to tell the whole truth to because it seems like he would be able to pick up the pieces of any situation. We sit down in two squishy plastic yellow chairs opposite each other, like one of us is the doctor about to give the other some bad news. "I think I should tell you that I already contacted your mother. Nice lady."

"Yes," I say. "She is. Did she seem, um . . ."

"Mad? I've heard worse. Nah, she was mostly worried about you. And of course she wants you to come home."

"I plan to," I said. "Go home, that is. I'm ready to go home." Part of me is hoping this admission will be enough for Officer Hanley.

"That's good to hear. If you don't mind, I'd like to know how your friend got hurt and how the two of you ended up here. It doesn't seem like the two of you are involved in any criminal wrongdoing but with you being a minor and all . . ."

I take a deep breath and tell G's story pretty much the way she told me to. I can't tell if Officer Hanley believes me or not, but he notes a few things down on a little pad of paper he pulls from his breast pocket and seems willing to accept my story for the truth.

"Okay," he says when I'm done. "So you don't know the names of the folks who gave you a ride?" I shake my head. "And they didn't stick around to see if you and your friend were okay?" I shake my head again.

"I think they were heading somewhere for the holidays," I offer lamely. And then a sudden burst of inspiration hits me. "Truthfully, I don't know what they were doing out there, but they smelled a little funny and they seemed kind of nervous about us being minors as well."

Now Officer Hanley nods his head like I've said something that makes sense. "There's a lot of oddballs out here. People like the weather and the desert. The area tends to attract some strange types. I'm just glad they were decent enough to give you and your friend a ride."

"Yeah, I don't know what would have happened if they hadn't come across us." I might be laying it on a little thick, so I change the subject. "Do you know if my mom is coming out here to get me?"

"Yup, she said she'd be on the first flight out. I imagine she'll get into Albuquerque sometime around noon. Of course, she'll need to rent a car and drive down here." I do a little mental math in my head and figure I have about seven to eight more hours until it's confrontation time. "You're lucky you have someone like your mom," Officer Hanley adds. "I haven't been able to contact anyone who's willing to take custody of your friend Maria. She'll have to go back to the state for at least one more year."

"G? But she's nineteen."

He picks up a manila file folder and flips through the pages. "Not according to the New Jersey Department of Social

Services. Your friend is sixteen until the end of the month. She probably just lied to you to protect herself. Most runaways aren't too trusting."

I flash back to the night of the meteor shower, when G told me the story of the trapeze in the sky and how she had ended up running away. *Is anything I know about her true?*

"Son?" Officer Hanley breaks my recollection. "Normally I'd have to stay with you until your mom gets here, but given what you told me about your willingness to go home, do you think you and I could agree that you're going to sit tight here at the hospital until she gets here?"

I nod, still a little stunned about G.

"Good." He grins. "Then I'll go home just long enough to eat some ham, miss out on church, and be back later this afternoon to check on you." He looks like he wants to ruffle my hair or maybe even hug me. I stick out my hand, which he shakes awkwardly before leaving. I hear him tell the nurses at the station that he doesn't think I'm a flight risk and to make sure I get some food.

It's only when he's gone that I notice the file he's left behind on the table next to him. Written in pencil on the manila tab are the words *Deluca, Maria Regina.* I know I shouldn't open it. I know what's in there is definitely none of my business. I know all these things, and still I open it up and look. The first page is just a brief description of G's injuries and the date and time that we showed up at the hospital. The next two pages have black lines along the edge indicating that they were probably sent through a fax machine. The letterhead is the New Jersey Department of Social Services. I've never seen a case file for a foster kid before, but it looks a lot like I imagine a criminal rap sheet would. There's an old picture of G in the upper right-hand corner where she's maybe ten or eleven. Her hair is messy and her eyes are dark and blank.

To the left of this is basic information like her date of birth, parents' and siblings' names and the words *relinquished into state custody.* There's a date, six years ago, when G would have been about the age she is in the photograph. Following this is a list of six foster families, and the dates that G lived with them show she wasn't anywhere for more than nine months. She lasted only three weeks with the last family. Underneath the list of names and dates is a short paragraph that suggests that the youth in custody, G, is a runaway risk and a possible arson risk. She should not be left alone in the house and should probably not be placed in a home with younger siblings.

I feel sick and close the file. I wish I'd never opened it. What I've read is so far from the person I've come to know in the last few weeks. I have a home to go home to; the last few weeks have been a blip in my life, a crazy adventure sure, a momentary rebellion maybe. But for G, this is her whole life. The Freegans were her whole life.

A FAMILY REUNION

The look on G's face in the moment after she hit the ground, right before she passed out from the pain, is something I don't want to remember but will probably never forget. Even worse than that was the sound. There was a thud and a snap. It's the snap I can't get out of my mind, worse than the sight of jagged bone poking through the wound in her thigh. Everyone swarmed around her as soon as she fell. Luckily there was a kid who had taken an EMT class, and he knew how to pull her leg into traction. I couldn't watch as he instructed one person to pull on her foot while the other held her hip. Then he tied long pieces of fabric around her leg to stanch the bleeding.

I stepped back away from the scene. People were crying, and some people were debating whether it was faster to drive her to the hospital or call an ambulance. Lyle was standing off to one side, holding the ropes in his hand. He was looking down at them as if there was an answer there. Bile rose up in the back of my throat. I went over the knots in my mind. I was certain I had done it correctly, and even G had checked it. Somehow I had screwed it up, but how?

That's when I looked up. Across the fire circle, on the

other side of the people kneeling down around G, I saw Emily's face. It was ashen. Our eyes met, and what I saw there is the only evidence of what I think I know about what happened that night.

***

I drop the file off at the nurses' desk and tell them that Officer Hanley left it behind. There's a lot in that file I wish I'd never seen. Particularly that last set of dates—the last family she stayed with where she lasted only three weeks before running away. I don't think I can ever tell G about it. It's a little like sneaking into someone's bedroom and reading her diary.

I sink back down into the chair next to her hospital bed. It's odd to think that I may never see Tim or Jesse or Lyle again. It's even more bizarre to think that I'll never see Emily again. I try to conjure all of the good images of her I have in my mind: Hula-Hooping in the bus station, our late-night chat in the bathtub, swimming in the hot springs pool, snuggling close to me in our Cub-Scout tent, but none of them last. The one that keeps returning is the sight of her face across the circle of people, her face filled with sorrow and shame. I want to tell her that when I think about the good things I already forgive her, and that I loved her, maybe I even still do. Because ultimately I think that's what Emily was looking for and wanting. Maybe she just didn't know it, or know how to ask for it. And then suddenly I have a weird feeling. It reminds me of the end of a stomach flu when you get your appetite back. I realize I'm actually looking forward to seeing Mom, and even Dad. And it hits me again, like it hasn't in days, that Mima is gone. There's a choking feeling in my throat, and a couple of hot tears roll down my face. When I brush them aside, the choking feeling is gone and I'm able to take a deep breath.

An orderly comes in with two trays of food: grilled cheese sandwiches and a watery-looking tomato soup. I gulp mine down and wait twenty minutes, staring at G's tray. When she doesn't stir, I polish off her food too. I figure she can always order some more. With my belly full of food, I twist the blinds shut and lie down on the plastic visitor's couch. I fall immediately into a heavy, dreamless sleep.

***

When I wake up I hear Mom speaking in hushed tones. I'm curled up on the couch with my back to the rest of the room, so I lie there for a minute, bracing myself for what I assume is going to be an onslaught of anger and guilt-tripping. But Mom sounds calm.

"I can't thank you enough for what you did, Maria," Mom is saying.

"It wasn't really that big a deal," G responds. "Just a couple of phone calls."

"Well, maybe not to you, but it meant the world to me to know that Andrew was okay." *Is that Mom crying?*

"I know what it's like to be cut off from your family," G says. "But if it's all right with you, I'd like to tell him myself when the time is right."

"Of course," Mom says. There's a pause, and I decide that now is a good time to pretend to wake up. I fake a big yawn and roll over dramatically on the couch to face the room. G is sitting up, eating off a hospital tray and looking better than she has since we got here. Mom is next to her with a large plastic cup of ice water in one hand.

"Hi, Mom. It's good to see you."

Her face is pink and tear-streaked. "It's good to see you too, Andrew," she sniffles. She walks over to the couch, and I scoot over to make room for her to sit. She runs her hand through my new shaggy hair and pats my head the way she did when I was home sick from school.

"Merry Christmas," I say. Mom rolls her eyes and smiles.

***

After G finishes her food she drifts off again, and Mom and I go for a walk around the hospital grounds. The air is crisp and about fifty degrees, which is the strangest Christmas weather I've ever experienced. Everything's quiet, and there are only a few cars in the parking lot. For a while we don't say anything at all. I'm not used to this with Mom. Usually she's going on about some student or parent or meeting she has to attend and I'm nodding along, all the while thinking about how I'm going to hide this quarter's grades from her. I take a deep breath.

"I know I owe you a really big apology."

"There'll be time for that," she says. "I think I owe you one too."

"About Mima?"

"Yes, about Mima. And the way you and I have been living, the things I've asked you to accept as normal."

"Things were never that bad," I say, thinking of Max and his wolf suit.

"Yeah, but they were never that great, Andrew. I've had some time to think about it." She makes a noise that's somewhere between a cough and a laugh. "I haven't slept much. It reminded me of when you were an infant, waking every couple hours. I remember how crazy I would get about your sleeping and eating and how much you were pooping."

"Come on, Mom," I say.

"Sorry, sweetie. But it's something you'll never know until you have kids. The unbelievable responsibility of it all. To be completely responsible for someone else's life. It was thrilling to me when you said your first words, or when you read a book back to us when you were only two. I wanted to take credit for it all—with your father, of course. But when it went badly with me and your dad, well, I didn't want to take credit or responsibility for that."

I take this in. Does she really see it all? Will anything really be different when I go home? Anything other than me. "Thanks, Mom. I appreciate you saying that, but I think it's okay if I'm responsible for me from now on. Like with school and stuff, like, whatever comes after. Life, I guess. You can still make me dinner sometimes if you want to."

Mom makes a little noise in her throat that's somewhere between a cough and a laugh. She stops walking and throws her arms around me in a big, uncharacteristically tight hug. I can tell she's crying because she's making little sniffly noises. It occurs to me that Mom needs to take responsibility for herself too, but I decide not to share this right then and there. It's funny, but in this moment, the person I'm thinking about the most is G.

I let her snurfle on for a little bit and then I pull away. "What's going to happen to G? She doesn't have anywhere to go. They'll send her back into state custody."

"Where she'll have a chance to finish school and maybe even go to college," Mom says.

I try and be patient. She doesn't know what I know now. "There's no way she'll stick around long enough for that, Mom." I take a deep breath. "What about St. Mary's?"

"What about it?"

"Well, don't they have scholarship funds? I mean, you run the place. Couldn't we find some money for G to go there? Or if they won't let her go for free, maybe I could help. Maybe Mima left me some money?"

"Oh, Andrew," Mom says. "What you're suggesting is very complicated. I mean, someone would have to become her legal guardian before she could go to St. Mary's. That's assuming of course I could convince the board to take on a scholarship student." She sounds skeptical, but I can tell by the way she's talking that she's really considering it.

"G doesn't have a home," I tell her. "And I don't mean she doesn't have a place to live. I mean she doesn't have a home." My voice gets a little scratchy here. "She kind of helped me see what a big deal that is."

Mom looks at me. Like, she really looks at me in a way that would make me squirm if I wasn't so sure about what I was saying. "I'll look into it," she says.

***

G didn't say much when I told her about the plan. She just turned her head and looked out the window.

After filling out paperwork with Officer Hanley, Mom spent the next several hours on the phone. First she contacted the guardian *ad litem*, who agreed to release G into Mom's custody until the state could find a new placement for her. After Mom gave her a serious headmistress-style lecture about neglecting her job and allowing the most vulnerable members of our society to drift about the country in near vagrancy. Then she set up meetings with the board at St. Mary's and called about renting a van in Albuquerque so that she could drive me and G back home without jostling G's leg too much.

The more the plan became a reality, the more nervous I got. And I dealt with my nerves by asking G over and over again if she was okay with the whole thing. Finally she started to get annoyed at me.

"What are my options?" she finally said. "I'm not going back to some foster home like this. I can't even imagine what kind of people would take on a teenager who needs help getting to the bathroom. What you and your mom are doing is incredible. I'll find a way to pay you guys back."

"I know you will," I said. "It seems like maybe you already have."

"Yeah, I made a few phone calls on the sly."

"How?"

"That day in Louisville when you called home, I memorized the numbers you dialed. I figured if you ever got to be real pain, I could just call Nancy and rat you out."

"Nice."

"So you're not mad? I just wanted her to know you were all right. And you were kind of busy dealing with other things."

It was the first time either of us even indirectly mentioned Emily. "No, I'm glad you did it. My mom would have been way more freaked out if you hadn't. It's really weird to hear you call her Nancy, though." But there was something else bothering me. "G, about the other night, about your fall." I paused and took a deep breath. "It could have been me. It could have been my fault."

"It's okay. Stuff happens. And anyway, I checked the ropes too. I think we both know it wasn't your fault."

"I know she didn't mean for you to really get hurt."

G sighed. "You know, it's weird. I'm not even that mad at her. I mean, this sucks." She wiggled her toes pointing out of the white plaster. "But it's probably my fault too. I mean I wasn't very nice to her a lot of the time. I thought she was using you. And it just seemed like a matter of time before she started drinking again. But maybe she wouldn't have if I hadn't been on her case all the time. If I'd really wanted to help her I could have gone about it some other way."

Her words are like a knife in my gut, reminding me about my own choices. How I could have gone after Emily and I didn't. I chose to stay. Not only that, but I was proud of myself, for the way I was finally making choices in my own life. G stared at me like she knew what I was thinking. "She made her own choices. I'm just saying I might have done things differently, you know, if I knew what I know now. Anyway, it's just a leg. I've got another one." She smiled weakly. "Like I said: stuff happens."

***

G couldn't be released until the next morning, so that night Mom and I found a motel room near the hospital and ate takeout from the only place in town that was open: a Chinese restaurant called Lucky Dragon. Afterwards we picked up two pints of Ben & Jerry's from the gas station convenience store and parked ourselves in vinyl chaise lounge chairs beside the empty motel pool. I was wearing a clean pair of jeans and a fleece jacket that Mom had packed in a suitcase full of my clothes. It felt great to be in clean clothes, especially clean socks. I kept wiggling my toes around in my shoes, relishing the feel of clean cotton. She'd also made sure to throw in a copy of *The Scarlet Letter*, which was on second semester's reading list. Mom was still Mom. "I figured you would want something to read on the drive home," she said.

That was the first time I *really* thought about it; the thirtysomething hours in a very different kind of van with a very different kind of purpose.

At first we didn't say much; we just shoveled ice cream into our mouths and stared into the chipped green concrete walls of the empty pool. "How was Mima's funeral?" I asked after I was halfway through my pint of chocolate fudge brownie and thoroughly buzzed from the sugar.

"Simple, classy, short. Just what she would have wanted. In fact, she left explicit instructions about what she wanted and who she wanted to be there." I expected Mom to go on and tell me about how my name was on that list and what a disappointment it was that I wasn't there, but she didn't. Instead she laughed. "She left a specific list of all the 'old bags' at the nursing home that she didn't want to attend. And she said not to let anyone speak who didn't really know her. And she wanted this one poem read. I've got a copy of it back at the house if you'd like it."

"How did Dad seem?"

"Appropriately sad. I think he missed having you there more than anyone. It meant a lot to him that you had such a close relationship with his mother, even though he didn't." It was good to hear Mom skip an opportunity to bash Dad for something. Mom sighed and stuck her spoon into the container of Chunky Monkey so that it was standing up straight. "I don't expect you to tell me everything that happened to you in the last month," she said. "But I hope when you feel ready, you'll tell me *something*." I wanted to tell her that I'd gladly tell her most of what's gone on while I was with the Freegans, that it's no big secret and that I haven't spent the last month feeling pissed at her. And that this trip hasn't been one big screw-you to her. But the sadness in her voice really choked me up, and I couldn't get the words out.

"Is Maria your girlfriend?" she asked after the silence stretched a bit too awkwardly.

I inhaled my ice cream too quickly, and a chocolate chip shot down the back of my throat, causing me to cough violently. "No, Mom, she's not."

"Oh good," Mom said quickly. "I mean, it would just make things awkward at home with your sleeping arrangements and everything." She waved her hand in front of her face quickly while I blushed deeply.

"But there was a girl," I added, finding that was all I could say. Answering Mom's questions honestly was harder than making up bullshit answers. But it felt a hell of a lot better.

Oh," Mom said. "Well, I hope you'll tell me more, when you're ready." She reached across to put her hand on my arm. Since I still couldn't speak, I just placed my hand on top of hers.

SKIPPING TOWN

I woke up early the next morning. Mom was still snoring with her earplugs in. I took a quick shower, threw a few things in my backpack, and left her this note.

Dear Mom,

First of all, I just want to tell you this is absolutely the last jerky selfish thing I will do for a long, long time. Second of all, thank you for everything you're doing for G and everything you've already done for me. I'm getting on a bus (for real this time) and I'll meet you guys back in Glens Falls. I might even beat you home, depending on what time they release G. I'm sure you guys will have plenty to talk about on the way home. I can't explain it exactly, but I really need to come home different than when I left.

I hitched a ride on this adventure with the Freegans, until it became my own. I'm still not sure exactly what I figured out, but I guess I'm hoping the bus ride will give me some time to sort it all out. Tell G

I said that. She'll get what I mean. And I want to come home on my own. See you back in New York.

Love,
Andrew

The bus station is only a few miles down the road from our motel. I'm able to board the first bus to Albuquerque, and using Mom's credit card I buy a series of tickets that will take me all the way back to Albany and then home to Glens Falls. The sky is turning from pink to a hazy blue, changing all the dusty buildings from a romantic rose color back to the tired sun-beat light brown. I have a seat to myself, but unfortunately someone has stuck gum in the outlet for the headphones. I watch a little bit of *Night at the Museum* without any sound before taking out my notebook and finishing what I started back in the hospital.

This will not be a list. This will be a real story with all the guts and juicy bits and bitter unrequited endings. I'm going to stare them all down until I know what they mean about my future. Or at least that's what I hope will happen. At the very least, I'll have some really good extra credit for Ms. Tuttle.

SOPHOMORE YEAR PART TWO

I'm not sure what I expected coming back to St. Mary's. It's kind of amazing how everything can be the same around me when I feel so different on the inside. It was all kind of shocking at first, like jumping into the ocean all at once and having the air squeezed out of you by the cold. But that wears off, and I'm a little bit afraid I could slip back to where I was before. Some things are different. Having G here is proof of that. Everyone's intrigued by how she broke her leg and came to be at St. Mary's. I've heard rumors that she's a mobster's daughter and part of the witness protection program, or that she's the heiress to a Middle Eastern oil fortune. Alex loves her. I asked him if it was because they're both gay, and he just laughed at me and said G was tuff. He spelled it out like that too. He said I should have my own support group and I could call it AMFAG—all my friends are gay.

Mom even bought me a car so that G wouldn't have to hobble back and forth to school. It's a used Ford Focus—nothing fancy—but it's a car and it's all mine. And of course some of the interest in her has rubbed off on me. Everyone speculates about whether we're "together" even though we've never said or indicated anything that would make it seem like we are.

Even Margaret and some of the other hot girls have started saying hi to me. They say "Hi, Andrew," even though I have no idea how they know my name because I'm pretty sure I never told them. A couple weeks after I got back Jennifer Barnes, in my history class, actually asked me to go to the movies. It wasn't really a big deal. There wasn't that much time to talk since it was a movie. We ate popcorn and made fun of the corny ads and quiz games that flash on the screen before the movie starts. Afterwards, when I dropped her off at her house, she sat in the car for a while after unbuckling her seatbelt, like she was expecting something. So I kissed her, just quickly, and told her I'd call her again sometime. But I haven't called. When I left her house that night I went home hoping G would be up and we could talk, but the lights were out in the guest room. I thought about opening the door to see if she would wake up. Instead I sat up for a while and thought about Emily and the things about being with her that made me really truly happy. Which of course makes me think about where I am now. It's not exactly the opposite of happy, but it's kind of like eating plain old white bread after you've had Alien Garlic Bread. You know you're missing something.

About a week after I went out with Jennifer, G asked me about it on the way to school.

"You going to call that girl again?"

"Who?"

"Whatsherface from history. What, you have so many dates these days you can't keep track?"

I snorted. "Nah, I don't think so."

"No sparks, huh?"

"Not really."

G paused for a minute. "Still thinking about Emily?"

"Maybe," I admitted. "You probably think I'm a total idiot."

G shook her head. "No, not at all. I think Emily's lucky to have met someone like you who sees the best in her."

"Really? After everything that happened, that's what you think?"

"I think you care about her a lot." She paused. "And I think she cares about you too. I think she's got kind of a messed-up way of showing it sometimes."

"So you don't think she was just using me to get back at Lyle anymore?"

"Maybe at first. But I think—no, I know she ended up caring about you a lot. Honestly, I think it ended up freaking her out a little."

"Yeah, well, not like it matters now. I'm probably never going to see her again."

G shrugged. "You never know. The universe works in mysterious ways sometimes."

I raised my eyebrows at her. "Now you *sound* like Emily."

G laughed. "Yeah, don't ever tell her I said that."

SPIDEY RETURNS

"Your grandmother left you some money in her will, Andrew," Mom said one night over dinner. "I hope you'll do something sensible with it, like put it in the bank for college." She paused. "But it's your money, so whatever you want to do with it is fine with me."

"Thanks, Mom," I said.

She was chewing on her lower lip like she had something else to say but wasn't sure if she should say it. "Anyway, I'm sure your grandmother would have preferred you take it to Vegas, go skydiving, or buy some hotrod car."

"It's okay, Mom," I said. "I don't mind putting it away for college." I took a deep breath. "I'm not sure I'll go right away, though. I mean, I'm not sure I see the point of just plunging headfirst into more education until I know what I want to be educated about." I expected her to flip out, but instead Mom finished chewing and placed her fork down next to her plate.

"I think a gap year can be very sensible for some students," she said.

"Or two," I said.

Mom sighed. "Yes, even two. You know this isn't about what *I* want. It's about having options."

"I know I have options, mom. What I want is a little more direction."

Mom looked a little stunned at my response and it took her a minute to gather her thoughts again. "Well there's more," she said. "Mima asked to be cremated."

"Oh."

"And she wanted you to decide what to do with her ashes." Before I could respond to this Mom quickly continued speaking. "Personally I think that's a bit of a ridiculous thing to ask a teenager. But she was very specific about it being your responsibility. I think she wanted you to go on some crazy adventure or something and leave them on top of a mountain. I don't know, she wasn't very specific. Just that you were to decide what to do with them and to be creative about it."

"Well, I guess I kind of already had the adventure part," I joked.

Mom grimaced. "You could say that."

"Don't worry, Mom. Whatever I do, I won't miss any more school this year. Mima can wait. I need to think about it anyway. Where is she now?"

"Her ashes? In an urn on top of the washing machine."

This was Mom's place for an infinite number of things that didn't seem to have any other set location: wrapping paper, phone books, VHS tapes for a VCR we no longer owned, and apparently ashes of the deceased.

One afternoon on my way home my stomach was growling more than usual. I stopped at Mr. Bagel in town to grab something to eat, but when I reached for the door handle I paused. Without really caring who was looking, I walked over to the side of the building and around the back to the alley, where there was a dark blue dumpster overstuffed with bags of trash. I lifted the lid and recoiled at the smell of rotting vegetables and sour dairy products. There was a brownish liquid pooling below the dumpster, and flies were buzzing around and landing in it. I grimaced and let the lid fall shut. I walked back around to the entrance, went inside, and mumbled my order to the cashier. She seemed overly sunny when giving me my change.

The experience reminded me of my really brief membership in the Boy Scouts. I went on exactly one scout outing. It was supposed to be a father-son trip, but at the last minute Dad bailed, and I had to get tacked on like a third wheel to some other father-son team. We hiked a little ways in to a shelter that was part of the Appalachian Trail and spent the afternoon clearing brush and tidying up the campsite as part of earning our community service badges. The best part of the whole trip was the beef stew we ate for dinner. Cooked in a pot over an open fire with the stars shining brightly above, every morsel tasted rich and delicious on my tongue. "What is this?" I remember asking my scout leader.

"Dinty Moore beef stew," he answered and tossed me an empty can. I memorized the label and begged Mom to buy it for me when I got back from the trip. She gave me a funny look but tossed a couple cans in the cart the next time we were at the supermarket. I raced home after school the next day and carefully opened and reheated a can of stew. When I tasted it, I was crushed. It smelled and tasted like dog food. Under the bright fluorescent track lights of our kitchen, it even looked a bit like dog food. I poured the rest in a plastic bag and hid it in the trash. I was never so disappointed in a meal or a memory until that dumpster behind Mr. Bagel.

After about a month, G moved into the dorms, Mom went back to her regular schedule, and I just kind of slipped under the radar again. I still see G every day. She's gotten super involved at St. Mary's, playing lacrosse and tutoring kids at the elementary school across the way. She even started an astronomy club. I thought about joining; maybe I still will.

Around the same time G moved into the dorms I got a package in the mail. It was my Spidey sack with my clothes and the rest of my things stuffed inside. The whole thing was rolled up and tied inside a supermarket paper bag that looked like it wouldn't have made it down the block in one piece, much less across the country. I couldn't figure out how they tracked me down until I looked inside my spare glasses case, where Mom had taped my name and address the last summer I went to sleep-away camp. Tucked into a pair of my boxer shorts was a postcard showing a bunch of people in '80s spandex lifting weights on the beach. "Venice Beach, California" was written in hot pink bubble letters across the bottom.

On the back Jesse had written the words *Peace and love* and simply signed his name. I looked the card over a few times, hoping there was something I had missed, some other detail that would tell me more about where they were and what they were doing, but that was it.

With G out of the house and everything else going back to normal, I was beginning to think my adventures with the Freegans had all been part of some strange dream. The whole thing seemed to be fading into memory until one extremely bitter day in mid-February when I got another postcard. I wouldn't have even known it was from Emily except that it was addressed to Drew West and she had doodled swirly lines and curlicues around the address. My name and address were the only things written on it. The front was a city scene of downtown San Francisco, and I knew it was Emily's way of saying hi. So I tacked it on my bulletin board, taking it down every once in a while when I felt like thinking about her.

That was when I started to hatch my plan. I knew I had to finish the school year, but if my grades were good enough Mom wouldn't hassle me about my summer plans. For the first time in my life I tried to do well in school. I know no one would ever believe this, but school isn't that hard if you listen in class and pay attention to a few basic rules. First off, always make sure your paper has your name, the date and a title on it. I swear, you could write ten pages of total BS, but if it has a nice header it will probably pass. Second, don't just study the night before an exam. I know this seems obvious and teachers have been telling me this for years. But seriously, twenty minutes of studying each day for a few days before a test makes the difference between a failing grade and a passing one. Thirdly, talk to your teachers. If you don't understand something, or even if you do, ask. Teachers will tell you pretty much exactly what they want to see on an assignment. They're probably just so jazzed that someone is making an effort that they'll practically write the thing for you.

Once I started doing these things, they just kind of became a habit. Third quarter I almost made the honor roll. Mom was so thrilled she took me and G out for a steak dinner. Well, steak for me and baked potato and salad for G. At dinner she talked herself blue about all the colleges I could get into if I kept up this kind of effort. I made a mental note to fail a couple things at the beginning of fourth quarter so she wouldn't make it her personal project to see that I got straight A's. I wasn't thinking about college, I was thinking about how I could get back on the road again, and of course there was Emily. But here's something else that I didn't expect. It felt good to do well. My teachers looked me in the eye when they handed back my work, raised their eyebrows like they were impressed, and occasionally (mostly Ms. Tuttle) even smirked like they'd known I could do it all along.

The next postcard came from Seattle.

Dear Drew, I'm in Seattle and I'm working and trying to get my shit together. I think I'll be here for a little while. I owe you more of an apology than can fit on this card. I think about you a lot. Your Emily

The last two words were the best part. It didn't say "Yours comma Emily" it said "Your Emily". Shortly after that card arrived I started researching airplane tickets to Seattle. The best part of my day every day was the approach to the mailbox. And the worst part was the walk up the driveway when it was empty.

The next card didn't come until mid-May and I had almost given up on hearing from her again. The writing was small and cramped and described a camping trip she had taken with some friends in the San Juan Islands off Seattle. It ended with the words "You should come visit." And a phone number.

That night I made dinner for Mom and me. When she got home from school she eyed the spaghetti in the strainer suspiciously. When we had both tucked in to a big plate of pasta I made my announcement. "I think I know where I'm going to scatter Mima's ashes."

"Really, where's that?"

"The Pacific Ocean."

"Hmm." Mom finished chewing and dabbed at her mouth with her napkin. "May I ask why? I mean, the Atlantic Ocean is certainly a lot more convenient to New York."

I was ready for this. "It came to me in a dream."

Mom dabbed at her mouth again with the napkin even though her face was clean. She looked to me like she was gearing up for a fight. So I was surprised when she said, "Okay."

"Okay?"

"Sure. It's your money. If you want to spend it on a plane ticket out west, I think I've learned I can't stop you."

She didn't mean it as a guilt trip, but immediately I felt bad. "That's not all," I said, deciding to come clean. "There's a girl I want to see. She's living in Seattle." Mom looked up, and I was surprised by how interested and, well, happy she looked. So I told her about Emily—kind of an edited-for-parents version. She asked a lot of questions. Good questions; the kind someone asks when they're really listening to you. So I kept going and I told her about Tim and Jesse and Lyle, about working for Gene in Hot Springs and living on Jeremiah's farm. It wasn't until Mom stifled a yawn with the back of her hand that I realized it was late and we'd been talking for a couple hours.

"I should go to bed," I said.

"It's late," Mom agreed.

"Yeah, but not too late."

***

G and I talked about my trip a few weeks before I left. "I heard you're going out west this summer," she said.

"Yeah, well, I heard there's this crazy hippie college out there called Evergreen State where you can basically study whatever you want and make up your own major."

G laughed. "Watch out for those hippies," she said. "You never know when they'll kidnap you and drag you around the country in some dirty van."

"And I guess the University of Washington has a pretty intense philosophy department that might be worth checking out."

Now G looked a bit more surprised. "You're serious," she said.

I nodded. "Don't tell Nancy. She thinks it's all about some girl."

"Well, there'll always be a girl," G said.

"If I'm lucky."

G shook her head, "You're a lot more than lucky, Andrew West."

***

When Mom dropped me off at the airport in June, we said our good-byes at the curbside. I had a plane to catch, and she had a meeting with the board of trustees. All I had for luggage was a hiking pack I bought with Mima's money and my Spidey sack strapped to the bottom. I promised to return in three weeks to the summer job I had lined up at the mini-golf place, but when I went to close the car door Mom threw the car into park and jumped out, nearly decapitating herself with the seatbelt strap. She ran around the front of the car and wrapped me in a huge hug. My cheek came just to her chin, and she pressed her lips to my forehead before getting back in the car without another word. I watched as she gave me a stilted headmistress-type wave and then pulled into traffic, cutting off a cab in the process.

I slept for most of the flight, and when I was awake I ignored the second-rate action movie flashing above my head and stared out the window at the changing landscape below. I flipped through the divorce diary, reading bits and pieces of my adventures. Certain moments, like running through the suburbs covered in finger paint, or kissing Emily's neck at the farm, made my pulse race. But I didn't want to just rehash the good stuff. I wanted to remember the ways I wanted to be different. As a symbolic act I ripped out the original pages of the notebook with their stupid lists, crumpled them up, and stuffed them in the tiny lavatory trash can.

Emily and I had talked only briefly when I told her I was coming out. She sounded excited and said she would try to meet me at the airport. If she wasn't there, she told me to call the house and someone would tell me which bus to get on. When I walked off the plane I peeked over shoulders and around heads, hoping I could see her before she saw me. When at last I came through the gate, I scanned the crowd and let out a disappointed sigh. A skinny boy with glasses was grinning excitedly at someone behind me. I moved to one side and then looked at him again. It was Emily. Her dreads were gone, and her hair was cropped short and pixie-like. When I got closer I saw her glasses were thick purple frames with no lenses. Everything else was pretty much the same. She was wearing baggy jeans and two or three sweaters layered on top. I dropped my carry-on and rubbed my eyes like I was seeing things. She threw back her head and laughed at my reaction. Then she jumped towards me and threw her arms around my neck. "Drew!" she screamed delightedly.

I pulled away and stuck my hand out, smiling but serious. "It's Andrew," I said.

ACKNOWLEDGEMENTS

There is the journey in the book and the journey of the book. In both cases I have had invaluable encouragement and collaboration from many people in bringing this story to the page. Kris White and Megan Frazer Blakemore lent a fantastic critical eye to early drafts. My super agent Lauren MacLeod helped me find *The Other Way Around* while showing endless patience and unflagging support. I am eternally grateful that this book found its home with the brilliant Andrew Karre; both for his editorial wizardry and dedication to telling the stories of adolescence.

To my fellow teachers and students both past and present—you are all in here. You are all a part of the story.

Thanks to Tara for the constant ear. You are my level. And to Carrie who is on whatever side I'm on. Thanks to all my friends who have shared with me their excitement, curiosity, and interest every step of the way.

To Mom and Dad, you were the first to hear my words. It is with you and because of you, that so many more are possible. With Noah and Ali, you are my Kaufmans. Thank you for loving and reading, sharing and eating.

Finally, thanks to Lance and Eliana for granting me time in "the cave." Lance, thank you for your unconditional love and support of my crazy monkey brain and the stories it spins. I know you think I did it without you, but you are wrong.

ABOUT THE AUTHOR

Sashi Kaufman is a middle-school teacher and an author. She lives in Portland, Maine, with her husband and daughter. Visit her online at www.sashikaufman.com.